The Waters of Star Lake

Other Books by Sara Rath

Novels

Night Sisters
Star Lake Saloon and Housekeeping Cottages

Nonfiction

H. H. Bennett, Photographer: His American Landscape
The Complete Pig
The Complete Cow
About Cows
Pioneer Photographer
Easy Going: Madison and Dane County

Poetry

Dancing with a Cowboy
Remembering the Wilderness
The Cosmic Virgin
Whatever Happened to Fats Domino and Other Poems

The Waters of Star Lake

A Novel

Sara Rath

Terrace Books
A trade imprint of the University of Wisconsin Press

Terrace Books, a trade imprint of the University of Wisconsin Press, takes its
name from the Memorial Union Terrace, located at the University of Wisconsin–
Madison. Since its inception in 1907, the Wisconsin Union has provided a
venue for students, faculty, staff, and alumni to debate art, music, politics, and
the issues of the day. It is a place where theater, music, drama, literature, dance, outdoor
activities, and major speakers are made available to the campus and the community. To
learn more about the Union, visit www.union.wisc.edu.

Terrace Books
A trade imprint of the University of Wisconsin Press
1930 Monroe Street, 3rd Floor
Madison, Wisconsin 53711-2059
uwpress.wisc.edu

3 Henrietta Street
London WCE 8LU, England
eurospanbookstore.com

Printed in the United States of America

Library of Congress Cataloging-in-Publication Data
Rath, Sara.
The waters of Star Lake: a novel / Sara Rath.
    p.   cm.
ISBN 978-0-299-28770-2 (cloth: alk. paper)
ISBN 978-0-299-28773-3 (e-book)
I. Wisconsin—Fiction.   I. Title.
PS3568.A718W38   2012
    813'.54—dc23
    2011042486

This is a work of fiction. Any references to historical events, to real people living or dead, to real
locales are intended only to give the fiction a setting in historical reality. Other names, characters,
places, and incidents are either the product of the author's imagination or are used fictitiously, and
their resemblance, if any, to real-life counterparts is entirely coincidental.

In memory of
my grandfather,
A. C. Lindsay,
who built Lindsay Lodge in July 1926
with my father and friends from Manawa, Wisconsin.

In its peaceful setting on Catherine Lake, our rustic cabin
has embraced five generations.

Come away, O human child!
To the waters and the wild
With a faery, hand in hand,
For the world's more full of weeping than you can understand.

W. B. Yeats, "The Stolen Child"

Acknowledgments

My family's cabin, Lindsay Lodge, was the genesis for this work, another visit to the imagined locale of *Star Lake Saloon and Housekeeping Cottages* and a place beloved not only by me but also by Art and Marsha Lindsay, my brother and sister.

I owe my deepest gratitude to Adrian Wydeven, mammalian ecologist and conservation biologist with the Bureau of Endangered Resources, Wisconsin Department of Natural Resources, who was a remarkable resource in my exploration for this novel. Thanks to my old friend David Gjestson, former biologist with the Wisconsin DNR, for facilitating this valuable connection with Adrian and his wife, Sarah Boles.

Russell Waters, a distant cousin, allowed me to borrow his name for Natalie's grandfather and thus the felicitous name of her family's cabin, Waters Edge. I recognize many special friends for their support: Ludmilla Bollow, who is always there with new ideas when I write myself into a corner; Judith Swartz Marcus, who heeds my frustrations and then takes me shopping; Susan Jannotta and Eileen Roeder, whose good-natured teasing and ultimate patience keep me grounded, Ben and Linda Bolton, who bring laughter to my life and cheer on my work. While completing this book, I lost a dear friend, Gail Petersen. She and her mother, Betty Irwin, have been sources of affection and camaraderie for many years. Gail's perceptive comments on my work are sadly missed.

Thanks to Jean Porter at the Spring Green Community Library, for obtaining obscure materials written by Billie Frechette. My granddaughter, Katie Lamont, said Minnow should be emo, explained what it meant, and helped me shape that character. Sadie Grace Lamont, our chocolate Labrador, stayed by my side during this journey. My son, Jay Rath, suggested the initial plot, and my daughter, Laura Beausire, will not let me fail—my children's stubborn insistence that I keep going has always helped me turn the next page in my life, no matter how daunting. The University of Wisconsin Press seems to have unfailing confidence in my inspirations, and I appreciate their efforts to help my work be the best that it can be. I'm proud to be one of their authors!

Finally, to my husband, Del Lamont, I owe my enduring gratitude. He allows me to pursue challenges I love, and I depend so greatly on the strength of his embrace.

1

Deep North

[T]he wolf knows he [is] not a dog and he does not have to be in a pack to give him dignity or confidence. He is hunted by everyone. Everyone is against him and he is on his own as an artist is.

Ernest Hemingway

1

Right off the bat, you've got to own up: the dog doesn't die.

Ginger Kovalcik,
bartender, Star Lake Saloon

*F*or one lingering moment, I had no idea where I was. Then, in the black abyss I heard the hysterical laughter of loons.

Molly nudged me with a cold, wet nose. She had to pee. Fumbling with items on the bench I'd shoved next to the bed last night, I knocked my glasses onto the floor. There went my journal. I finally found my flashlight and flicked it on. Of course, the new batteries were still in one of the grocery bags so only a stream of light hit the rustic interior of the one-room cabin.

"This better be fast," I warned the Lab. "I'm still asleep . . ."

The first night at the cabin was always a restless one, riddled with skitterings of mice (soon to meet their doom) and the loons, of course, and sometimes disembodied voices of fishermen out on the lake, so I had swallowed a couple of sleeping pills before blowing out the oil lamp. In time, the nocturnal Northwoods activity would become familiar again.

With some effort, I elbowed myself to a sitting position and waited until the dizziness went away. My Birkenstocks were somewhere on the filthy throw rug. After the sun was up I would definitely have to clean this place. Last evening when I slid the padlock from the hinge and pushed the heavy front door open, the interior of the cabin was an oven and it smelled like it always did. I expected that. Throughout my almost sixty years the cabin remained a constant. My parents had moved several times during my childhood, and Charlie and I had lived in several homes in Madison, but the cabin never changed. Here it was always November 1927 and smelled like mothballs and mouse urine.

By the time I had unloaded my supplies from the car, I was sweaty and didn't give a hoot about mouse droppings and spider webs, or about porch furniture piled and scattered inside. It was getting too dark to see. In a cabinet drawer I found a roll of paper towels that hadn't been chewed to bits and swiped the oilcloth on the long wooden table where I set down the bags of groceries. I turned up the wick of an oil lamp, scratched a match, and replaced the glass chimney. Then, before I collapsed, I grabbed the yellow plastic bucket and made my way to the shore so I could at least wash my face. The lake was low, and I had to kneel on the pier to dip the bucket between the weeds to fill it. The effort of bringing it back up and rising from my knees was a discouraging reminder of age. Molly splashed in the lake, got out, ran to the end of the pier, and splashed again.

"I'll be sleeping with a wet dog," I mourned aloud, but she was entitled to some joy after a six-hour ride in the car.

The cabin hadn't been opened since a year before Charlie died. You were in greater danger of dying in an accident on the way to your cabin than from hantavirus, I'd read somewhere. Inhaling deer-mouse feces was not my preferred cause of death. Not that I *had* a preferred cause. Charlie certainly would not have chosen prostate cancer. And swallowing a bottle of sleeping pills wasn't guaranteed unless you also took Tylenol and washed everything down with alcohol. I had researched such arcane subjects on Google during Charlie's last days in hospice.

Now Molly was desperately dancing at the back door. A leg on the old pot-bellied stove in the middle of the room seemed to reach out and grab my left foot. Then my right foot kicked over the enamel chamber pot I'd placed a few convenient steps away from the bed, just in case. Thank goodness it was empty, because the cover clattered and the pot rolled across the floor where it banged into the wall; there was no way I'd venture out to the outhouse after dark. If there was no way around it, I used to have Charlie come with me and stand watch.

By this time Molly was yipping and shrieking, and after an array of expletives (for which I later felt very guilty), I yelled at her to hold it, I'd be there in a goddamned minute!

When I unhooked the screen door, Molly nosed it open, leaped down the steps, and ran into the woods.

Still woozy, I shuffled over, pulled a chair out from beneath the long wooden table that ran half the length of the room, and sat down. None of the chairs matched—they were old Windsor chairs, one painted green, two gray, but I knew by the duct tape holding the bow together that this was my favorite: faded red with a crack in the seat. I slid a grocery bag and my purse aside on the table so I could brace my elbows and rest my head in my hands.

It was still uncomfortably warm, although I had opened all four windows and had been covered with only a sheet in bed. Usually I closed the wooden doors, but last night the only protection Molly and I had from wilderness critters were rusty screens. I'd hooked the screen doors, pretending that predators would have more respect for an unlocked door rather than plunge through worn-out mesh. That might have been after the sleeping pills began to kick in.

It was sometimes a nuisance not having any electricity or plumbing, but that had also been one of our cabin's attractions through the years: the simplicity. Charlie and I laughed when it became trendy to live off the grid. Grandpa Waters built the place with my dad and pals from Little Wolf in the mid-1920s. All the materials were brought up by train and then hauled on big sleds, over the ice. The 24-by-24-foot building was never meant to be anything more than a hunting and fishing cabin.

5

No one ever referred to it as a "cottage," and Grandpa Waters, who sometimes called it a shanty, would be surprised to see it still standing. And much loved. Next to the front door, sheltered by the screened porch, was a wooden sign upon which Grandpa Waters had printed "Waters Edge." He had surrounded the words with painted images meant to resemble muskies and a few bucks with impossible antlers. More than once I had been tempted to carve an apostrophe after Waters but Charlie insisted the sign should not be altered and belonged right there just as it was, next to the cabin door where the children's cane poles were propped and their treasured clam shells and other finds were still displayed.

The sign was deceiving, because beneath "Waters Edge" Grandpa Waters had burned in the words "Star Lake." Our cabin was not actually on Star Lake. It was on Sundog, a smaller lake that was part of the Star Lake Chain: Star Lake, Sundog, the Lost Arrow River, and Lake Sickle Moon. Since Grandpa built the cabin, however, the chain had been re-christened "The Celestial Chain" by a bunch of hippies, according to Max, my younger sister, who said she'd heard it from somebody over at the Star Lake Saloon. When anyone asked where our family's North-woods cabin was, we always said "Star Lake." It was too confusing to explain, and nobody had heard of little Lake Sundog.

Charlie bought out my siblings' interest in the cabin years ago, but Max and my brother, Alan, still came up north once in a while. I'd already informed them that this summer I'd be there until Labor Day.

One item in the cabin *was* comparatively new. When Charlie became ill, I surprised him with a new bed to make his visits more comfortable. The old metal double bunk bed with squeaky springs—no doubt hauled over frozen lakes and through snowbanks by resolute ancestors—had been dismantled and set out in back, behind the lean-to. In its place was a lovely double bed made of logs, with a new mattress. Last night, I'd only had to fold back the protective plastic covering laid over it at the close of our last visit to reveal a clean mattress pad.

Recently, I'd seen this part of Wisconsin referred to in a travel magazine as the "Deep North." It doesn't get much deeper, I mused, nodding.

After a few more minutes, Molly's absence began to seem ominous. Deep North, overcast moon, sinister, not a single neighbor on this side of Sundog. During the day, Molly would ram open the back screen door whenever she wanted and push her way back in through the front. But at night she usually went outdoors, peed, and that was that.

I checked the door to the porch, but she wasn't waiting there. At the back door, I whistled. That's when I heard the growls.

Was she tangling with a porcupine? Please, not a skunk!

"Molly, *come!*"

I was annoyed and barged into the night toward the scuffle. Behind me the screen door slammed like a gunshot. The flashlight barely lit the overgrown path to the open space between birch trees where I'd parked the car.

"Molly! Get back here!" My order began to carry more distress than demand as I grew closer to what sounded like dogs fighting. "Get back here, *now!*"

As I came upon them, I could see the shadowy figures more clearly. It was not two dogs fighting. It was a chocolate Labrador retriever and something that might be a timber wolf.

It was a wolf.

I screamed and threw the flashlight at the wolf. Everything immediately went dark. The wolf snarled and backed off a few steps.

From the edge of the woods, the animal's almond eyes still caught the feeble beam of my flashlight where it had bounced off a tree, blinked, and now lay nearly within my grasp. The wolf gave a low warning growl, from deep in its throat, when I reached for Molly.

"Oh, my God! Oh, Molly! Ohmygod!" I repeated this, like a prayer.

I retrieved my flashlight, worried that the wolf might attack me next.

"Go!" I yelled. "Get out of here!"

Once, I had fought to defend these beautiful beasts, their pack loyalty a trait I deeply admired. Timber wolves in Wisconsin had been nearly exterminated twenty years ago, but their numbers were increasing now.

"*Go! Go away!*"

Its yellow eyes stayed on me. I had a sick feeling that it wanted to finish with Molly and had no taste for me.

My dog lay nearly lifeless at my feet, in the bracken and undergrowth.

I found a branch and flung it into the trees. Then I scrabbled around on the ground and finally found a rock. I threw that too. "*Get the hell out of here!*" I found another rock, and another. "Goddammit, *Go!*"

Molly was still panting, fast and shallow. I didn't want to leave, but I had to run back to the cabin. No, I knew I must not run, or to the wolf I'd look like prey. But I walked damned fast and took less than a minute to grab my purse and some towels and hurry back. The wolf could have been surveying the scene from the shadows; I didn't care.

Tenderly, I wrapped several clean bath towels around my dog. I managed to carry her to the car, where I placed her on the back seat with strength that came from an unknown source.

The towels were quickly soaked with her blood.

Without thinking, I pulled my cell phone out, and then slid it back in my purse. There was never a signal out here.

Wolves this close to the cabin! Jesus Christ!

"It's going to be all right," I told Molly, trying to soothe her with one backward hand while I started the SUV and clumsily backed it between two stumps, then went forward, climbing the overgrown path up to the logging road while dodging fallen birch, twisted pines, and protruding rocks. My headlights carved a bright corridor that identified the lane only by tracks made when tires had bent the ferns and tall grasses yesterday afternoon as we drove in.

Molly was breathing in low, weak whimpers.

"Don't let her die, Charlie! Please let her be okay."

Over a year since his death, and I sometimes still talked to Charlie. Right now, the focus was more a desperate combination of Charlie and God.

"I knew the wolf count had gone up, but I never imagined they'd be on our property. Now Molly can't pee outside after dark! And why didn't I grab my glasses? Yes, I'm sure it was a wolf—I could see that much. It was not a coyote, it was bigger—it *was* a wolf! But if I had my glasses now, I could drive a lot faster. And I'm sure it must be illegal to drive when you've taken sleeping pills. I'm all over the road. Oh, Charlie, let this be a bad dream. Let me wake up with everything okay, okay?"

I reached the gravel that announced the junction with the county highway and stopped to rummage through my purse. My sunglasses had prescription lenses, so I put them on, but my mind was a raging mess and things seemed to have changed since the last time I'd been there, and even with diminished 20/20 I couldn't remember the short-cut to Star Lake Saloon, where I knew I could find friends. The clock in the car said it was almost two in the morning. Did bars stay open until two? Or was it two-thirty? I needed to find someone who was awake. Hopefully, someone who wasn't drunk.

"Just get me to a telephone and a veterinarian," I begged aloud.

The road snaked, curving when I least expected. "Star Lake Saloon" was not on any of the white arrows nailed higgledy-piggledy to signposts. *Lost Resort.* Neon beer signs for the roadside bar flared on my right so abruptly that I jammed on the brakes. Then I backed up and made a sharp right turn into the parking lot. People were still there. I made certain Molly was still alive and had not fallen off the back seat, then left the car with the motor on and rushed inside the tavern.

"I need help," I announced to the smoky din. No one heard me.

The place was gritty, disorderly, and raucous. Walls and ceiling were covered with marked up dollar bills stapled there. Everyone was singing along to "Luckenbach Texas" on the jukebox and drunkenly waving their beer cans back and forth.

"*Help me, please!*" I hollered, waving my arms to get attention,

9

Why couldn't anyone see me? I knew my hair was wild and I was wearing an old white T-shirt of Charlie's with a pair of his blue plaid boxer shorts. My face, arms, and clothing were freshly smeared with Molly's blood. What more did I need to stand out in this crowd of rowdies? I took off my sunglasses and jumped up and down, screaming.

"*Help!*"

Then, except for Waylon Jennings, there was sudden silence.

"Holy shit, lady, what happened? You been in a accident?"

"Honey, you got blood all over yourself!"

Two women put down their cigarettes. "Sweetie, you're in shock! You better take it easy!" one said.

The other asked, "Where's your boyfriend at?" And they tried to get me to sit on a barstool.

"Hey! Somebody call 911."

I wrenched my arms away from the women.

"It's not me! A wolf attacked my dog! She's outside, in my car. I have to find a vet!"

Immediately, the bar emptied. Dazed, I watched the crowd swarm into the parking lot.

"Don't touch her!" I yelled, rushing out. "Just tell me where to take her."

"I'll take you," a man said, calmly. He placed a reassuring hand on my arm when I tried to slide back behind the wheel. "Let me drive. I'm the only sober one here. You sit with your dog."

"Yeah, Bud don't drink," someone else said, snickering.

"Bud'll take good care of you," one of the women assured me with an awkward, beery hug.

"We'll call Doc Baker and tell him you're on your way. Fucking wolves! Christ!"

"Oughta kill every last goddamn one of the sons a bitches."

The crowd was reconvening indoors when I slid next to Molly and gently cradled her wounded head.

"Thank you," I told the man at the wheel. "I didn't know . . . I didn't . . ."

"Doc Baker's seen all this before. He'll treat her just fine. He'll look her over, stitch her up, give her some antibiotics, then in a day or so she'll be okay. I've seen dogs bit by wolves in worse shape than this and survive. You take it easy."

That was little comfort. I was trapped in the back seat of my car with my dying dog and a stranger driving us God knows where in the Deep North surrounded by wilderness and wolves. I bent to brush Molly's sleek head with my lips, fondled her velvety ears.

"Poor baby," I whispered. "My poor baby, poor baby . . ."

"You visiting here?" the driver asked at last.

I wiped my nose on my T-shirt. "We have a cabin in a little bay on Sundog. Family cabin. I drove up yesterday. Haven't been here for a couple of years . . . my husband died . . ."

That was too much information. I didn't want this stranger knowing where I was staying or that I was alone. And now he could pull the car over and rape me and my word wouldn't mean a thing up here because he was a local and I was a stranger and Molly would die because we didn't get her to the vet.

"You the ones who have that little green cabin back over on the north side? Kind of hidden, wouldn't know it was there if you weren't looking for it? Been there forever?"

"Yes."

"Are you one of the Waters, then?"

"Um, I used to be Natalie Waters, but then I married Charles Lindquist. So I'm really Natalie Lindquist, but sometimes I use the name Waters, too. Natalie Waters Lindquist. Natalie."

Again, way too much information. TMI. TMI. TMI. Next thing, he'll ask for my social security number and I'll blab it out to him. How about my MasterCard number; I've memorized that, too.

What did this guy look like, anyway? All I could see by the dash light was his silhouette—a big guy with a crew cut.

Oh, Natalie!—just shut the fuck up!

If this was a nightmare, then it was a really serious one. Charlie did not approve of coarse language, and I almost never used the "F" word.

Well, sometimes, when I was talking to myself, but not when I was talking to Charlie, even if it was Dead Charlie. But then I'd never shouted "Jesus Christ," either, like I had during the encounter with the wolf.

"Natalie, huh? Hello, Natalie. I'm Bud Foster," the driver said. "That's my bar, back there."

Molly moaned softly and tried to lick my hand. I put my face down next to hers and murmured more soft words of comfort.

"My husband gave me this dog," I told Bud. "Charlie knew he was dying, and he didn't want me to be alone."

Although I really didn't want the extra burden of a new puppy just then, he insisted on getting me the dog. And he told me what to name it. "Molly. Her name is going to be Molly," he said when he proudly placed the squirming seven-week-old chocolate Lab in my lap.

"So I thought I'd be safe, coming up here with Molly." Again, I brushed my lips against Molly's soft fur. "She's two years old. And a wonderful, loving companion. And now—"

"Whoa . . ." Bud said. "I told you Molly's going to be all right, and I meant it. I'll make you a bet."

He paused at a stop sign and turned onto a road I thought I recognized. It led into Antler.

"It's not a joking matter," I said flatly.

"I'm not joking, I'm serious. After Doc Baker fixes up Molly and she's back with you again, I'll take you out to dinner. You name the place. Steak, lobster, whatever you want. It'll be on me."

"And . . . and if she . . . if Molly . . ." I couldn't spit it out.

"Then I'm an idiot. Shoot me. That's how sure I am that she's going to be all right."

Bud pulled into a driveway where yard lights illuminated a house with a small building attached: "Antler Animal Clinic." The sign on the front was big enough that I could read it with sunglasses in the middle of the night. A man emerged from the front door when the car came to a stop.

"Let's see this poor critter," Dr. Baker said after introducing himself. He was young, slim, balding, and had pulled on a pair of jeans but still wore a striped pajama top. He and Bud carried Molly into the clinic and placed her on an examining table under bright lights. Molly didn't put up any resistance. Her tongue was lolling out the side of her mouth like it does in pictures of dead animals, but her ribcage was still expanding and contracting.

Dr. Baker peeled away the bloody towels. "You sure it was a wolf? You saw it yourself?"

I could only nod my head. The blood, Molly's lethargy and labored breathing, the wounds—it was too much to take in now that I could see it all more clearly.

"I can't tell how serious the wounds are right away, but I don't think she'll lose the leg. Might have hit an artery with these puncture wounds on her neck; that'd account for all the blood.

"Wolves usually go for the hindquarters. Sometimes we'll see a few neck injuries like these, but more often than not they go for the flanks. Sometimes they go for the groin and around the base of the tail."

"Will she be all right?"

Dr. Baker was still examining Molly, but his words were heartening.

"When you scared that wolf off, you probably saved her life."

I grabbed the side of the steel table, but my hands, wet with Molly's blood, slipped on the cold, metal surface. Bud caught my arm.

"Why don't you take a seat out in the waiting room while I get down to business here," Dr. Baker suggested. "I've got to shave off some of Molly's fur, give her some painkillers, clean her up, suture the lacerations, and give her some antibiotics. You can relax now and catch your breath; you've done all you can. Bud, you might get your friend some of that special 'medicine' I keep in the cabinet over the sink."

Bud guided me to the adjacent room.

"Sit down, put your head between your knees, and take a few deep breaths. Everything's going to be okay. Just like I said."

"I have to—" I said. "I think I'm going to—" All of a sudden I was overwhelmed by nausea, surrendering the terror I had been suppressing.

Bud placed a wastebasket in front of me, just in time.

"I'm sorry, it's just that—"

13

"It's okay," Bud said. "It's okay." He gently wiped my face with a damp towel and held me close, rocking me in his arms.

I didn't know this man, but I really welcomed his embrace.

What a fucking night. All because of those goddamned loons.

I hadn't even cried.

2

My head ached, my stomach hurt, and the sky was pale and sallow by the time Bud drove me back to the tavern from the veterinary clinic. He offered to fix a pot of coffee. All I wanted was to sleep for hours and when I woke up realize with enormous relief that the terrifying episode had been a bad dream. Only that.

"Sure you can find your way back to your place?"

"I shouldn't have a problem, now that it's almost light."

I went around to take Bud's place behind the wheel.

"Keep an eye out for that wolf," he warned. "Once they get a taste of canine blood, they'll show up again."

I wanted to tell Bud that I'd always thought "keep an eye out" was a curious thing to imagine, like pulling out an eyeball so it could flop around and stare this way and that. Boy, I was getting punchy. Bud was still speaking. Something about a pack of wolves seeing Molly as encroaching on their territory, if no one had visited the cabin in a while.

"It's against the law to kill one, but a lot of guys up here subscribe to the 'shoot, shovel, and shut up' philosophy. They think the only good wolf is a dead wolf. When news of Molly's injuries gets around, you might be hearing from them."

I was barely hearing what Bud was saying, and whatever it was, I didn't want it to register. Once I was locked safely inside my cabin, got some rest, and then found out how Molly was doing, I'd get things sorted out.

"Give me a call if you need anything, okay?" Bud handed me a business card that said "Last Resort." So it wasn't "Lost Resort," as I'd read the sign in the dark in my panic.

"Does your cell phone work up here? Got a number I can reach you at?"

Damn. I had to admit that I couldn't get a signal.

"This is your place?"

"Yup. You're welcome to stop in any time. But it might be easier to come by boat. You know the tube?"

Sure, I knew the tube; it was a huge metal culvert that connected Star Lake with Sundog and the rest of the chain.

"From Sundog, aim your boat straight ahead through the tube and keep going until you run into the shore. Look for the Miller Lite sign next to the pier."

The boat was too heavy for me to put in the water by myself, but I would not tell Bud. I also didn't want to let him know I couldn't carry the five-horsepower motor down to the lake, either, or that I was certain there wasn't any gas. Or that I was unequivocally sure I would never set foot in his sleazy tavern again.

Instead, I said, "See you soon" and managed a watery smile. The man who'd rescued Molly (and me) was pleasant looking. He had dark hair, slightly graying and cut short; brown eyes; and glasses with round metal frames. Maybe he lifted weights to stay in shape. His faded jeans had a rip in the knee. This was someone you wouldn't want to start a fight with. He was certainly younger than I was.

"You take care of yourself," he said, extending his hand.

Without thinking, I went in for a quick hug instead. Then I reconsidered, because of my blood-soaked shirt. "I can't tell you how grateful I am for your help," I told him, arms still extended. "If I hadn't found you . . ." my voice withered.

Bud held my shoulders and pulled me so close to him that he didn't seem to mind how disgusting I must have been. My cheek touched his, and I could smell cigarettes and a trace of shaving cream—a man smell I hadn't realized I missed so dearly.

"Everything's going to be all right," he whispered, comforting me. He patted my back and with a tender brush of his lips gently kissed my forehead. "I may stop by later today to see how you're doing. In the meantime, get some sleep."

That was a nice touch, the kiss, but I was too drained to say I didn't want him to show up at my cabin. When I reached it, I drove down the rutted logging road and went past my usual parking space, navigating as close to the building as I could—ten feet from the screen door in back, which was still unhooked.

Before sliding into bed, I stuffed Charlie's bloody T-shirt and shorts inside the potbellied stove. My body was also stained with Molly's blood, but that helped me feel closer to her and her suffering.

I figured I'd hit the pillow and immediately collapse, but the adrenaline rush of the past few hours refused to subside. Eyes wide open, I watched the interior of the cabin gradually resolve itself as darkness fled the shadows. I hadn't slept without Molly snuggled tightly against my side since Charlie had given her to me.

Crying came easily now as I replayed again and again the trauma of finding my nearly lifeless dog with the snarling wolf. I half-expected, deeply wished, I could hear Charlie reassure me that it wasn't my fault. How *could* it have been my fault? You've got a cabin out in the woods where packs of wolves are proliferating, and if one shows up it's not your fault when your dog gets attacked. How can you keep them at bay? "At bay," why did that seem so familiar? *Keep the wolves at bay. Keep the wolves away from the door.* Those were metaphorical wolves, not real ones.

I thumped my pillows and tried to let go. When Charlie said he wanted his ashes sprinkled in the pines in front of the cabin, I argued that was unwise because our sons were no longer interested in coming there. "What does that matter?" he'd argued. "It's where I want to be!" So we carried out his wishes when our boys and their wives were in Madison for the memorial service. We drove to Antler, spread his ashes in the ferns and grasses, and tossed the rest off the end of the dock. I drove Harry and Camille, Seth and Avianna, to the Rhinelander airport so they could fly back to their homes from there. Then I stayed in a Rhinelander hotel and returned to Madison alone the next day.

The cabin wasn't opened then and had not been since the weekend before Charlie's surgery when I'd surprised him with the new bed. We'd shared a bottle of wine and made love for the last time. It was a bittersweet visit. Eighteen months later, Charlie was gone.

That memory brought a cleansing interval of tears, after which I found myself focusing on the Lydia Pinkham calendar nailed on the wall. The top half featured a black and white lithograph of a stern yet pleasant woman's face encircled with the words *Lydia E. Pinkham's Vegetable Compound.* At the cabin, it was always November 1927, because the calendar (if not the old metal bunk beds) had been there forever and was sacrosanct; Grandpa Waters's name was at the bottom:

~Waters Pharmacy~
Russell Waters, R.Ph.

My earliest trips to the cabin were with my grandparents, as I was their first grandchild. When it rained, Grandma Waters taught me how to knit. If I promised to be quiet, they would take me fishing for an afternoon. I was shown how to bait a hook, put a sinker on the line, and tie on the bobber—then instructed to keep my eye on the red-and-white bobber at all times. I only caught panfish, but Grandpa praised me for them, and after he filleted them, Grandma fried the tiny bits for my delicious supper.

Despite Grandma's playful protests, when I asked Grandpa who Lydia Pinkham was, which I did during every visit, he could be easily encouraged to sing a comic song about the infamous Lydia. It wasn't long before I had memorized every verse:

> Then we'll sing, we'll sing, we'll sing
> Of Lydia Pinkham, Pinkham, Pinkham
> The savior of the human race.
> For she's invented a vegetable compound
> And the papers, papers, papers
> Published her face.

That was the chorus. There were a number of hilarious versions, some of which he and I could sing in front of Grandma.

> Mary McCarty, hale and hearty
> > Suffered for years from hair on the brain.
> Now she's bald and free of all dandruff.
> > Lydia Pinkham, Pinkham, Pinkham triumphs again!
> > (She triumphs again!)

> Widow Brown, she had no children,
> > Though she loved them very dear,
> So she took she swallowed, she gargled
> > Some vegetable compound,
> And now she has them twice a year.

But if we happened to be out on the lake, or somewhere Grandma was not, Grandpa and I sang a bawdier account.

> Now Mrs. Brown had an invisible bosom,
> > It barely showed beneath her blouse.
> She rubbed her chest with
> > the vegetable compound,
> And now they milk her with the cows.
> > (With the cows!)

When they were old enough, I taught the songs to Maxine and Alan and we'd march through the woods shouting the lyrics. They especially enjoyed the line about milking Mrs. Brown with the cows. But Dad and Mom didn't bring us up to the cabin as often as I'd visited there with my grandparents, and my sons were not fond of the rustic lifestyle . . . no television, no indoor toilet, no friends next door. Their wives, Camille and Avianna? Well, just forget it. They were grossed out by the thought of a lone mouse, to say nothing of a deer fly or a wood tick. They'd joined me and Charlie once for the Fourth of July but stayed at the

Yank 'Em Inn in town. Harry and Camille had a daughter, now a teenager, but she had never been up north. They lived in New York, Seth and Avianna in Phoenix.

Dammit, this was not a good time to indulge myself in self-pity over the indifference of my children. I grabbed a handful of Kleenex from the box on the bench next to the bed and blew my nose, wiped away the tears.

"Billy Black lacked hair on his balls," I managed to sing in a feeble voice. "And his pecker wouldn't peck. So he took, he swallowed . . ."

I paused to recall the next few words. " . . . he gargled some vegetable compound . . ."

After blowing my nose again, I shouted out: "Now it's as long as a gy-raffe's neck."

I laughed until I began sobbing again. Oh, God, please let Molly be okay, and let last night's terror subside in the happy memories of this place!

I got out of bed to use the chamber pot. The outhouse was still padlocked, and there was no way I was going to take a chance sitting in there all day with a wolf at the door (that wasn't even funny). As long as I was up, I took a sleeping pill. It might not put me to sleep, but maybe it would help put the skids on my manic brain.

Rustic as the cabin was, it possessed million-dollar views: four big windows, two doors, roughly fashioned but with magnificent vistas of the woods or the lake . . . or the woods *and* the lake; you weren't allowed to build so close to the water anymore. The cabin was grandfathered in (coincidental term, considering).

It was sheltered by white birch and balsam; tall pines silhouetted against the sunrise through the window on my left. The scene was fuzzy without my glasses, but I knew the landscape by heart. I knew everything in this cabin by heart, the watermarks on the ceiling, the handwritten messages on the walls, the petrified fungus upon which I'd used a nail to carve the date of a visit with my parents and Max and Alan in the 1950s.

We came to the cabin even less frequently with our parents as the years went by, seldom for more than one night. Mother complained that she didn't like roughing it. She didn't know how to swim. We didn't have a road then, and it wasn't a treat for her to haul everything from the car down to the shore by the tube while Dad and Alan hiked through the woods to the cabin to get the boat and then come and pick up the rest of us. We'd have to load up the boat with drinking water, bedding, groceries, and everything else a family of five would need for our short stay. And when we reached the cabin, Mother complained it was not fun for her to clean up after creatures that nested between the screens and the windows—making the cabin dark even at noon—and sleep on mattresses that smelled of mold and mice.

Dad sometimes came up with fishing buddies to play poker and drink beer (one summer, Alan and I found a buried cache of beer cans back in the woods but never told), and he knew Hal Larkin over at the Star Lake Saloon—they had been in the same class in Little Wolf. When he went over there by boat, returning long after dark, Mother became extremely anxious, especially if there was a threat of a storm. She was not a happy camper. We were more likely to stop briefly at the cabin just to see that it was still standing, then spend a week at a Northwoods resort where clean little cottages lined up side by side with hot water and electricity and perhaps even a dining room so Mother wouldn't have to cook.

So Charlie bought out my siblings and insisted on breathing life back into the neglected place. I got into the spirit as we scrubbed and painted and made multiple trips to the dump. It was a big effort. He tried to get the boys to help out, but they were in high school then and chose to stay in Madison with their friends so they wouldn't miss soccer practice or baseball. Uncomfortable with confrontation, I'd seldom argued with my own parents or with Charlie. When I thought Harry or Seth needed discipline, I let my husband handle it. I worried I'd lose the love of my boys for being too tough. In retrospect, I saw they might have more respect for me now if I'd been firmer.

Charlie built the screened porch on the front. He hired a carpenter to shore up the floor and fill in the cracks around the doors and windows. The mice were mostly eliminated. The logging road was leveled and graveled. My brother and sister were guaranteed lifetime visitation rights.

After that there were times I tried suggesting a vacation in Europe or New England, but Charlie was frugal (I'm being generous with that designation), and he'd argue, "We already own a perfectly lovely vacation paradise." I didn't really mind, although I'd always hoped the boys would find it more appealing. I treasured their carefully printed entries in the cabin journal "Cot a fish," Seth had written when he was five. "Ait it to."

Harry wrote, "I hate it here. Boooooringgg."

Maxine still tried to visit every summer with her husband, but Alan, out in Oregon, wasn't able get away as often as he'd like. We all felt a special kinship with the cabin, though. There was no family home to return to in Little Wolf—that had been sold by our parents when they moved into an assisted living facility, where they'd eventually passed away. So at Waters Edge, ancestral spirits mingled with our own as in no other place. Because of happy visits with my grandparents and then with Charlie, I knew I must feel this intimate connection most deeply of all.

Sleepy now, I lay in bed, closed my eyes, and did a mental inventory. The rafters above my bed were unpainted and held nails from which necessities hung: life preservers, baseball caps, plastic garbage bags that protected fresh toilet paper from mice. Flat awnings outside each window were held up with perpendicular logs you had to stand in place. Inside, each large twelve-light window swung open inside and up, held by a wooden latch, to reveal a nailed-in screen. There was an army cot against the front wall, below one of the windows. It was wooden and wobbly, now supporting my suitcase, a duffel bag, and shopping bags of books.

At the foot of my bed stood a huge and weighty wooden blanket chest that held Grandma Waters's mothballed quilts. The door in the center of the front wall led to the porch but was now and for the rest of the summer would be closed and barred against unwanted intruders! No more sleeping at night with only the rickety defense of flimsy screen doors and hooks and eyes.

Another window, to the right of the door, opened onto the porch. Below that, in the interior, was the eight-foot table with its unmatched chairs at each end and on one side and a bench against the wall.

In the center of the room stood the old pot-bellied woodstove that had not yet burned the cabin to the ground but had come close several times. When it was blazing, flames were visible through the cracks. When fired up, the stove would roar and the crooked stovepipe glowed red-hot. One summer, Harry's wet sneakers, hung next to it, melted from the heat.

Beneath the window, off to my right, was a sink and propane-stove combination taken from an old pop-up camper. The fuel tank underneath was probably empty; I had yet to check. Two burners were sufficient, and dishes were washed in the sink with heated lake water.

There was a dented metal kitchen cabinet Charlie had boldly rescued from a neighbor's curb one garbage day. It held more toilet paper, paper towels, a gallon jug of bleach, sweeping compound, bug spray.

Then the heavy back door in the corner, now latched, covered the screen door Molly had exited through last night.

Along the back wall (far from the head of my bed) hung various tools—push broom, regular broom worn to a point on one end, axe, metal dustpan, hatchet, handsaw, claw hammer, and splitting maul. Upon a wire plant stand, a gray enamel basin served as a sink for washing hands with a tin dipper to dunk into the nearby bucket that was filled from the lake morning and night.

And then there was the display of dog photographs. On the wall beside the cracked mirror over the washbasin (crack sealed with silver duct tape) were snapshots held with tacks. Below each, written in carpenter pencil, were the names of the dogs with dates of birth and death and in my childish printing, "THESE DOGS LOVED WATERS EDGE." Grandpa's English Setter, "Doc." That was before my time. So was "Beau," a little Boston Terrier. I recalled "Penny," Max's Cocker Spaniel who loved to swim. And Alan's mongrel, "Butch." who'd had his short life curtailed by a car in the street in front of our house. More recently, there was "Maggie," a sleek black Lab that Charlie and I had loved almost as much as we loved our boys, who'd grown up with her. And "Molly," who was . . . well, improving every minute, I hoped. I had taken Molly's snapshot the last time Charlie and I visited the cabin — the two of them were sitting at the end of the dock and I captured them in that golden hour of almost sunset. Molly was still a puppy. At home, I had a framed enlargement on my desk.

Most of the dogs—or their ashes—were here on the property, buried in a pet cemetery marked with crude crosses lovingly fashioned from branches and fishing line. Maggie's grave had a granite stone with her name engraved on it.

Next to the washbasin, four long shelves built into the back wall held glasses, cups, plates, pots and pans, Grandma's rolling pin, and odds and ends of utensils accumulated through the decades, most of them useless (an eggbeater that was stuck and wouldn't turn, a rusty fish scaler, a glass baby-food jar of lead sinkers, boxes of wooden matches— some of which were empty). Lamp wicks, a peanut-butter jar filled with paper matchbooks and candles, a jar of instant Maxwell House coffee that had been there at least a decade, OFF, Raid, plastic wine glasses, nibbled bars of soap that reminded me to add mouse traps to my list of things to get.

I opened my eyes and attempted to focus on the long table. My grocery bags, still packed, nearly hid an oblong tin breadbox, tan with red-and-green flowered trim and green lid, wooden knob. Papers were inside, clippings. Next to it, a round Campfire Marshmallow tin, white, with much wear, held numerous cabin journals.

CAMPFIRE
MARSHMALLOWS
THE ORIGINAL FOOD
Made By THE CAMPFIRE CO.
Milwaukee, Wis., Cambridge, Mass.
For Baking, Topping, Eating and Toasting
FINEST QUALITY

On the first, a tan composition book, Grandpa had written, "Please register in this book." The first page had the notation, "Cabin was erected July 12–17, 1926. Saw 10 deer. Heard wolves first night only." Thereafter followed notes from everyone who'd enjoyed the cabin's hospitality, except for those who'd inconsiderately chosen to record their stay on the walls. One entry in Dad's hand said, "Someone broke in cottage and took all heavy blankets and nothing else." Another, from the Little Wolf Boy Scouts, said, "Food sure tastes good up here and we have been taking care of plenty of it. This is a grand spot for the boys to explore, and we wish to thank Mr. Waters for making this possible."

Grandpa had always intended the cabin to be a retreat for family and friends, and the entries made through the years were fun to read on rainy days. I would do that again, surely, but I would refrain from reading Charlie's final entry, made years ago. It was his goodbye to the lake, a farewell to all the memories. I had not read it after he wrote it and knew I never could.

A glance at my alarm clock revealed it was only quarter after five. I was not going to fall asleep.

At six o'clock, I stumbled out of bed, pulled another of Charlie's old T-shirts from my duffel bag, took a metal pot and a big wooden spoon to scare away inquisitive wolves, and ventured to the outhouse. Behind the cabin, there was a one-holer with tin walls and roof. It listed at a slight angle. I unlocked the padlock and opened the door with furtive dread.

Charlie used to tackle this disgusting job. Dusty spider webs cloaked the corners, and a ragged roll of TP swung from a bent coat hanger—mice had been here, too. Almost at once, the little building swarmed with hungry mosquitoes.

I brushed the webs away with a broom and swept down the walls, cleared the floor. Then I sprayed everything with Lysol disinfectant—ceiling, walls, plastic toilet seat—until it was dripping wet. Finally, I gave it all a good rubdown with a roll of paper towels, and I dropped the wet towels into the gaping hole. I paid special attention to the toilet seat and the cavity beneath it that led to . . . the *underworld*, as Charlie and I used to refer to it when it got smelly. ("The underworld could use another layer of ashes.") A doctor had once told me that almost all the black widow spider bites he'd seen had come from people sitting in privies. I tried not to think of that each morning because it guaranteed constipation. Sometimes I took a stick and knocked it around the hole to scare any spiders away.

After I cleaned the outhouse, I went down to the lake with my improvised drum and plastic pail. My intention was to dip the pail into the lake and bring more water back up to the cabin so I could bathe, but standing on the dock I abruptly changed my mind.

Mist rose from the glossy surface of the water where no fisherman's boat had yet disturbed the sheen. I'd haul the Adirondack chairs down later, because I loved to watch the mist rise from the lake while sipping my coffee and breathing deeply of the brand-new day. In July, water lilies would open each morning to reveal golden centers, as if releasing the pure joy they'd enchanted every night. Sometimes we'd see the resident eagle that nested in a tall pine east of the cabin. It was an incomparable thrill to see that majestic bird circle high above and then dive swiftly, catch a pike in its talons, and fly away. Equally thrilling, but not as enjoyable, was the time the eagle swooped down to snatch an as-yet uncooked slab of sirloin from our charcoal grill. Memories.

If Molly were here, she would be splashing in the lake with blissful abandon. My eyes teared up again. I set the pail on the dock, kicked off my sandals, and cautiously stepped into the shallows to avoid any sharp rocks on the sandy bottom. The water was warm and only up to my knees, so I pulled off my shirt and made my way out to where the long grass was no longer floating. Then I scrubbed my skin with sand, scrubbed until it stung. I scoured Molly's blood from my breasts and my thighs, rinsed my hair in the lake, and again climbed up the hill to the cabin, with enough water in the pail to dip into throughout the day for washing dishes or my hands.

Towel-dried, dressed in clean clothes, I poured bottled water into the teakettle and heated it over the stove. I made a thick cup of instant coffee that tasted like poison. It settled with a punishing bitterness on my empty stomach and completed the penance begun with my brutal attack on the outhouse and my harsh morning bath. I couldn't stop blaming myself for Molly. She was so trusting. So full of energy and affection, absolutely nonjudgmental with her love. Surely I would know in my heart if she had died, but I worried that she was in pain.

I sat in my favorite red chair. I ran my fingertips over the chipped enamel finish of the breadbox. The lid didn't fit soundly anymore and the wooden knob on top was wobbly. Charlie spent many hours reading and rereading the yellowed clippings and curled paperback books tucked inside, all of them relating to John Dillinger. Grandpa Waters had been fascinated with the gangster and said he knew Carl Christensen, one of the innocent men who G-Men had accidentally shot during the raid at Little Bohemia, resulting in Dillinger's escape. It had taken place not far from here. Charlie loved to quiz Ginger, the bartender over at the Star Lake Saloon, about the Little Bohemia fracas. She apparently was acquainted with people who'd had connections to those involved.

Ginger Kovalcik, with her frizzy dyed saffron-colored hair and her feisty personality. I hoped she was still tending bar at the Star Lake Saloon. The little woman would be well into her seventies now, an orange hand grenade with a razor-sharp tongue. Was Ginger the reason why, in my panic, I instinctively headed for the Star Lake Saloon late last night when I needed help? She had always seemed so independent; nothing would frighten her.

Dr. Baker had said to wait until ten o'clock if I wanted to visit Molly. It was still too early to drive into Antler. My stomach cramped from the coffee with no food, but the thought of a fried egg made me gag. Perishables were still packed in a cooler, and they'd stay fresh for another day if I left it sealed. I would need ice.

One of the bags of groceries held a box of Entenmann's doughnuts. They had a nice crust of glazed sugar that made a satisfying crunch when you bit into them. After three donuts, I crawled into bed and took a nap.

❧

"Oh, for cripes sake, if it isn't Tallie Waters!" Ginger exclaimed later that afternoon when I stepped into the porch of the Star Lake Saloon. "My gosh, I haven't seen you since Hector was a pup!"

Not far from the sign along the gravel road that still declared "Thank Your Lucky Stars," the dark brown, two-story log building sat at the edge of Star Lake and hugged the slope of the shore, as if to keep from falling into the water. How could I have forgotten the unmatched chrome dinette sets against the outside wall, or the chorus of deer heads lined up opposite them? The bristling antlers and blindly staring glass eyes had terrified me as a child, when I was convinced the vacant eyes followed my every move.

"I'm so glad you're still hanging around," I admitted, with a surprising gush of tears. This was the same old Ginger, and she had not changed a bit. She still favored baggy blue jeans and sweatshirts with silly slogans like today's black one, which said "Does This Make My Aura Look Fat?"

"Where's the hubby?" Ginger asked with a warm hug of enthusiasm, looking around for Charlie.

"My husband passed away. I'm up here by myself this time."

"Oh, Tallie, I'm so sorry!" Ginger pulled back from the clumsy embrace. "Sorry I asked, even. That's just too bad. *Really* too bad. Charlie was always such a sweetheart, wasn't he? How'd he go? Oh, never mind. Was he sick for a very long time?"

I told her it was prostate cancer, but declined to go into detail. She probably attributed my tears to Charlie's death.

"Well, we've seen a lot of big changes at this place, too," Ginger offered sympathetically. She patted my shoulder. "Maybe you didn't notice, but this here's a brand new porch, right where you're standing. That's because the old one you'd remember was blown up a couple winters ago. You must've read about that. C'mon, sit down, Tallie. Take a load off. You look bushed!"

Ginger punched the faded cushions in the familiar metal glider and sat down there herself with a grunt. "Yup, blown to smithereens, and, long-story-short, we had a heck of a mess on our hands. I'll have to fill you in on the brouhaha sometime.

Just then a shiny black Labrador came padding out to the porch from inside the Saloon.

"Ah, Babe, . . . this here's Tallie Waters!" Ginger clapped her hands and the dog came over to her. "I'm sorry, I meant Tallie Lindquist."

I really lost it then and reached for Babe as though she were my own. The musky scent of her coat had me sobbing. I missed my Molly. Babe kindly responded by licking my salty tears with her soft, warm tongue.

Ginger, speechless for a change, didn't seem to know what to say.

"I'm sorry," I mumbled, hunting in my purse for a tissue. Ginger grabbed a stack of paper napkins from a dinette table.

"Well, as I was saying," she continued, "we had a great big environmental whoop-de-do here, and we sustained a bunch of damage. It wasn't all bad, though. Up there on the hill, you probably saw our brand-new Star Lake Inn. It's already gotten to be real popular. I'll show you around in just a minute. The loyal old folks still love our cute little housekeeping cottages, and we're full to the brim again this year, but the Inn's got some schmancy rooms like you wouldn't believe. Hand-made quilts and handmade furniture, and the food! Well, it's nothin' like the frozen pizza and hamburgers you still get down here at the bar, I'll tell you. A young couple runs the place. I know you'll like 'em. Oh, and this over here is Lily."

As if she were an afterthought, Ginger indicated a well-groomed, white-haired woman in light-blue nylon pants and matching jacket. Lily nodded hello. Narrow reading glasses perched low on her delicate nose while she dealt a game of solitaire on one of the tables. Charlie and I had enjoyed many Friday fish fries out here, perch and walleye, seated on this porch.

"Oh! I brought you something."

Ginger had been eyeing the large item I carried in my arms. "What you got there, a bunch of rubbish you want me to take off your hands?"

She briskly grabbed the tin breadbox and lifted the lid. "For cripes sakes, Tallie, it's all that Dillinger stuff of your Grandpa's. After saving it all these years, you're giving it away?"

"Ginger, what would I do with that?"

"But these clippings are originals! They'd bring a fortune on eBay!"

"She's big into eBay these days," Lily commented dryly, dealing cards from her deck without looking up.

"Lily's a relation by marriage to Hal Larkin, my old buddy who owned this place way back when," Ginger nodded toward Lily, much distracted by the clippings. "Your daddy knew Hal, remember? And your grandpa knew Hal's folks."

"Lily?" Ginger turned from the breadbox and announced in a loud voice, "This here's Tallie Waters. The Waterses have that slumpy green cabin over on Sundog. I've pointed it out to you lots of times. It kind of blends into the trees." To me, Ginger added, "Lily is Hannah's mother. You never met Hannah, I don't think. She was here when we had that commotion I mentioned earlier but she's off gadding about right now. And Hannah's daughter, Chloe, she's the young woman who runs the Inn with her husband, Eric. Hal Larkin, Hannah's uncle, he left the resort to her when he died. Well, Chloe and Eric have the cutest little baby. She just turned two. I don't know how Hannah can go away and not dote on Miriam. But Lily and I make up for it, don't we? Lily?"

My mind was wandering during Ginger's friendly chatter. The squeal of the porch glider was bringing back soothing recollections. My grandparents would bring me over here by boat after supper for an Eskimo Pie. While they visited, I would sit here obediently, trying to nibble chocolate from my ice cream bar before it began to melt and land on my pajamas.

"I bet you've got grandkids of your own by now," Ginger remarked. "Those two good-looking sons of yours must be all grown up with families of their own."

I nodded. There was an uncomfortable silence, so I added, "Yes, the boys are grown, and they're married. I have a granddaughter. I don't see any of them often; they live rather far away." I guess I sighed, because Ginger, who had an uncanny talent for reading people, interrupted my thoughts.

"Oh, sweetheart, is it Charlie?" she asked, massaging my arm. "Are you missing him a lot, being up here by yourself? Your eyes are so bloodshot, it looks like you hung one on. What's the matter, sweetie?"

"Well, I'm not really alone. I brought my dog, Molly. She looks a lot like Babe, actually—except she's brown."

"A chocolate Lab," Ginger said softly. "They're so pretty. Like a big Hershey bar."

"But last night, she was attacked by a wolf, right behind our cottage."

"NO!" Ginger slapped my arm rather painfully. "You can't be serious!" The bread box slid from her lap, crashed to the floor, and spilled its contents.

I found a photo of Molly in my handbag. Then I explained my blind and desperate race on unfamiliar roads and the eventual kindness of Bud Foster.

"How in the heck did you come across *Bud*?" Ginger asked, curiously. "Where'd you think you were headed for, anyway?"

"Here!" I replied. I decided not to mention the sleeping pills.

"Bud's a good enough guy, I guess," Ginger said warily. "Used to be the football coach in Antler. So you came across the Last Resort, huh?"

"I thought it was 'Lost Resort,'" I confessed. "But I was wearing my sunglasses. It was the middle of the night, and I was kind of a mess."

"Of course you were," Ginger grunted as she bent over to scoop up the clippings. "Good thing it wasn't one of them little dogs, you know, the yippy kind. Little appeteasers those are, to the timber wolves. At least a big dog like a Lab has got a fighting chance!"

I began to tell her that Charlie had insisted on giving Molly to me, but she interrupted, "Bud's kind of cute. The gals all like him."

"The girl's a new widow, Ginger. Don't go playing Cupid!"

"Over one year isn't new anymore, "Ginger muttered to Lily under her breath. But she squinted to carefully review each of the Dillinger pieces as she picked them up, one by one. "Now he'll for sure invite you to his Road Kill Picnic if you're here on the Fourth of July."

"Nauseating," Lily muttered. "The man throws a dinner with dead animals he finds along the road. I cannot imagine anything more repugnant."

"You've never gone," Ginger snorted. "I wouldn't miss it. Sure, it's a different kind of meal, but Bud can make a fricassee out of a beaver. When's the last time you ate raccoon, Tallie? Or woodchuck?"

"Or muskrat," Lily shivered. "I heard one time he even served skunk. Although it may have been an apocryphal skunk . . ." Her voice drifted off.

"Tallie knows we got ourselves some certified characters up here," Ginger nodded. She must be aware that she qualified as one of them, herself.

"I ate squirrel once, when I was a child," Lily added in a dreamy tone. "Pansy Colgate, a little classmate of mine who lived out on a farm, invited me to stay overnight. I suppose it was considered a treat to be served squirrel. I ate it to be polite. She said squirrel tasted similar to rabbit, but of course I'd never eaten rabbit before, either. I thought it might taste a bit nutty and have a flavor of acorn, but that could have been all in my mind. Not lot of meat as I recall, but a great many little bones. Rather a trial to pick them out. Gravy and bones, that's what eating squirrel was like. At least there were mashed potatoes."

Ginger clucked her tongue and shook her head, as Lily continued.

"Then Pansy's father cracked a raw egg in a glass of beer and drank it down in one draw. The whole egg, the whole beer. He gulped rudely when he reached the yolk at the bottom, then slammed his glass on the table and belched. When he smiled I could see he was missing his front teeth."

"Lily—" Ginger interrupted.

"A *wolf*, you said?" Lily asked, returning to the present. "Well, it won't be long before Bud serves wolf at one of those meals. Wolf rarebit. Wolf stew. Marinated wolf with macerated mushrooms . . ."

"Lily, that's enough." Ginger said. "Yes, we got more wolves up here now than we used to," she turned to me, "but it's not such a big deal. We've got to learn to live with 'em just like anything else. It's the North-woods, right? Not Milwaukee or Chicago."

"And how is your dog today, Tallie?" Lily continued, ignoring Ginger. "Have you contacted the veterinary clinic?"

"Actually, I'm just on my way back from there. Molly's still sedated, but Dr. Baker says she's doing well. Her wounds weren't as severe as they could have been, and I may be able to pick her up tomorrow."

"Tomorrow and tomorrow and tomorrow," Lily proclaimed, shuf-fling the deck.

"That one's turned into a regular poetess since she moved here," Ginger remarked under her breath. "Be careful not to let your guard down, or she'll share some of her original verses."

"And that one," Lily pointed a manicured red fingernail at Ginger, "still swears like a pirate and dyes her hair that hideous pumpkin color that matches a monk's robe. And of all things, she insists on having C-SPAN on the TV constantly. With all due respect—"

"Oh, for Pete's sake," Ginger snapped. "With all due respect, pretty soon you'll say I snore louder than you."

"Well, that's definitely true," Lily sniffed, dealing another game. "I'm surprised the people who live across the lake have not complained of the roar. The roar of your snore. We live up on Lake Sickle Moon," she explained to me. "We built a cottage there together a couple years ago. An experiment in insanity."

"Oh, we bitch a lot, but we get along just fine," Ginger laughed. "Lots of teasing."

"And lots of Canasta. We play a lot of Canasta."

"For money," Ginger added.

"We keep track," Lily said. "Thus far no currency has changed hands, in point of fact." Then she added, "With all due respect," and sent me a sly little smile.

"That's because you're so far in the hole," Ginger muttered. "Oh for cripes sake, look at this! I forgot all about it."

I took the paper she handed me and saw a letter from the Smithsonian Institution. "In response to your recent inquiry, we can assure you that anatomical specimens of John Dillinger are not, and have never been, in the collections of the Smithsonian Institution."

"You know what that's about?" Ginger asked, her black penciled eyebrows arched nearly up to her hairline. "It's about his joy stick."

"Excuse me?" Lily interrupted, "Are you referring to someone's penis?"

"John Dillinger's," Ginger responded heatedly. "His schlong was supposed to be eighteen inches long."

I burst into laughter.

"Go ahead and laugh," Ginger said with a serious expression. "There's probably a picture of it in here somewhere. It's sticking up with a hard-on like you wouldn't believe. He was covered up with a sheet, but his cock made a pole for a pup-tent big enough for a midget. The Smithsonian Institution in Washington, D.C., pickled it, and J. Edgar Hoover kept it in a jar on his desk. Well, that's what the gossip said at the time, anyway. Now that would've been a real *Washington monument!*"

She was paging even more enthusiastically through the clippings.

"And here's a clip that says his penis measured twenty-three inches!"

"Oh, mercy," Lily said, covering her eyes and putting down her cards.

"Twenty-three inches long. That's one heck of a pecker!" Ginger began reading aloud, "*Hoosier Folk Legends*, 1982, includes a tale that Dillinger's penis was twenty-three inches long and a genuine handicap to lovemaking, because the amount of blood it took to maintain an erection often caused him to pass out."

"Like a giraffe's neck," I said, recalling the Lydia Pinkham account of Billy Black and his tribulations.

"Excuse me," Lily said. She went inside the Saloon and closed the door.

"Delicate flower," Ginger wisecracked. "Probably has to clear her throat."

"This isn't serious, right?" I asked.

"Of course not," Ginger chuckled. "It was the way the arm was bent and sticking up under the sheet when they took the corpse to the morgue. The newspapers got a picture of it, and tall tales started to grow taller. I just can't help teasing Lily sometimes; she's a good soul but gullible as all get-out."

I had to blow my nose again, this time from laughing so hard.

"They did take his brain, though," Ginger said. "But I heard it got lost."

"Dillinger's brain?"

"I guess they wanted to study it. His father supposedly sold it. But the brain got misplaced somehow."

"Is this another joke?"

"Nope, not this time. The coroner's office said they divided it up for science. And then their tests destroyed the whole thing, except for part that was placed in his stomach and buried by mistake."

I leaned back on the glider and relaxed. It felt so good to laugh.

"You're good medicine, Ginger," I said, grasping her freckled hand and bringing it to my cheek.

"Tell me about the wolf," she asked. "Did you really see it?"

I assured her I did. "A wildlife specialist from the USDA will investigate the area behind the cabin where she was attacked, along with the DNR warden. There's some paperwork, apparently. It's a big deal."

"Paperwork?" Lily inquired, returning to the porch.

"About the wolves! She's talking about *wolves,*" Ginger explained, impatiently. "You know, it's those wolves we got up here. *Woooo, woooooooOOoooo.*" She imitated a howl. "Those three or four wolves, probably; the Sickle Moon Pack. A lot of the wolves now wear radio collars," Ginger explained to me. "Any given day, the Department of Natural Resources can tell you almost exactly where the pack is at. The DNR does flyovers every week to track them."

"Flying wolves," Lily said. She again took her seat and adjusted the colorful silk scarf she had knotted artfully around her neck. "That's what they call what they do, 'flying wolves.' I find it a very poetic term. Are you now concerned about staying alone at your cabin because of the wolves? If you would feel any safer, there's a vacant cottage here—we had a cancellation just yesterday. And pets are allowed."

"We've even got a spare bedroom at our place, LilyPad, if you and Molly want to bunk with two old geezers," Ginger offered.

Lily looked up from her solitaire, and Ginger was watching me.

"I'm going to stay at my cabin for now," I said. "But thank you."

Ginger decided it was time to show me around the Inn, so the two of us wandered up the hill while Lily dealt yet another layout and kept an eye out for customers—most of whom were doubtlessly fishing out on the lake. As we left the porch and began climbing up the steps, we could hear Lily proclaiming: "Flying wolves. Furious wolves. They leap, take wing, and soar through our decadent dreams."

"The poetess is off and running," Ginger muttered. "We got out of there just in time."

❧

The Star Lake Inn stood on a hill above and behind the building that was the Saloon and lodge. Built of light-colored logs, the center of the building extended toward the water like a prow of glass and rose several stories to "bring the outdoors in," as decorators liked to crow. A dining room, also suitable for meetings, was located on one half of the prow; on the other side was a gathering room with a massive stone fireplace, leather sofas, coffee tables, and a bar. The kitchen was behind the dining room part of the structure. Guest rooms were behind the other and above—they could accommodate over a hundred guests, Ginger said.

We found Chloe Swann in the kitchen, rolling out a piecrust. A folded red bandana held her short, dark hair with a touch of natural curl off her forehead. She reminded me of a childhood friend, although taller and more composed than my old pal Hannah, and she smiled more readily. In fact, Hannah Larkin Swann, who had been several years behind me in school at Little Wolf, was Chloe's mother. Now I knew why Lily had looked familiar! Hannah was currently in Iceland and would not be back until after Labor Day, when I'd be gone. I told Chloe to give Hannah my regards and to tell her how impressed I was with her resort. "My father knew your Grandpa Larkin," I told Chloe. "He was named Russell, like my grandpa, but his nickname was Rusty, to tell them apart."

"Rusty was a pharmacist, too," Ginger said. "What's Eric up to right now?

By then I was entertained by little Miriam, who stood on a chair next to Chloe, playing with a piece of dough. I wiped her runny nose with a towel, then washed my hands and helped her roll out a little tart to fill with jam.

"I have a granddaughter," I told Chloe, "but I never see her. She lives in New York, and her parents have never brought her up here."

"You're welcome to come over and play with Miriam any time you'd like," Chloe offered. "I have my hands full! Right now, I think she needs changing."

Chloe pulled her floury apron over her head, took Miriam from me, and left the room.

"Be right back," she said over her shoulder.

I grabbed Chloe's apron and continued with the piecrust, because it seemed like a normal thing to do and I didn't want it to dry out. One of my few talents: I can whip up a pie with only a moment's notice. Apples, already peeled and sliced, were in a nearby bowl. I added them to the crust, measured sugar, cinnamon, and nutmeg; sprinkled the mixture over the apples; topped it with a few dabs of butter; and rolled out the top crust and crimped it in place before Chloe returned.

"You're a chef!" Chloe exclaimed.

"After my husband died, I did a little catering," I said. "But I began cutting back. I only had one wedding reception to get out of the way before I came up here."

Ginger brought Chloe's husband, Eric, into the kitchen—he'd been doing some work on the new fish-cleaning station. He was taller than Chloe, slim but well-muscled and wore jeans torn off at the knee. He removed his faded Green Bay Packers cap to reveal a receding hairline and reached out with a well-calloused hand. He was friendly, but it was clear he wanted to get back to his carpentry. I could see why he and Chloe were a boon to the resort; they had energy and imagination and were an attractive couple.

⚮

Bud stopped over in late afternoon, as he'd said he might. He came by boat. I was glad to see him but tried to suppress the still-warm memory of being encircled in his arms.

"To tell you the truth, I'm not sure I could find your place by land," he admitted. "Besides, it's closer this way."

He told me Dr. Baker called him after I left the clinic that morning, and I could pick up Molly tomorrow afternoon around two.

"The game warden will be there too, Dave Jensen. He'll talk with the doc and inspect Molly's wounds, no doubt have a few questions for you. The thing is, the State of Wisconsin will pay the vet's bills if it's a proven wolf injury. That's standard procedure."

He'd brought along a pizza from the bar that wasn't exactly hot, and I had no way of reheating it, but we sat on the porch, away from the mosquitoes, and enjoyed the meal anyway. I had some cold Pepsi in my cooler and some beer, but Bud didn't drink alcohol.

"So this is your way of taking me out to dinner?" I joked.

He blushed. That was cute. He was so much younger, yet I could make him blush. I felt kind of empowered. And it didn't even matter if Charlie was watching; the pizza was just a neighborly gesture, a friendly thing to do.

Another nice gesture was the cell phone that Bud brought for me to use. He said it would work in the woods and had something to do with the tower or the company or the speed—I wasn't sure. He had already put his phone number in it on speed-dial so I could call if I needed help. "I don't want you to be out here without a phone," he said. "Not like you were last night."

We were finished with our pizza then, so I took Bud back behind the cabin to show him where I found Molly on the ground.

"Do you have a gun?" he asked.

"No," I laughed. "Of course we've had lots of hunters here, but we've never needed a gun for protection."

"You should have a gun," Bud said. "Just to make a noise and scare off predators, if nothing else. Let me see what I can find."

I noticed that he'd left a manila envelope on the porch table. "Some information about wildlife," he said, pointing. "Things you ought to know about wolves and what the local opinions are." Now he seemed to be in a hurry to get away.

He gave me a swift kiss on the cheek when he said goodbye. I stood on the dock and waved as he swung the boat out into the lake. I waited until the wake stopped lapping the dock before I went in to my darkening room, where I had neglected to leave a lantern lit and forgotten to bait the mousetraps. Skittering mice along the rafters would embroider all sides of my lonely night.

3

If you closed the door, three bullet holes provided the only light. It was also claustrophobic in there, so I usually sat in the outhouse with the door slightly ajar. Not very wide, in case fishermen trolled the bay west of the cabin for walleyes, but just enough to view the balsam and hemlock and the pet cemetery on a rise of land nearby.

Now, of course, I'd left it open to watch for wolves. At my feet was my improvised "wolf drum," the wooden spoon and metal pot. I didn't know if it would scare away a wolf, but it made me feel more at ease.

The space smelled of disinfectant and mosquito repellant—another reason for the open door, despite the rain; it was probably poisonous to breathe. I liked the sound of rain on the metal roof, but my feet were getting wet.

Under cover, mosquitoes swarmed thicker than ever. I was constantly waving them away and getting more itchy bites on my bare thighs. I heard a boat motor approach suspiciously close. Then the motor was killed, and Ginger's voice called, "Yoo hoo, Tallie! Anybody home?"

As usual, I reached behind to flush and, as usual, felt foolish. Why was the act of flushing so satisfying? Was it the sense of closure? Merely standing, pulling up my pants and walking away, seemed sort of indecent. And I had to go inside the cabin to wash my hands.

Ginger and Lily were making their way up the path from the dock. There are certain friendly conventions of casual lake life: it is customary to wave a greeting at everyone you see on the water, and they always wave back. People are laid back about dropping in when they're floating past, or calling out helloooos, or asking "What's for supper?" if you are seen using your outdoor grill.

In their wind-flipped plastic ponchos, the two women resembled yellow angels, fluttering toward the cabin. Ginger said she'd never been inside and eagerly surveyed every detail after she shucked her poncho on the porch. Lily, dripping, eyed the still filled grocery bags before she stared at my unmade bed and its bloodstained sheets.

"I'm going to the Laundromat when I pick up Molly, this afternoon," I explained. "I know the bed's a mess. The whole cabin is. I haven't had much time to clean, or even unpack."

"Gloomy in here," Ginger commented bluntly, poking around. "And you sure could use one of them scented candles. I suppose I could survive like this without indoor plumbing and so forth, but I'd get me some skylights so it's not so dark when it rains, like today. Help circulate fresh air when it's hot, too. Eric and his buddies could fix you up with a couple of skylights from Home Depot. Might be a good idea to slap a new roof on while they're at it."

Water was dripping down along the stovepipe and onto the floor. I placed a basin in the center of the puddle.

Then I set a couple of Coleman lamps on the table. I found their noisy hiss objectionable, but their white brightness did illuminate the room. I dug a package of Oreos out of my groceries and a fresh box of teabags.

"Take off your wrap, Lily, and have a seat," Ginger said gruffly. She and Lily each pulled out a chair. "We'll be here a while. Raining outside like a cow pissin' on a flat rock."

I was heating fresh water in the teakettle when Ginger revealed the topic that was on her mind.

"Now, this probably isn't the best time to bring this up, Tallie, what with your problem with the wolf and your dog and all, but I got something I want to propose, and I don't want you to say no until you hear me out, okay?"

She tugged a folded bundle of papers from under her sweatshirt and slapped it on the table while I blew dust out of three mugs and added hot water from the kettle.

"It's about those Dillinger papers you brought over yesterday. I got to reading through them again last night and got a terrific idea. It's a humdinger, if I do say so myself. All you have to do is agree to go along with it, and we'll be all set."

"A bringer of a humdinger," Lily pointed at Ginger and smiled at me. "Is she a singer? The one I'm indicating with my finger?"

"Zip it," Ginger told Lily. "Tallie, close a window—it's getting chilly in here."

The rain was now accompanied by gusts of cool air. I shut the window behind the table. The pot-bellied stove was an iffy measure, but I crumpled a newspaper, threw in some kindling, and struck a match. Briefly, I caught a glimpse of the bloody clothes I'd thrown in there the night of Molly's attack. Then everything suddenly went up in flames with a very loud whoosh. It didn't take long before the metal chimney was glowing bright red. We could see flames through the cracks in the stove, and when the chimney shifted slightly, a shower of rust fell down.

"Put it out!" Lily shouted. "Throw some water on it!"

I didn't hesitate very long before doing just that.

"Cripes, you better invest in a decent fireplace or a safer stove," Ginger complained. "You could have burnt this place down and us with it!"

"You're full of all kinds of helpful suggestions this morning," I said, sourly. "Are you warmer?"

I passed out the teabags and tore open the Oreos.

"Dillinger," I said eventually. Impassively. "How silly of me. I thought with Charlie gone that tiresome subject was out of the way. What do you have in mind?"

"Sugar, please? Without ants?" Lily had investigated the sugar bowl in the center of the table.

"I'm sorry," I replied. "I didn't buy any fresh sugar."

"Scrape off some of that filling from your Oreo, Lil," Ginger offered. "You won't know the difference. Tallie, you got a clean knife around here?"

I pulled a knife from the silverware drawer of the cabinet and furtively checked my watch. How long before I could say I had an appointment in town?

"I may have told you before that I knew Billie Frechette," Ginger began.

"Lily did not meet Billie," Lily said, "I know it sounds silly—"

"Not now, we've got business to discuss." Ginger was impatient. She made a space to flatten out her papers, and I observed a hand-drawn map.

"Billie Frechette. She was a girlfriend of John Dillinger's."

I told her I was aware of that.

"At what time?" Lily asked.

"When they were robbing those banks," Ginger responded. "Drink that hot tea, Lily, you're shivering like a dog passing peach pits."

Lily obediently sipped her tea. Ginger's eagerness to explain her idea was spilling over.

"Billie was a girl?" Lily asked.

"I don't give a hoot if it's raining tomcats and Shih Tzus, Lily, I'm about ready to make you wait in the rain."

"Let's all slow down and take a deep breath," I suggested with a sigh. "I know Billie Frechette hung around with the Dillinger gang." My face grew hot as I explained, but I could not reveal why. "These gangsters were like rock stars. And molls like Billie were their groupies."

Ginger helped herself to another Oreo and explained she'd done some Googling last night and discovered that "moll" had originally been a name for female pickpockets. During Prohibition, women who hung out with gangsters were called "gun molls."

I didn't know the word's origin. Interesting. I tore open a package of prunes.

Lily stirred more Oreo filling into her tea.

43

"Well, these molls who hung out with the Dillinger gang, some folks thought they were floozies," Ginger continued. "Some girls thought it was sexy and glamorous to consort with gangsters and live it up, you know? And attitudes toward bank robbers were more lenient then, because during the Depression some of the banks royally screwed their customers. Robbers who took on the banks were looked on as heroes. Charlie, being a banker, must've known all about that, Tallie. Maybe that's why he liked to read those gangster stories your grandpa held onto.

"When John Dillinger and Baby Face Nelson and the rest of the gangs made their getaways, everybody watched and kept track because the whole shebang was a real-life adventure serial. Or so I've been told. Naturally, it was before my time."

"Naturally," Lily cracked. "And then there was J. Edgar Hoover. He naturally became perturbed."

"Hoover got obsessed, all right. Everywhere you looked, you saw a poster with Dillinger's face on it, smiling that crooked smile. The problem was, Dillinger wasn't such a bad-looking guy and lots of folks encouraged him on to keep on going."

"And the molls?" I asked, trying to move things along.

"When things got too hot and their men took off, well, too bad for the molls. They were usually the ones who got captured and put in jail. Cops called 'em whores because the gangsters paid for everything, even abortions. Sad thing was, the first thing the molls did when they had some money was to get their teeth fixed."

I began chewing another prune, then washed it down with tea.

"Tallie, how many are going to be enough, and how many will be too many? I never know," Lily said.

"Just one more," I remarked with my mouth full, and then I closed the bag. "Want one?"

"No, thank you, Natalie," Lily replied. "But at my age, a good BM in the morning is very satisfying."

"With all due respect, I had the floor." Ginger glared at Lily.

"I'm sorry, Ginger. Did your friend Billie have bad teeth?"

Ginger chided her friend. "Did you take your pills this morning?"

"Somebody get up on the wrong side of the bed?" I rolled my eyes.

Ginger muttered a few more words under her breath, then inquired, "Where's a deck of cards?" I found one in the metal cabinet, hoping it was complete. Ginger got Lily started with a hand of solitaire.

"Okay, now let's get down to the really important stuff." Ginger's voice assumed a conspiratorial tone.

"Billie Frechette wasn't at Little Bohemia when the FBI flushed out the gang; she was stuck in a federal jail. Got caught in a sting in Chicago a year before, and it was the last time she saw her Johnny alive. He went up to Michigan to break her out, but she warned him it was a fortress, and when he saw the place, he knew for sure that it was."

I wondered where Ginger was going with this story, but I had an hour to kill.

"I'm getting the impression you knew her well," I told Ginger.

"Well, that's what I'm getting at, Tallie. Hold your horses. Okay. Billie's real name was Evelyn. Evelyn Frechette, and she was only twenty-five when she met John Dillinger. She said it happened like it did in the movies: they fell in love on the north side of Chicago at a cabaret. Evelyn said she liked his eyes."

"His eyes," I said. "What about them?"

"That they had a 'carefree twinkle,' or something like that. And they seemed to go right through her. Then he smiled a little bit with the corner of his mouth, you know, like in his pictures?"

"You read this on the Internet?"

"Oh, for Pete's sake, the woman told me herself! And then he said, 'Where have you been all my life?'"

That was rather impressive, I had to admit.

"I guess I'll have to cut to the chase," Ginger said, slapping the table and shaking her head, as if she'd hoped to draw out the suspense as long as possible. "For a long time, Billie—or Evelyn—thought his name was Jack Harris. That's how he'd been introduced to her, and she didn't read newspapers. Evelyn said she fell in love with what he was, not because of who he was, and you can't argue yourself out of falling in love."

"I thought she called him 'The Big Bad Wolf.'" Apparently Lily was not totally absorbed in solitaire.

"That was when Evelyn was being hauled off to jail, Lily. The feds were putting her on a plane and she turned around and said, 'Watch out for John. He's the big, bad wolf, you know.' She liked to play with their heads. Anyways, she told me all sorts of stuff. You know how women are when they confide in you, after awhile? They begin to trust you and tell you all kinds of things. This 'Jack Harris' always seemed to have plenty of money: he bought her jewelry and pets and fancy clothes, things she'd never had, because her family was very poor. But when she asked him what he did, he just said he had a little racket and let it go at that. So she did, too. They went places and saw things, and she had a dreamy look in her eyes when she told me that, even then after all those years. I think she still loved him."

"This is cutting to the chase?" Lily remarked.

"With all due respect, Lily, I wish you'd shut up! Evelyn and Jack Harris went dancing every night, and she wondered why he was such a poor dancer, but he'd been in prison and hadn't learned to dance. When they didn't go dancing, they went to the movies. His favorite movie was *The Three Little Pigs*."

I couldn't help interrupting. "Do you think he really saw himself as the Big Bad Wolf?"

Ginger pointedly ignored my query.

"One night after a movie, 'Jack Harris' finally told Evelyn he was John Dillinger and asked her if she'd like to set up housekeeping with him."

I didn't want to disrupt Ginger's tale, but it was taking a long time to get to the point.

"*Evelyn*, after all was said and done—and by that, I mean Dillinger was eventually sent to prison in Indiana, where he broke out with a gun he carved out of wood, and the gang had to hide out in Florida and then in Tucson and St. Paul and I won't go into that—"

I was relieved.

"Evelyn walked into that trap in Chicago and was sent off to prison. Later she published a memoir and went on the road with a vaudeville show featuring her as 'John Dillinger's Famous Gun Moll Sweetheart' where she lectured on why crime doesn't pay. When I met her, years later, she was married to a very nice man from Shawano. Art Tic."

"Tic," I said.

"Yes. And the Tics spent their summer vacations at Star Lake."

Now Ginger's story was beginning to make sense.

"Evelyn married Art when she was fifty-eight. He was a quiet gentle-man, maybe twenty years older than her. He was a state game warden and also a barber. He was very protective. Never wanted her to work outside the home. They lived on Shawano Lake, but they liked to come up here, and they always took the same cottage, Arcturus, way down on the south end. So I got to know her. We enjoyed the Tics' visits to the resort. They always paid their bills right on time and cleaned up their cabin real nice before they left. Evelyn and I had some long talks while Art was out fishing and sometimes late at night. Of course, I asked her plenty of questions because the subject of gangsters always fascinated me. And some of the things she told me came back to me last night and got me to thinking. 'I've had one hell of a life,' she used to say. Then she'd tell me another tidbit about all she'd been through."

"Evelyn Tic," Lily said, sweeping up a completed solitaire spread and tapping the closed deck on the oilcloth. "Evelyn Tic. I suppose that's better than 'Woody.'"

I was anxious to get cleaned up and go into Antler to pick up Molly, and this seemed like a convenient break.

"I'm really sorry, ladies," I told them both. "I have to bathe and get dressed so I can get to the vet by two. The conservation warden will have some questions, and—"

"No problem," Ginger said archly, backing her chair away from the table. "We took a chance, just dropping in on you like this. Looks like the rain's let up now so we can make our getaway, Lily!"

Okay, there was something not quite right. Obviously, Ginger had come by with more than just a recount of the Life and Times of John Dillinger and Billie Frechette. I'd hurt her feelings.

"You said you had an idea," I reminded her.

"A humdinger," Lily replied.

"I'll just spill the beans right now, and you can mull it over."

Ginger leaned forward again, arms firmly crossed in front of her on the table.

"Evelyn wrote to me from her home in Shawano, in the 1950s. In one her letters, she asked if she could bring her little dog along that summer and swore it was well-behaved and wouldn't pee or poop in the cottage. She said she had a little dog like that once before but it got lost when Dillinger's gang was at Little Bohemia and got flushed. One of the other girls was supposed to be caring for it because she was in prison, but it got scared by the bullets from all the machine guns and ran away. So, of course, we said, 'Sure, bring the little dog along.'"

"And this has to do with *what*?"

"A clipping that she sent me with that particular letter. I found it last night among some other stuff I saved in my top dresser drawer. Here it is."

Ginger placed a yellowed piece of newspaper in front of me.

"Don't take the time to read it; I'll tell you what it says."

But I was already skimming the news item:

Dillinger chuckled as he told about making monkeys out of the federal agents. "I heard the shots down by the highway and knew Hoover's little helpers were out there. So I grabbed a pistol and the suitcase of money. I ran 500 yards straight north of the lodge. There was a semi-circle formed by three trees, and I dug a hole in the ground and shoved the suitcase into it. I threw some dirt and leaves on top of the suitcase. It won't look like I was ever there."

"Where did this come from?" I asked.

"Hell's bells, I got no idea. I forgot all about it. But Evelyn sent it to me. And when I found it last night, I got this flash of revelation."

"She wants to search for buried treasure," Lily said.

"Dammit, Lily!"

"Treasure?" I echoed.

"The loot. The missing suitcase," Ginger said, annoyed, her surprise balloon had been burst. "There were lots of rumors at the time that Dillinger buried some loot on his way outta there, but this is the first I've seen it in his own words. And the loot has never been found," she asserted, her voice rising. "Three trees in a semicircle. The three of us could find where that was! It's just waiting for us! Three trees, three of us! If that's not a sign, I don't know what is!"

"Oh . . . I don't think so," I replied with sincerity after blowing my nose in a square of paper towel to cover my amusement at the absurdity of Ginger's harebrained notion. "After Molly's encounter with the wolf, I'm not going to venture out into the woods. And the mosquitoes are ferocious, not to mention the deer flies and wood ticks! I'm sorry. Count me out. You and Lily can split the loot in half, instead of three ways."

Ginger's animated expression collapsed, so I added, "Besides, if Dillinger buried a cardboard suitcase, your 'treasure' will only be crumbs, after seventy years in the ground."

"What if it wasn't cardboard?" Lily inquired idly, again gathering her cards.

"It could've been a leather valise," Ginger said, "or a metal one. The museum upstairs at Little Bohemia has some personal stuff they left behind."

"I've been to the Dillinger museum," I argued. "I've seen it several times."

The "museum" was a pathetic but oddly fascinating display laid out in a glass case in a room still riddled with bullet holes. At one time, the resort had exhibited the relics in a separate cottage and hired John

Dillinger's father as its caretaker. I'd seen an old postcard with a photo of the man and the original museum; admission was then 25 cents.

"I have never seen the museum," Lily declared. "And I would very much like to see it one day."

"How about this Friday night?" Ginger asked, pleading now. "They got a really good fish fry. Not as good as ours, of course, but you want to meet us there, Tallie? We can talk about it some more. You might even change your mind by then."

She seemed so determined, so hopeful, that I really hated to turn her down. After all, I'd been the one to dump the Dillinger clippings on her, causing this resurgence of interest in the subject.

"Molly's still going to be pretty fragile, and I won't want to leave her here."

"Well, by the looks of the weather forecast, it won't be too hot to let her rest in the car," Ginger replied. "Snug as a bug. She likes riding in the car, doesn't she? And by Friday, I'll bet she's feeling almost her old self again."

"I need to speak with the conservation warden and some guy who's a wildlife specialist."

"Just how long do you plan on having them stick around? All week?"

"I'd like to see the museum," Lily repeated softly.

"I'm absolutely not in favor," I said, "of joining you in any treasure hunt. Let's make that clear. But the fish fry at Little Bohemia, I know it's very good. And I suppose it wouldn't hurt to get together and listen to the rest of your crazy proposal."

"We won't have to make any definite decisions until after dessert," Ginger agreed, smiling. "Maybe Eric can tend bar for me a couple of hours that night."

She folded her papers and stuck them back beneath her sweatshirt. "Then it's all set. Six o'clock okay? Tie your plastic rain scarf back on Lily, we're going back to the boat."

I offered to give them a ride on my way into town, but Ginger insisted they were tough old birds, and the rain had, indeed, diminished.

Little Bohemia. The supper club had held special significance for Charlie and me, but I could never share our private personal history with anyone else. Charlie liked to play fantasy games. On the outside, he may have resembled a stuffy banker, but he had a fondness for imaginative foreplay. At Little Bohemia, Charlie would become one of Dillinger's mob and I would pretend to be his gangster moll. Oh, I knew all about molls. Somewhere in this cabin, in the blanket chest beneath Grandma Waters's hand-sewn quilts, was a plastic storage box that held my "moll" clothes: a wide variety of sexy outfits from Victoria's Secret, all with garter belts—including a black lace teddy with a push-up bra and split crotch, fishnet stockings, a pair of killer high-heeled pumps and dangly earrings studded with rhinestones. I enjoyed our fantasy as much as he. In bed after our Little Bohemia rendezvous, Charlie was a vigorous and dynamic lover like he never was in our four-poster at home. "Molly"? Of course her name was an allusion to "moll."

❧

I washed my hair (with shampoo this time) so I would appear a little more civilized. I even wore clothing of my own instead of Charlie's—clean jeans, fresh shirt.

Conservation Warden Dave Jensen had finished examining Molly's wounds and was writing up his report when I arrived at the clinic. He seemed like a nice man, behind his aviator glasses and big moustache. His impressive uniform was comprised of dark gray pants, light gray shirt, silver badge, and handgun. With him was Tom Scott, wildlife specialist from the US Department of Agriculture, who also wore a gray shirt, though with a pair of jeans. Scott told me he'd been a fur trapper before he was hired to do this job. "I'm the guy who follows the tracks and signs and tells the story," he said.

I was also introduced to Dr. Baker's veterinary assistant, who went by the name of "Beemer." Seems he was fond of BMW motorcycles, when almost everyone up north drove Harleys. I'd probably have guessed Beemer rode a motorcycle. He was tall and gangly, with a shaved head, wore two "diamond" earrings, and had a tattoo of a snake around his neck. "Do you wear a helmet?" I asked (because HOGs were notorious for not wearing helmets). Beemer shrugged. I took that for an embarrassed yes and gathered he took some flak for doing so.

Molly's beautiful chocolate coat had been shaved around her wounds, revealing brown skin beneath. The sutured wounds were ragged and lined with dried blood. She was excited to see me, hopping and slapping her tail. "Try to keep her calm," Dr. Baker advised. "She shouldn't be running or jumping for a week or two."

With Labs, was there anything more impossible than trying to keep them still? Molly wore a large, white plastic cone around her neck to keep her from licking her injuries. "If you find it's bothering her, you can remove it in a day or two, then watch and see if she's licking her wounds. If she isn't, then you can just leave it off."

Beemer filled a plastic bag with antibiotics and tranquilizers—to keep her quiet. I noticed he tossed in a dog biscuit, which was a nice touch.

To write up his report for the Department of Natural Resources, Warden Jensen needed some specifics about the attack. I told him what had happened. This is what he wrote:

Chocolate Lab—$800 vet bill:
Comments: On Monday, June 7 at 1:45 a.m., Natalie Waters Lindquist put her Labrador retriever outside her cabin on Lake Sundog, and when the dog did not return she went out to find her, at around 2:00 a.m. The dog was fighting with something in the woods about 50 yards from the cabin, where Lindquist usually parks her car. When she approached the site with a flashlight, she saw her dog, and approximately 15 feet away she saw a wolf, which she was able to scare away. The dog was behaving submissively and had punctures on the left flank, right groin, left lateral hindquarter, a 3 inch cut on the right lateral hindquarter, and a deep canine puncture in the neck that was

bleeding profusely. Lindquist was able to intervene before the dog sustained a more serious injury.

Warden Jensen said Molly's wounds appeared to have been caused by a wolf, and if the DNR agreed, they would pay for her care. He and Scott followed Molly and me back to the cabin so I could show them the site where the attack occurred. When I parked and let her out, Molly immediately headed for the lake. I had her on a leash, but she pulled so hard that I tripped over a root, fell flat on my face, and let go. I had to yell angrily at Molly (which made me feel stupid in front of the men and sorry for Molly), and my good dog obediently returned, content to sniff around the area where the wolf had been. I had to call Molly again when she started to head off into the woods "on the trail."

"You're going to think I have no control over my dog," I tried to joke. "*And* Dr. Baker said I should keep her quiet for a couple of days!"

Warden Jensen and Scott took a while to look around the site of the attack. After the men discussed it, the following was added to the official report:

> The area is heavily forested. Wolf tracks were not plainly visible. With Dr. Baker's description of the injuries when the dog was brought in and Lindquist's description of the canine she witnessed attacking her dog, the location of injuries, and the diameter of the canine punctures, this complaint is classified as a probable wolf injury. Because of the remoteness of this location, adjacent large blocks of contiguous forest-land, and low density of livestock and other domestic animals, I recommend not implementing lethal control at this site.
> —D. Jensen. T. Scott.

Scott gave me a form to submit to the Wisconsin DNR Wolf Program Coordinator for possible reimbursement for Molly's wounds.

I had made notes of questions I wanted to ask, like how to keep wolves off my land. I told the men that I'd emptied the chamber pot that morning by sprinkling urine around the perimeter of the cabin. But Jensen said that probably wouldn't scare any wolves, just indicate someone had been there. He did say yelling, shouting, and shooting guns in the air might scare a wolf if I saw one. But I wanted something more substantial, something I could count on. Maybe a fence?

"Wolves and coyotes can leap over a fence," Scott said.

"So what's the point of going to my cabin to be free, when I have to fence myself in?" I objected with a wry smile.

There was a method called fladry, or flagging, that I might use to surround the cabin, Jensen said, at least temporarily. It would involve stringing a wire and hanging from it fabric or some other material that would flap in a breeze and keep wolves from traversing the line. Fladry would work for a while, probably all summer, until the wolves got used to it and it just became part of the landscape.

He said if I was serious about trying to keep wolves away, I could get more detailed answers from Will Davis, a former wolf biologist from Minnesota who now lived in the area. If I'd like, Jensen said he could contact Will and set up a time for us to meet. He had to get to another meeting just then, but after I met Will I might have more questions for him, so he gave me his card.

"Don't let Will put you off," Tom Scott warned. "He's got a reputation for being kind of an introvert, a very private person. Very quiet."

I thanked the men and said the fladry suggestion sounded promising. "Please have Mr. Davis get in touch with me."

I had to do something, obviously! I gave them both my new cell phone number.

Then I had time for a nap and a welcome snuggle with Molly. Maybe now our summer would return to normal. All I had to do was get out of Ginger's preposterous treasure-hunting scheme.

4

$\mathcal{L}$ittle Bohemia had been given a cosmetic makeover for the dramatic movie scenes shot there a few years ago, and a banner over the front door featured a close-up of its charismatic star. But it still appeared to be just a typical Northwoods lodge (no rooms rented now, just a supper club) built of dark, heavy logs on the ground level, with a few hints of Swiss chalet on the tan colored upper floor.

Northern Wisconsin cherishes its idiosyncratic history as a safe haven for Chicago gangsters; tourists enjoy the titillation of Prohibition, bootleggers, rumrunners, and hideouts for Al Capone and others. Little Bohemia never tried to disguise its extraordinary past, and now, of course, its owners were exploiting it as much as they could. In the entrance hall beyond the massive front door, framed yellowed old newspapers bore headlines of the FBI shootout of the Dillinger gang. Some city papers called it a roadhouse, which wasn't quite right.

I had seen the movie, and the filmmakers got it wrong. The shootout, worthy of a Keystone Kops comedy, took place during a mid-April blizzard in 1934, not in mid-summer with leaves on the trees. The hurried G-Men landed in Rhinelander in the snow, then rode on the running boards of two urgently borrowed cars in the icy storm (because three other cars broke down along the way and were abandoned) arriving, fairly frozen, at the darkened lodge to surprise Hoover's Public Enemy No. 1. The movie also made too much of the melee; from all I'd read (or Charlie had read to me), the initial gunfight ended within a few seconds.

Instead of Dillinger and his gang, the FBI shot three customers who chose to leave the bar at the wrong time: a gas station attendant and two Civilian Conservation Corps workers.

The botched attack encouraged calls for J. Edgar Hoover's resignation. His agents should have realized that a gang as slippery as Dillinger's would have laid out a careful getaway plan as soon as they'd arrived at the lodge. When escape became necessary, Dillinger and another gang member slipped out a window toward the lake in back and turned to the right. Baby Face Nelson made his way to the left. In their haste to blast the car they witnessed leaving the bar, the FBI agents fell into a drainage ditch on one side of the driveway and became entangled in barbed wire on the other. The movie neglected to include those awkward details as well. Eventually Baby Face Nelson shot eight bullets into Constable Carl Christensen, Grandpa Waters's acquaintance, who had been on the job less than a month.

Now tourists wandered around, pointing out to their children windows and exterior locations, mostly the spot between the rear dining room porch and the dock and the lake. "Yup, this is a historic site," one dad said to his son. "Remember this when you're older 'cause we probably won't get back here again."

We enjoyed a fine fish fry of perch—a Wisconsin tradition—on the back porch overlooking Little Star Lake. The walls were dark stained pine, and a door crowned by a buffalo-head trophy mount led out to a stairway down to the beach, while a stuffed elk head and a moose with antlers like wings guarded the entrance to the main dining room.

Since the movie's release, the museum was no longer free. Having seen it so often, I opted out, and so did Ginger, but she gave Lily $5 to look around at the windows with cracks and bullet holes and review items displayed in the glass case where faded typewritten labels identified the residue of that fateful ambush.

Ginger and I waited for Lily out in back on a park bench near the steep shore, and Ginger enjoyed a cigarette. Little Star Lake, about 125 feet away and 10 feet down to the shore, was a peaceful shimmer in the early twilight. I estimated the pines that sheltered us were at least fourteen inches in diameter. Without a doubt, those trees had witnessed the momentous confrontation. I pointed to an upstairs window of the lodge, located just behind our bench and asked, "Is that where Dillinger escaped?"

"Him and Homer Van Meter. They jumped from that window, down onto a pile of snow that was up against the building here, and then slid down that steep embankment toward the lake. They made a turn and ran along the edge. Went into the woods. Remember in the clipping he said"—and here she removed the rumpled clipping from her purse—"'I ran 500 yards straight north of the lodge. There was a semicircle formed by three trees, and I dug a hole in the ground and shoved the suitcase into it. I threw some dirt and leaves on top of the suitcase.' And here we sit, at the very spot of their getaway. Can you believe it? I always get chicken skin." She rubbed her bare arms.

Over dinner, Ginger had continued relating her friendship with Evelyn Frechette.

"I don't doubt Evelyn was glad to be away from that rough-and-tumble kind of life, but she said that from the very first night she met her Johnny there was never anybody else. Can't imagine she confided that in Art Tic. She got cancer and died in 1969, poor thing."

Emphasizing once more that "it was well before my time," Ginger mentioned that she had obtained even more particulars to enhance the spectacle—like the fact that three of the molls hiding here in the basement had refused to come out when the FBI ordered them to. And apparently after Dillinger's escape, there had been sporadic bursts of shooting by the FBI and others that took out windows from the lodge and caused considerable commotion until tear gas was lobbed indoors.

"After the skirmish, the molls came upstairs because of the tear gas, got arrested, and were taken to Madison, where they pled guilty and were given eighteen months of probation. Evelyn would've been here if she hadn't been in prison, like I said."

"Do you think Lily's okay, wandering around in there by herself?"

"Oh, she has her ups and downs. She's failed a bit this last year, can't deny that, but she's very sweet-hearted and usually congenial. She'll behave herself. In fact she's in pretty good shape, today. I watched her take her pills."

Ginger's proposition had, by now, grown even more ambitious. The entire concept was ludicrous! I could come up with more reasons John Dillinger would not have buried a valise of cash while running away on that wintry April evening than why he would have. But Ginger, convinced by now, was actually asking me to purchase unusual items for our pursuit. Still waiting for Lily, she handed me a list and some catalogs and asked if I'd please place an order online.

"I made a note of our shoe sizes, mine and Lily's," she said. "So you add yours, and after everything gets here we'll give you a check for our share."

"Hey, wait a minute," I intruded. "You're presuming I've agreed to go along with this!"

"Oh for cripes sake, Tallie! Don't be a such a party pooper! I got my heart set on this project, and there's no way I can take it on all by myself—you know that. Doing it with Lily, I might as well do it with a porcupine strapped on my bare back. And you know darned well you're bound to have an adventure like you've never had before. Maybe there's a reason I came across that clipping stuck in Evelyn's letter right now, ever think of that? Maybe it's meant to be, that we look for the loot!

"What in the heck do you think Charlie'd want you to do up here all summer? Sit in that dark cabin up to your chin in mouse turds and read until you go blind? With all due respect, Tallie, I know for sure he'd be chompin' at the bit to search for Dillinger's treasure. Let yourself go and do this for him! Or Grandpa Waters, who knew that poor guy Christensen who got all shot up by Baby Face Nelson. It's your responsibility as a Waters! Look at yourself, girl—it's later than you think!"

There was a certain kookiness about Ginger's idea; a daft, wacky, zany, screwball conception that might be slightly appealing, despite the sure plague of mosquitoes and the unknown consequence of wolves and other unfamiliar wildlife. What was keeping me from playing along for a couple hours, at least? She did have a point about carrying on the family tradition, although I had never been enthusiastic about Dillinger—except during my make-believe trysts with Charlie, which were pretty erotic.

I paged through the Cabela's catalogs and grudgingly agreed to place an order for the items marked with Post-it notes. Who doesn't need a pair of camouflage cargo overalls? I also spotted a pepper spray gun that might be handy to have around the cabin with my lurking wolf.

According to Ginger's list, I was to place an order for three of each:

Insect repellent shirts to ward off ticks, mosquitoes, and chiggers
Insect repellent scarves, ditto
Camo cargo overalls, two mediums and a petite XL for Ginger
Hiking boots (individual sizes)
Three different backpacks with varying capacities and uses
Compass (1)
Walkie-talkies (x3)
GPS (optional)
And 2 hiking staffs.

Ginger said she'd order a metal detector herself, over the phone. We'd only need one of those and she had selected the $299.99 "Treasure Hunter," which included a digital readout, headphones, and a handy carrying case. "Detects coins to 9 inches deep and larger objects to 4 feet," the catalog said. "That should be sufficient for our needs, don't you think?"

"What about a shovel?" I asked. "After we discover the loot, won't we need a shovel to dig it up?" I bit my lip to keep from laughing; the prospect was so preposterous.

"On the first try, I expect we'll be busy enough just trying to figure out where to dig," Ginger replied. "Don't want to call attention to ourselves or give away our intentions, in case we run into any of these treasure-hunting types out hiking and trying to figure out the getaway trails. There's been plenty of them, so I've heard."

"But isn't that just what we're going to be doing?"

"Oh, sure," Ginger replied. "But with all due respect, those greenhorns don't have my commonsensical directions or trustworthy information direct from the horse's mouth."

I decided to add a folding shovel for $49.99 to the list and pay for it myself. I could always use it in my car during the winter. I was tempted to mention to Ginger that three old(er) women in camouflage overalls, hiking boots, backpacks, with walkie-talkies and a metal detector would create a sensation before they even left the parking lot. But Lily emerged from the back door just then, her eyes darting around suspiciously and a curious smile on her lips. She joined us on the park bench and wouldn't stop chattering about what she saw.

"It's like a shrine in there! There's even a big rusty tin can the gang used for target practice! And the tiniest little high-heeled shoes, very delicate, in this glass display case." Lily indicated the shoe size. "One of the molls must've been a fragile little girl. And there were bullets, a book, some neckties, a striped man's shirt folded like it just came from a Chinese laundry, and a crimped tube of shaving cream. And the bullet holes! You'd think it was an army that ambushed this place, instead of a few agents from the FBI!"

"It was more than a few," Ginger said. "In the end, quite a crowd congregated, cops from around the area, a bunch of self-appointed deputies . . ."

"And there was a leather satchel, Ginger," Lily said excitedly. "A thick, leather valise that looked very sturdy. Maybe that's the kind that John Dillinger buried with the loot. But it was quite large and would have needed a very big hole!"

"I read in one account he might've used a knapsack, instead of a valise," Ginger told Lily. "Don't know how deep he could dig, because it was in the middle of April, remember. Snow on the ground. Lake still froze up."

"I saw a postcard with a sign that used to be out on front saying they served steak, duck, and chicken dinners," Lily said. "'Dine, Dance, Swim.' It must've been quite the romantic retreat."

"Duck and cover, I'd say," Ginger added. "I also forgot to mention that I found out it might be $210,000 that was buried. More than I figured. Divide that by three!"

"Did you know when he was killed by that movie theater, witnesses soaked their handkerchiefs in his blood?" Lily asked.

"If it was Dillinger that was killed," Ginger remarked. "I've got my suspicions about that, too."

When my cell phone rang, I was startled to realize what that foreign sound was. I seldom carried it along, since it didn't work up there. I walked down to the beach, for privacy.

"Mom, I've been trying to reach you for days. Didn't you get my messages?"

"I've been at the cabin, and my cell doesn't usually work out there. Right now I'm at Little Bohemia. Remember when your dad and I brought you and Seth here to see the Dillinger museum?"

"Sorry, this has to be quick," Harry said, interrupting.

"I haven't been at the cabin since we brought your dad's ashes to the lake."

"Mom, Camille and I are leaving for Budapest in a couple of days. Have to be there all summer. Business. We've rented an apartment—"

"That's wonderful, honey! What a great experience for you!"

"But Minnow . . ."

"Yes?"

"Camille wants to know if she can stay with you."

"What? Minnow?"

"Stay with you. In Madison. I told Camille it was too much to ask, but we've had some serious . . . *issues* with her."

"Like what?"

Harry sighed. "Too many to go through now." He laughed ruefully. "Teenage stuff, probably normal these days, or at least it is here, but

61

Camille feels Minnow would be safer in the Midwest without so many temptations."

"Like what, Harry?"

"Oh God, Mom—you know, the usual. Then she met some guy online and tried to run away. An older guy. Supposed to meet him in Miami last week, and we caught her going out the door. Camille wants you to enroll her in volunteer work or something. Madison must have lots of opportunities. Get her thinking about something besides herself."

"Oh, Harry—what can I say? I told you, I'm up north."

"I know. But when you get home—"

"I'm planning to stay all summer."

Silence.

"You never stay all summer."

"I am, this year."

"Well, we're leaving this weekend," Harry said, his voice regressing to a familiar little-boy whine I'd always hated.

"I know I told you I'd be at the cabin. Perhaps you and Camille forgot. I realize your schedules are very busy. Cell phone service here is unreliable, so I have to drive into the Antler Library to check my e-mail. I only caught your call because I'm within range, I suppose."

"But I'm leaving for Europe with Cam next week. The summer camps we looked into, well, they didn't appeal to Minnow. Most of them were already filled, anyway. Honest to God, Mom, we're at our wits' ends. Camille's been chewing my ass because I haven't been able to reach you."

"Harry, listen to me: *I'm up north, at the cabin.*"

"Well . . . Minnow could fly into Rhinelander, right? I can change her tickets. Look, I wouldn't ask you to do this for us, but it's really urgent. There's nowhere else she can go, and she can't stay home alone—and she will not allow us to hire someone to stay here with her. We don't know how we can guarantee her safety."

"Harry . . . honey . . ."

"If I change her reservations, can you meet Minnow's plane? I'll get back to you with details. Plan to pick her up on Monday. I gotta run."

⌦✗⌫

"That's all I know," I said, relating the phone call to Ginger and Lily while I drove them back to their LilyPad. "I haven't seen my granddaughter in a very long time, more than ten years at least. Harry and Camille didn't bring her to Charlie's memorial service, and the kids weren't with me then for more than forty-eight hours. That includes the trip up here to scatter Charlie's ashes at the lake. I was kind of a mess anyway, as you'd imagine. And now I'm supposed to pick up Minnow on Monday and look after her all summer! I can't believe Harry expects that of me. Why didn't I just say no?"

"Minnow?" Lily repeated. "Like a baby fish?"

"I remember when Minnow was born," Ginger said, "and, Tallie, you had a few choice comments about her name."

"I still have comments," I said. "But I keep them to myself."

"Oh what the heck, kids use all kinds of names these days. Apple, Sunday Rose, Feather, Toot-Sweet, Gargle, Twink . . ."

"Twink, Twink, Little Star." Even Lily was trying to amuse me. Or herself. Sometimes it was hard to tell.

"Stop at the lodge with her on your way back from the airport so we can meet her," Ginger said. "I'll have Chloe send a couple pizzas down from the Inn, their good ones, with the crispy crust. Is she a vegetarian?"

Molly had been asleep in the back seat all this time. I said goodbye to the women and reached our cabin before the sun began to set. I'd been doing a lot of thinking about my sons.

When Charlie died, I'd been fraught with sorrow and beleaguered by well-meaning friends and unable to even appreciate the companionship of my family. It was annoying, since I saw the boys so seldom, but I had to hold my chin up and contend with the funeral routine. And the

63

boys and their wives were in a big rush, as always. Every time I called either of them I always got, "I'm just leaving, Mom," or "I'm in the middle of something, can I call you back?" which made me feel so second-class and disposable. Dispensable. They hadn't stayed with me when they were in Madison, either—booked hotel rooms, saying they didn't want me to be inconvenienced. Although I'd hoped, even pleaded (as much as was proper) for them all to stay in our home. The kitchen was heaped with food from friends, and the house was so silent without Charlie's presence. Camille and Avianna insisted they were doing me a favor. I didn't argue. I just let it go, like so many other times.

Rather than disagree with Charlie, it had always been easier to lean on him for decisions and direction. Usually we agreed, but I wasn't exactly "creating my own life path," as they say. I usually immersed myself in my husband's identity—I was the perfect "banker's wife" and almost always deferred to him. We had a nice bungalow in the Vilas Park neighborhood. Belonged to a country club, where I played golf with the lady's league on Wednesdays. It was like he took care of all the planning and thinking, and I'd have all the feelings. Just like buying out my brother and sister, and the work he did with the cabin.

The stars began their spectacle as the sky was turning dark. The night sky at Waters Edge has never failed to thrill me. I've always found it a reminder of how inconsequential we are, with our petty battles and trivial outbursts. People who live in cities polluted with ambient light can't possibly realize the amazing vastness of the universe, the Milky Way, the glowing planets, the millions of stars spilled like stirred-up sparks that intensify our true insignificance. Molly and I sat on the dock for a few minutes, taking it all in. My anger over Harry's phone call began to dissolve while I watched the rippling reflection of the stars in the water, heard the loons begin their evensong.

"If you have to pee, do it now," I told Molly before we went inside. "You're not going out in the middle of the night anymore, so this is it!"

I wanted to pretend we were starting all over again. Molly made herself comfortable on the bed as if nothing had happened, head on my pillow, brown eyes looking up at me with her usual sweet innocence. The plastic cone around her neck must be uncomfortable. Since Dr. Baker said it could be removed if she did not show any tendency to lick her wounds, I took it off.

I paged idly through Ginger's catalogues again as my sleeping pill kicked in, but my mind was occupied with the concept of having a teenage girl living here with me. I'd need another bed—she couldn't sleep on that ratty old army cot. Tomorrow I'd call the craftsman who'd made this larger one and have a matching twin bed delivered.

But teenagers were different now than in my time or when my boys were growing up. "Issues," Harry said. They'd had *issues* with her. That could mean alcohol, drugs, sex, running away, who knows what. He and Camille were asking a hell of a lot of me. I was willing to share summer with my grandchild, but this didn't sound like it was going to be a lot of fun.

Then again, who knew? Maybe she would enjoy some of the things I had when I came up here as a kid. The landscape was exceptionally beautiful right now. There'd been many reports of newborn fawns being spied. Turtles were laying eggs in the sand along the road. Bullfrogs were calling at twilight, making their goofy croaking sounds. I had seen Jack-in-the-pulpits in the woods and wild geranium, yarrow, and columbine. The lupine blooms along some of the roadsides were beautiful. How could she not be impressed?

She could take the canoe out onto the lake. I'd show her how to use the boat and motor, and we could go up to Lake Sickle Moon or over to the Star Lake Lodge. Maybe she'd be content just lying on the dock in the sun with a good book. Did she like to read? If she had a camera (I'd get her a camera), she might become absorbed in nature photography. Then again, she could be upset because we had no electricity, no indoor plumbing, no neighbors, no TV, no internet.

"But we do have Molly," I whispered as I blew out the lamp. I hugged my dog and sniffed the pads of her feet. I suspected I had a fetish—I enjoyed the funky musky-smell of my dog's toes.

5

*A*t least Bud waited until nearly noon to stop by on Saturday morning. I was up and washed and dressed, had enjoyed a solitary cup of coffee on the dock while I summarized recent events in my journal, and then I'd even fixed a decent breakfast for myself, including stewed prunes and Raisin Bran that weren't really necessary, as the dread and anxiety of Minnow's visit had been incorporated into my digestive system.

Bud brought Madison and Milwaukee newspapers that carried accounts of Molly's attack. There were interviews with hunters who complained of wolves spoiling their hunting. Northwoods residents charged the growing packs of wolves for attacking their dogs and taking down too many deer. A recent study by Will Davis was cited, regarding the escalating number of wolves in Wisconsin. The article closed with my comments to Warden Jensen: "Natalie Lindquist said that since she had not been on the Waterses' family land for several years, her dog may have surprised a wolf who assumed it was his territory."

If my friends in Madison saw this, they would be concerned about me and make a fuss over my safety. My e-mail in-box was probably already clogged with anxious messages that I couldn't access until I went to the library. Well, that visit could wait.

Bud asked if I'd read the literature he'd given me the other day. He wanted to know if, now that Molly had been attacked, I was willing to join the locals and take a public stand on wolf predation. Oh crap. I had actually studied the materials closely and wondered if this was at the heart of his proffered friendship. I didn't want it to be, but I may have been too trusting. To Bud, I admitted that I had mixed feelings on the subject.

"I'm not saying wolves aren't a problem up here, and I'm sure a lot of their bad hype goes back for centuries—to the Bible, actually. Isn't there a verse warning about wolves in sheep's clothing?" (Maybe someone like Bud, a sheep who was only pretending to be my friend.)

I was going to mention Romulus and Remus, but I didn't want to sound pretentious, and chances were that Bud was unfamiliar with the founders of Rome, who were raised by a wolf.

"And wolves have been demonized in fiction and folklore—like *White Fang*, for instance, or 'The Three Little Pigs' (I was thinking of Dillinger) or in 'Little Red Riding Hood'; they're almost always cast as the villains. And for a long time they were hunted for bounty. Look at Sarah Palin," I shrugged. "When she became governor of Alaska, she encouraged the hunting of wolves from planes. The pack was chased by planes, the wolves were shot from the planes, and then the hunters would land, and the hacked-off left forelegs would be delivered for $150 each. I'm not sure that's fair."

In defense, Bud pointed to a newspaper article inspired by Molly's attack to prove his point. "I don't know about Alaska, but it's common knowledge up here that timber wolves were brought in on purpose from Minnesota. They didn't migrate like the DNR claims. They'll deny it's so, but the DNR wanted to reestablish our packs, and Minnesota had way more wolves than they needed."

I glanced at the article he referred to. It contained a quote from a letter a wolf activist sent to Will Davis:

I truly do not think you would like to be culled, shot, collared, and controlled, Mr. Davis. But since wolves aren't human, you think it's ok to do whatever you want to them—which of course is unethical. And so are you. And you can think I am just spouting, but you being a cold calculating scientist with no ethics, this isn't surprising.

Apparently convictions released a broad range of emotions. I didn't want to argue with Bud. And Molly, to my relief, was doing her best to change the subject. She was making a fool of herself over him. We had coffee on the porch while Molly pestered Bud to rub her ears and scratch her back. He was gentle, careful to avoid the black-threaded sutures and the areas where she'd been shaved. Molly clearly relished the absence of her plastic Elizabethan collar, which had limited her mobility and ability to be stroked.

"Looks like Molly's doing pretty well. Now, what about that dinner I owe you?" Bud asked with a grin. "Where'd you like to go?"

"I guess you're serious."

"I guess your dog is doing okay now."

While Bud was there, I had a call from Warden Jensen on the cell phone Bud had given me. He said Will Davis would be in town that afternoon and could meet me at the Antler Library.

I'd wandered indoors to take the call, then lied to Bud about it when I returned. I was not sure why, but I sensed that Bud wouldn't approve of my speaking with Will Davis, or even Warden Jensen. It was just intuition.

Before he left, Bud went down to the boat to get a shotgun. It was in three pieces, and he demonstrated how to put it together. "It's just a single-shot 410, but you'll sleep better with this under your pillow." He was dead serious, so I didn't comment on how lumpy my pillow would be. He handed over a box of shotgun shells, said they were filled with pellets, and showed me how to load the gun. Then he insisted that I try it out. I did as he said, and it was really loud! The kick from the recoil nearly knocked me over. I still felt the urge to make a joke, but refrained.

"Just shoot it in the air if you see a wolf," he said. "Whatever you do, *don't* shoot the wolf! I've heard of guys getting fined as much as $2,500 for killing a wolf, and they lose their hunting and trapping privileges for three years. You could even get up to six months in jail. So be sure you just shoot up in the air. Or at least, not right at the wolf. Okay?"

After Bud left, I felt disgusted with myself. I worried I might be cheating on Charlie by having dinner with Bud. Not that I hadn't had dinner with another man since Charlie's death, but that had been a close friend of Charlie's, a widower, a director at the bank. A debacle, too. I didn't count my dinner with Howard Eberhart (disastrous as it was) as a date. It was a complete catastrophe.

"It's not a date, Molly," I insisted. "Just a deal we made while taking you to the vet!"

Molly replied by hopping up on the bed for a nap. After a few more minutes, I joined her there. But first, I called the man who'd built the new bed and asked if he could have a twin-sized one ready by the time Minnow arrived next Monday. He had no problem with that.

⚬⚬

I left in early afternoon for the Antler Library because I wanted to plug in my laptop and place the online order with Cabela's. There would be e-mails to sort through, and after meeting Will Davis I needed to pick up more fresh water and a couple blocks of ice. I also wanted to have another propane tank filled. I considered purchasing a few more newspapers so I could send copies to Harry and Seth but then decided against it. Harry and Camille would be in Budapest by the time my letter arrived, so it wouldn't change their minds about sending Minnow. Seth? I hadn't heard from him or Avianna in months, despite my weekly letters to them. A mother wanted her children to develop lives of their own, but not be seen as ancient history. I guess I missed the page about how to prevent becoming irrelevant in my dog-eared volume of Dr. Spock.

I plugged in my laptop. The battery was nearly exhausted, so it took more than a few minutes to boot up. I had the catalogs with me, pages carefully marked. It took a half-hour or more online to locate all the items on Ginger's list, specify each by size and number, and finally arrange for payment.

Then I checked my e-mail and, no surprise, found anticipated messages of concern from friends (although not as many as I'd imagined, which made me wonder if my friends cared about me as much as I'd presumed). I took swift action to send a hasty response to Charlie's old friend Howard Eberhart, who strongly hinted at joining me at the cabin so I wouldn't be on my own. That had to be halted, immediately! I marked it "urgent."

Then I saw e-mails from people I did not know.

How had my address been so easily obtained? And why was I suddenly the target of so much hate?

I believe Mother Nature took out the wolves for a reason, and the DNR introduced them back to eliminate Wisconsin's deer herds. When they run out of deer, what are they going to turn too next? Dogs, cats, and even humans will be on the menu if we support wolves procreating. I saw a picture of a large cougar in someone's yard next to a child's swing set, and I don't believe he was smelling around the play area because he wanted his turn on the swing or teeter-totter.

When will we say "enough is enough"? Now that our north woods has been taken over by marauding gangs of vicious wolf packs we need to stop this. In WW II troops of German submarines were dubbed wolf packs. Why? Because they were hunter/killer gangs that preyed on allied commercial shipping. Now we have real wolf packs in our backyards that have been inflicting their terror on dogs and deer and who knows what else. I can appreciate the months of love and training that have gone into your dog, not to mention the friendship that is kindled in your pet that means the world to you. It's time we stop this get rid of all of them with a hunting season on wolves.

I know what you're going through, believe me. Not far from where I live, there was a grandmother who had her grandkids out playing with the small family dog. For whatever reason, the kids went in the house, and five minutes later the grandpa walked out of the garage and saw two wolves—one carrying off Jingles, the small family dog—still in the

70

yard. The man started to yell and run after the wolves in hopes of saving their small family pet. Instead of the wolves running off and away from a human, the wolves stopped, turned around and stood there in a defiant manner. The grandmother heard the yelling and came out of the house. The dog later died from its wounds. We can only wonder what may have happened if the children had remained outside alone. It truly is a possibility that Jingles gave his life to save the lives of his best friends. The grandmother told me they were paid for the dog but not the love that is missing. She said she and her husband were just saying the other day that this would be their first Christmas without Jingles.

One e-mail contained a brutal photograph of a doe with two unborn fawns pulled from her and fed upon. The caption said this was due to an attack by a wolf.

Another revealed a grotesque photo of a dog's bloody skeleton with head and collar attached at the neck. The remains were being held by two men—one with his hand in the collar, the other holding the rear paws. "The attached photo is not for the weak stomached," the letter warned.

I was so emotionally shaken that I left my laptop plugged in and went back out to my car, where I could take some deep breaths and close my eyes. I was parked in the shade with the windows cracked—a humid day, but Molly was comfortable there. I ducked down and hid so no one could see me crying. What was I supposed to do? Become a spokesperson against wolves because Molly had been attacked? That was ludicrous. I deeply regretted Molly's injuries with all my heart, but this was the wilderness, an element of the Northwoods that was part of the attraction for me, had always been. I didn't want to eliminate all the wolves; I wanted to learn how to coexist with them.

So of course, despite my best intentions, I was late for my appointment with Will Davis, even though I was only steps away. The librarian directed me to the reading room; it was through a short hall to the left.

I hoped Davis hadn't already given up on me or that I'd create a bad impression with my lack of punctuality and reddened eyes.

Oh. My. God. There was only one person in there, and if that man was Will Davis, I had to catch my breath. I backed away silently and slid into the ladies' room.

I was a mess. After my crying jag I had fussed just a bit with my hair in the car's rear-view mirror, but humidity had made it go flat. Could I fluff it up a bit? Tease it with a comb? (No comb in my purse.) I needed some "product," as my hairdresser called it. Desperate, I rubbed a generous chunk of ChapStick on my palms and then rubbed my palms on my hair—which then stuck up weirdly in large, sticky, cherry-scented points. Maybe he'd think it was a "sassy" look. My hairdresser was always promoting "sassy," which sounded like something you'd persuade a middle-(to-later)-aged woman to try, someone who would not let her hair naturally go gray and still insisted on highlights. Now I added a little lipstick, and just a dab of it on my cheeks for blush. Can you say "clown"? All I needed was a bulbous red nose that squeaked when it was squeezed. I found my sunglasses (but it was a cloudy day!) so he wouldn't see my red eyes or lack of mascara. The clock was ticking.

Surely the Antler Library had some of his books. Wouldn't I be better prepared if I at least perused a flap on the back of a book with some biographical information? I quickly checked the stacks in the library: Nonfiction: wildlife. Nothing. Nonfiction: animals. Nothing. Local authors: the shelf was bare.

Then I noticed local authors featured on a display shelf up in front near the checkout. I hastily grabbed two by Will Davis and withdrew to a corner to scan an inside flap:

Will Davis, recent winner of the US Fish and Wildlife Service prestigious Bruce Nelson Award, is recognized for his biological expertise coupled with his work in wolf recovery and management. These have earned him the respect of the scientific community, landowners within recovery areas, and the many other government entities and interest groups involved. Throughout his thirty years of leadership, he has made significant contributions to wildlife conservation through the implementation of new approaches and techniques. During Davis's career he has worked for the Forest Service and the Bureau of Land Management, in addition to the US Fish and Wildlife Service. He has been a certified wildlife biologist since 1982.

This book was called *Life in the Shadow of Civilization*. His picture was on the cover: curly white hair, a slender man, dressed in black turtleneck and pants. Handsome. Indecently handsome. With dark eyes, serious but behind them a kind edge that gave me a shiver similar to the one Billie Frechette must have got from Dillinger, and this was just a photograph. It was definitely the man in the reading room who'd made me want to swoon.

Now it was the man standing right next to me this very minute as I knelt to replace the books.

"Excuse me, have you seen a woman named Natalie Lindquist? I expected her to meet me here twenty minutes ago."

I blushed furiously, replaced the books on the local authors shelf (one upside-down, which he corrected) and then I grabbed them again. "I thought I'd read some of your work," I mumbled as I pulled myself upright. "I'm Natalie."

"You might enjoy my latest," he added wryly, pulling another from the top shelf and placing it on the library's checkout counter.

He was probably in his sixties, tall, smelled wonderful—some kind of woodsy cologne.

"Do you have a library card?" the young library assistant asked me.

"No . . ."

"Well, you can fill out this form," she said, slapping one down with a pen.

"I don't have time right now," I remarked awkwardly. My voice seemed unusually high.

Will said gruffly, "I can wait a little longer."

I quickly scribbled on the forms and waited while the girl checked out my books. But I couldn't look up at Will when I took my seat in one of the chairs near the fireplace. "I'm sorry," I apologized. Then I asked, *stupidly*, "What are you wearing?"

"Jeans," he said abruptly. "Jeans and a blue plaid shirt. Is this what you came here to talk to me about?" He was brusque and cool.

An appalling beginning. I was falling apart. I had to explain.

"I meant your cologne. You smell very nice. I like men's cologne."

"Are you all right?"

"Yes," I said, finally looking him in the eye. "I'm sorry. I'm really sorry. I apologize. I'm not myself. No, that's not true, I *am* myself, I mean, this is who I am, but—Can we start over?" I pleaded. "I'm Natalie Waters. Lindquist. But I may be taking back my maiden name, 'Waters.' I've been thinking about that lately. Except then I might feel I was abandoning Charlie, my husband, who died recently, but I do like 'Waters' better, I always have. I never felt 'Lindquist' fit who I really am."

"Okay, that was awkward. Let's begin again."

Was that a glint of amusement in Will Davis's eye, or was it exasperation? I didn't know him well enough to tell.

Deep breath. I reached out my right hand. "I'm Natalie Waters. I'm very pleased to meet you."

"Will Davis," he said soberly, taking my hand in his. A solid grip.

"And it's something my daughter gave me, probably for Father's Day. She always asks what I need, and I always say, 'Nothing,' so I end up with a dozen kinds of cologne and usually grab whatever is closest when I leave the house."

"Charlie and I had two sons. I always wanted a daughter. As the years have gone by, Mother's Day has become pretty much ignored. Now I consider myself lucky if I receive a card. But I do recall fondly the rubbery eggs served with breakfast in bed, and the boys in their pajamas standing there expectantly until I've swallowed every bite."

"I can assure you daughters also serve rubbery eggs." He smiled. "What can I do for you?"

74

"Everything," I wanted to shout! But I said instead, "I just read some abusive e-mail messages, and my mind's kind of numb. E-mails like that were totally unexpected."

"What did they say?"

I retrieved my recharged laptop and read the angry notes to him. I showed him the photographs, too.

"There's a roughneck group up here, loosely organized. They're fanatically opposed to wolves." Davis said, "Call themselves the Howlers. They want to start hunting them, not to control the wolf population in a healthy way, but just to kill for the sake of killing. Howlers love their guns.

"Some of those photos are bogus, I can tell you that. Pull up that one again of the one of the dead doe with two fetuses drawn out. It's hard to tell if this is even a wolf kill. Looks more like a vehicle kill to me, with both the doe and fawns fed on by scavengers. The amount of consumption seems too low for wolves, who'd more likely have eaten everything."

I turned off my laptop, folded it, and tried again to casually fluff my weird hair.

The reading room would be a cozy place to read in winter, with its fieldstone fireplace, framed watercolors of local scenes on the log walls, colorful woven rugs, and comfortable wing chairs. A coffee pot and pitcher of lemonade were set out on a table by the window next to a plate that held a plentiful pile of homemade chocolate chip cookies. I poured myself a cup of lemonade. Will declined. My back turned to him, I quickly downed one cookie, then stacked a significant number on a napkin and returned to my chair.

As usual when I'm nervous, I talked fast and rambled a lot. I told him about Molly's injuries, which he'd previously learned about from Warden Jensen and the newspapers. I said Molly was in the car, that Warden Jensen checked the wound sites and agreed it was a wolf attack, and I gave lots more information that Davis already knew.

"But I'm interested in something called 'fladry,' and how to use it. Is

75

it expensive? Can I install it myself? Do you think it might work? And what supplies would I need to set it up?"

"If you're heading back now, I could follow you," he said. "I brought some brochures about it, and directions. Wouldn't hurt to take a look at the attack site, either."

I explained that I had to get a few supplies—propane, ice, and water. Will said he had to stop at the grocery store. So we met in the IGA parking lot, and he followed me back to my place.

After I parked my car, Will beckoned for me to follow him back up the hill. He pointed to something and said it was wolf scat.

"Scat," I said. "That's not a word I've heard a lot except related to jazz."

"Well, you should learn about it in relation to wolves, and learn how to identify it—especially scat like this."

The pile of excrement looked like something a dog might have left, but bigger.

"These can vary quite a bit, depending on what the wolves have ingested," Will said. "If their diet is composed mostly of hair and bone—they last the longest here in the wild—then you'll find examples like this, twisted and tapered ropes with pointy ends. Bone shards, probably from deer, are surrounded by hide and hair that keep the wolf's intestines from being shredded."

I poked it with a stick.

"You'll find wolf scat in the middle of a road, like this, or at trail junctions. They also mark their territory with urine on low stumps and foliage."

I asked Will to recommend a book with illustrations of tracks and scat and signs, and he said he had one in his truck I could borrow. Then, while he was surveying where the wolf got Molly, Eric arrived with his pickup to deliver Minnow's new bed.

I was pleased to learn that the men knew one another. Eric told me Will was going to be the keynote speaker at an environmental conference to be held at the Star Lake Inn in July. I didn't mind Will seeing my rustic cabin, but I had not imagined that he and Eric would set up the new bed and mattress for me.

"Natalie, you're in the way," Eric said. "Take Molly and wait on the porch."

When they were finished, we each had a cold beer, thanks to the chilled six-pack I'd bought in Antler. The new bed looked great.

"We have eighty acres here," I explained, and told them both about coming to the cabin with my grandparents. Eric took measurements for two skylights and a new roof before he left. Will seemed interested in the cabin's history, so I showed him snapshots from the early days, kept in the Campfire Marshmallow tin with the journals, pictures of my siblings with fishing poles and sunfish and of Charlie and the boys. He laughed at Lydia Pinkham, and I found myself revealing how it hurt that my boys had not inherited my affection for the cabin.

"You wouldn't like to live closer to them?" he asked. "I moved to Wisconsin to be near my daughter and my grandkids."

"No," I answered, too brusquely, I realized. "I mean, they definitely have lives of their own. Seth is in Phoenix, and I don't like Phoenix; everything is so new. Nothing has much original character, and I feel sucked dry out there, pinched like a raisin. I like moodier weather. For me, there's nothing more boring than sunshine and blue skies every day.

"Then Harry and Camille and their daughter, Minnow, live in New York. I can't see myself living in Westchester."

I mentioned Minnow's pending arrival. "I'm more than a little worried about that. I can't go back to Madison until late August because I rented out my house to a visiting professor from Uruguay and his family. They'll be there until the end of the summer session. I'm afraid Minnow will find this place a complete bore."

Will said he loved it up here, too. He liked being in sync with the natural rhythms, getting up at sunrise and going to sleep at sunset. He enjoyed experiencing the change of seasons so intimately, as well. The attributes of living an unpretentious life, close to nature. "It's people

I've had problems with, and cities would have more of them," he admitted. "Phoenix and New York? You've got my votes there; I agree with you."

I confessed that I'd told my friends I had to get away from home for a time because of Charlie's death. And that *was* true—the memories, the closets that still needed cleaning, Charlie's clothes I still had to sort and put away or send to Goodwill. "I said I was going to spend a therapeutic summer at 'our cottage.' At least I didn't say 'lake house.'" We both had to chuckle at that.

"Well, I may have mentioned 'lake house' to two of the wives of Charlie's vice presidents. They have plush condos in Door County and would be horrified to learn that not only do I lack granite countertops and stainless steel appliances in my kitchen, I don't have a hot tub on my deck. Or even a deck."

"Those condos don't have your family's rich history," Will reminded me.

"Or my outhouse," I added. "Or Ginger Kowalski, my dear friend at the Star Lake Saloon. If you know Eric, I'm sure you've met her. And now I find that I'm being courted by this group of Howler guys to speak out in favor of exterminating all the wolves. So this is my summer. It's gotten totally out of control."

I wondered why Tom Scott had warned me about Will; he didn't seem aloof or introverted.

"Let's talk about fladry," Will suggested after a lengthy pause, and he told me what the fencing would involve.

"It's been used for centuries in Eastern Europe and Russia, but mainly for *hunting* wolves. Here we use it to keep wolves from certain areas for at least sixty days."

"That would get me close to the end of summer," I said.

"Right. It provides a visual barrier that wolves usually won't cross. What you do is install some rebar—do you know what that is? Those thin steel posts that are used to strengthen concrete?"

I said I knew.

"You pound one in every ten feet or less, around the entire perimeter of the fence you want to achieve. Then you string the line to the posts—it's just strong wire—and it has to remain consistent and taut. After that you tie red flags to the wire every eighteen inches or so. I suppose you could make part of it as a gate, so you could have it enclose your car."

He'd brought some computer printouts about tests with fladry in Michigan and other states. "The only problem is, eventually the wolves get accustomed to it. And it works better with wolves than with coyotes."

I was incredibly relieved! There was a better solution to my problem than a metal pot and a wooden spoon.

"Does your wife share your appreciation of the Northwoods?" I asked, before giving it a thought. Risky question. Too personal. Definitely none of my business. Or maybe it was information I subconsciously wanted.

Will looked off at the lake for a few moments, then caught my eyes with a level glance.

I quickly apologized: "I have a habit of putting my foot in my mouth. You may have noticed."

Will just shrugged. "You said you were a widow, so I expect you'll understand. I stay by myself a lot," he replied. "I had cancer, and it made a mess of a lot of things, including my personal life. I'm writing another book, and that's a solitary occupation, so I can use that as an excuse."

"You don't have to explain."

"My last place of residence was northern Minnesota. Lots of wolves there, too, as you know. Some idiots think we moved them over here. And when I got cancer in my leg, I started getting even worse flack than you did. Rumors got around. I was supposed to be the Minnesota wolf expert, but I got bit in the leg by a wolf and it became infected. A wolf mauled it so badly, my leg wouldn't heal. A wolf took off so much of my leg, there was nothing left but the thigh. Of course, all of this was damned foolishness."

Will pulled up his left pant leg, and I noticed his metal prosthesis.

"One thing led to another; you know how that goes. My wife had a problem with the rumors. And taking care of an invalid wasn't easy for her. We parted amicably, as soon as I could get around on my own, but I knew she'd be more comfortable with a *normal* husband, one who didn't have cancer and did have two good legs."

That was enough. I really didn't want to know more about how he'd been hurt.

"I'm okay with it now, but I felt my body had betrayed me, too. My leg was amputated, the cancer went into remission, and I moved across the border because I'd lost my trust in a lot of things. My daughter has a nice husband and three kids, and they check in on me once in awhile. Still run into my ex-wife because of them, and that's okay—we're still friends. I have a couple dogs and a cat, some little creatures I feed from my deck. I have a deck." He smiled.

"Designed and built my own house, by the way. Not a cabin like yours, or a 'summer house,' I guess it's a comfortable cottage. I could get a better leg, one that looks real, but why bother? At least I don't need a crutch or a wheelchair. I don't feel sorry for myself. But I do like my privacy."

Silence. The blissful silence of the Northwoods when your ears begin to ache because it feels like all the sound has been sucked away.

"I didn't mean to be intrusive," I explained. "I ask too many questions."

"I'll ask one of you now, and it's a personal question, too. Is there a possibility that you're upset over the arrival of your granddaughter because her presence might disrupt the solitude you need for grieving?"

Damn. Those tears were really close to the surface.

After Will left, I felt ashamed by my timidity. If he could get around on only one good leg, I could hike through the woods on two. Especially now that I had Bud's shotgun. I figured out how to put the gun together and carried some shells in my pocket—feeling a bit like Barney Fife, but more confident than with a pot and wooden spoon. Dr. Baker didn't want Molly going into the water until her wounds were healed, but he'd prescribed gradual exercise for her strained tendons. I wanted to get some exercise, too.

This was my first time this season on the path that led back to the far end of our eighty, and toward the end of the trail I came across a puzzling sight. I did not understand why dozens of donuts and pails of cherry pie filling had been dumped there, near a big stump. The sticky mess was surrounded by flies, and I had to harshly order Molly to keep away.

When I got back to the cabin, I tried calling Bud. The woman who answered the phone at the bar said Bud wasn't there.

Then, embarrassed by calling him so soon after leaving my place, I called Will Davis to describe what I'd found. He explained that I had stumbled upon bear bait. Someone was obviously trying to lure bears to that spot, for hunting. The season for hunting bears with hounds was in early September, but training the hounds to tree them began in early July.

"The bait might be drawing wolves there, too. Look for tracks."

"And scat," I added, as though I knew what I was talking about.

"Where there's bait, you'll usually find a trail camera," Will explained. "So whoever put that bait out has you on record now. He's going to eventually know that you found the bait placed on your land."

"Not good," I agreed. "They're not allowed to hunt here!"

"You need to get rid of the picture, or there could be repercussions."

"What do you suggest?"

I was angry, seething really, and trembling with fear as well.

"If I were you, I'd go back to where you saw the bait and look for the camera. Then I'd remove the memory card."

"It's going to be obvious that a bear didn't do that—"

"And the camera may be locked."

"I don't know," I said, thinking of the perils I could be in for.

"Would you rather have the hunter know you're aware he's unlawfully hunting your land?"

"I have a shotgun," I said. "Would that work?"

"I suspect a bullet or two would probably take care of the lock. It would also destroy the camera. Let me know how it turns out."

When I was finished, there wasn't much left hanging on that tree. I'd retrieved the memory card from the camera before blasting the whole thing to hell one final time. I deposited the empty shotgun shells in the outhouse underworld and carefully wrapped the memory card in Kleenex before tucking it in my checkbook, in my purse.

I felt strange, like the time I had a bad case of poison ivy and the doctor gave me a prescription for prednisone. "One of the possible side effects," she said, "is inappropriate happiness."

That's exactly what I felt: inappropriate happiness. My shoulder ached and my ears rang, but I felt smug and satisfied that I was taking charge.

2

Thundersnow

It was the worst thing that ever happened to me since I had a brand new pair of boots burned off in a forest fire.

Constable Carl Christensen,
shot by Baby Face Nelson during escape
from Little Bohemia Lodge

6

The Rhinelander/Oneida County Airport has two runways, a long one and a short one, and a modest but modern terminal that serves Delta and Frontier. So even though I arrived ten minutes after Minnow's plane was scheduled to land, I thought I'd have no trouble finding her. But almost no one was inside, and the Flyby Cafe and Lounge was closed for the day.

The airport had a couple of vending machines, a fountain, and music piped in from a local radio station. A rental car desk offered the usual cars for hire. According to the arrivals board, Minnow's Delta flight had landed on time, but I didn't see a fourteen-year-old girl traveling alone, a slender girl of moderate height with light brown hair, perhaps pulled back in a ponytail. Wearing jeans or shorts? Or maybe something more chic; Minnow lived in New York, after all. Had she missed her Milwaukee connection? Harry had given me her cell number, so I punched the numbers into my phone.

"Outside," a girl answered dully. Not even "Hello."

"Issues," Harry said over the phone. Probably more than sexting some strange guy over the Web and trying to run away. Bulimia? Anorexia? Maybe she'd had her tongue pierced; a lot of girls did that these days. I was even prepared for a tiny diamond stud in her nostril; that wouldn't break my heart.

I saw her as soon as I went back outdoors, leaning against the wall at the far end of the terminal, smoking a cigarette. Her dull black hair was ragged, as if she'd dyed and tried to cut it herself. A glaring purple layer began at the crown and swept down on one side, covering her right eye. Despite her dark glasses, I couldn't help noticing the makeup: neon-pink eye shadow, eyes thickly rimmed with kohl. What the hell? There was a silver nose ring like a barbell, a knob on each end. And two silver rings pierced her bottom lip. Beneath her right eye, a blue tattoo of a tear was strikingly bright.

What had happened to the sweet little toddler I'd snuggled on my lap? Surely her black hoodie was oppressive in this humidity. It bore some wild rock-band design that I couldn't possibly interpret. Beneath that were a tight black tank top tucked into skinny jeans and a thick studded belt. Black nail polish. Laced-up high-top sneakers (again, too hot for summer wear), fingerless crocheted gloves, and a thin green scarf wrapped several times and knotted around her neck. My initial impression: it must take a lot of effort to accumulate such a costume.

"Minnow." I said.

The girl pulled earbuds from her ears and stuck her iPod in a pocket of her sweatshirt.

"Your little Minnow," she said listlessly. "Banished to the wilderness." It sounded like a much-practiced line. The droop of her head also seemed rehearsed.

I took a deep breath and reached out for an awkward hug. Minnow pulled away and flipped her head sideways to shift her purple bangs.

"So, what's the deal?" I asked.

"Meaning what?"

"This getup. The makeup, the hair, the *costume*. Help me understand."

"You can't understand," Minnow said, soberly.

"Well, try me," I replied.

"I'm ready to go," she said mournfully, tossing her cigarette to the asphalt.

"Your luggage?"

"This is it," Minnow said. She dragged a heavy backpack.

Issues, I thought to myself. Right. Thanks a lot, Harry.

"Well?" I asked.

"What?"

"Don't you want to put it out?"

"What for?"

I ground the butt with the toe of my sandal. "My car's over there."

I was grateful I'd left Molly at the cabin.

Absorbed in her music, Minnow said little as I drove. Finally, she spoke.

"I'm not goth. I'm emo."

"It doesn't matter to me," I said. Goth. Emo. (Was that like the bird, I wondered? Did she say emu?) Whatever. It was simply teen rebellion, and I refused to be impressed.

"EMO. E. M. O. It stands for 'emotional.' Like emotionally deprived."

"You're emotionally deprived," I repeated, flatly.

"I knew you wouldn't understand. Nobody gets me."

"I thought the look was goth," I offered for the sake of argument. "Sorry."

"What would you know, anyway?" Minnow whined. "Goths hate everyone."

"And do you hate me?"

"Hate *you*? Why should I?"

"Doesn't sound like you're too happy."

"I hate myself."

Well, that was enough for a while, I decided.

"I'm not trying to *be* anything. I just *am*. My life sucks."

"I'm sorry—"

"F. M. L.," Minnow said, despondent.

"What?"

"Fuck My Life."

"I have those days, too," I agreed with all my heart.

❧

"Where is this cottage, anyway?" Minnow asked after we'd driven silently for forty-five minutes. I stopped in Antler to pick up some gas for the boat, then we eventually emerged on the county highway, heading farther north.

"It's more of a . . . cabin," I said. "I wouldn't call it a cottage."

"Meaning . . . ?"

"It's not a cottage. It lacks, um, amenities."

"Like it has only one bedroom?"

"Like it has only one room. And no bathroom."

Silence again. Minnow pulled a pack of cigarettes from her jacket pocket, along with a lighter.

"No smoking in my car," I said. "That's a rule."

"Fuck."

"Or in my house. My cabin," I amended. "And be careful where you drop your butts, because you can start a forest fire. And I'd appreciate not hearing that F-bomb emerge from your mouth quite so often."

I realized I was bordering on bitchy, so I added, in a more jovial voice, "These flowers along the road are lupines. The pink spikes and purple ones? They bloom up here this time of year. I think they're really pretty. Lupine is from Latin—for 'wolf-like.'"

No response.

"'Wolf-like,' because the plants were thought to ravish the soil."

"Ravishing," said Minnow.

"Right now we're going to have supper with some friends."

"Supper. I forgot. Out here in the wasteland of flyover country, you call it 'supper.'"

"Actually, it's pizza. And you'll be meeting my friends Ginger and Lily."

I took the next corner a little too fast.

Ginger and Lily were polite, if a bit taken aback. "So this is *Minnow*," Ginger said, tsk-tsking. "I'd never have guessed that she was one of yours."

It was six o'clock by then.

"Do you have a bathroom?" Minnow asked.

Ginger guided her to the ladies' room off the bar, her eyes making several complete rotations when she returned.

"Tallie, what in the heck happened with that girl?" she whispered.

"And what do you plan to do with her?" Lily asked.

I closed my eyes and shrugged. I had no idea.

"Um . . . do you have a Band-Aid or something?" It was Minnow. She had her sweatshirt tucked under one arm and was holding a wet paper towel over a bare shoulder. Her chest was flat beneath the skinny straps of her tank; she was thinner than I had thought. Her shoulder blades resembled sprouting wings.

"Sure, honey," Ginger said. "What size you need? C'mon, let's go look in the first aid kit."

Minnow glanced at me with a guilty look. What was going on?

Lily and I followed them into the kitchen, where Ginger removed the paper towel from Minnow's shoulder. An angry red tattoo of a weeping heart was bleeding there.

"I think it got infected," Minnow mumbled. "The sleeve of my hoodie was rubbing it on the plane."

"When did you have this done?" Ginger asked gently. "Looks pretty fresh."

"Day before yesterday. It's really sore."

"I have some salve," Lily offered. "I keep it here in the kitchen because it's very effective for healing burns."

"She can burn herself trying to flip a burger," Ginger remarked with a sympathetic smile. "Get your salve, Lily. We'll doctor this up tonight, and if it's not better tomorrow, we'll take Minnow to the clinic."

Ginger soothed the raw tattoo with liniment and tenderly bandaged it. Minnow squeezed her eyes shut and bit her lip; I thought she might be trying not to cry. When we returned to the porch of the Saloon, two fresh pizzas had been set on a table, by Chloe no doubt, along with napkins and paper plates.

Whatever issues Minnow had, problems with her appetite were not included. That was a relief; I was definitely not prepared to handle an eating disorder. Even feeding a vegetarian (I noticed she'd chosen the veggie pizza) would be a stretch, with my limited pantry.

Following a fad in appearance or behavior was temporary, I hoped. Smoking, well, every kid thinks it looks sophisticated to smoke. But Minnow still had to be introduced to Waters Edge.

❧

"What. The. Fuck." Minnow said. "I'm sorry about 'fuck,' but *this* is where you're staying?"

"This is where *we* are staying," I said. "It's our family cabin. Your great-great-grandfather Waters built Waters Edge eighty years ago, and one day it will belong to you."

"Jesus, fuck, no," she said. "God, this is like the end of the freaking earth! You pick me up at that random airport, take me to a stupiculous old resort with those two wackadoos, feed me revolting pizza, and now this!"

I got out of the car, but Minnow refused to budge. I went around the front and opened the passenger door.

"In the first place, *Minnow*," I spewed, "I had plans of my own for this summer. The Rhinelander Airport is perfectly serviceable, and we're fortunate to have a connection up here. Ginger and Lily have hearts of gold and would do anything for me. Or for you, for that matter. They patched up your botched tattoo, didn't they? The pizza was made at the Inn, where they have a gourmet chef. It was delicious. And I'm wondering, how could you get a tattoo and all that metal crap when you're fourteen and underage?"

"How do you know the legal age in New York?"

"I was prepared for your arrival. I know how to Google. Duh."

"I've got friends."

"And they do a great job, obviously. Let's just hope you don't get an infection from defacing your body like that."

Okay, I was coming off as the worst grandma in the world, but I hadn't had much practice. I slammed the car door on Minnow and walked toward the back door of the cabin, where Molly was whining.

90

"As far as I'm concerned," I yelled over my shoulder, "you can start walking back to New York whenever you want."

Of course, Molly bounded out of the cabin and immediately ran over to the car, eager to greet the newcomer, furiously wagging her tail, Minnow turned away, huddled into her seat, afraid.

"She won't hurt you," I said, following Molly. "She's very loving. Harmless, really."

"She looks weird," Minnow yelled. "Like she's got some fugacking disease."

Well, yes, she did look strange with patches of fur shaved from her body and sutures from the wolf assault.

"She was attacked by a wolf," I replied, without thinking.

Minnow shrieked, "Wolves?"

I kicked myself for revealing that so soon.

"Do my parents know you've got wolves? They sent me here into this fucking goddamn backwoods where there's wolves and shit?"

"Bears, too," I added, truthfully. "We have black bears. And bobcats. If you have sharp eyes you might even spy a cougar!"

"Fuck," Minnow said, shutting her eyes so tight that I could see tears emerge. "Fuck, fuck, fuck, fuck. I'm so fucked."

I left her to sort out her curses, and went inside. The cougar comment was a bit of a stretch, but I couldn't resist.

When I heard the car door slam, I figured Minnow would appear indoors any minute. I made up the new bed, put one of Grandma Waters's quilts on top, and went out on the front porch. Still no sign of Minnow or Molly either, for that matter. They weren't out behind the cabin or in the car.

The sun was low in the west, and the hot, humid front that had moved in during the day was grossly uncomfortable. I was eager for the skylights I'd talked to Eric about. Deer flies swarmed when I walked out onto the dock with a glass of red wine. Why did they always burrow into one's hair and take a bite out of the scalp? The whine of mosquitoes made me wonder how Minnow would manage in her tank top if she removed her hoodie in this heat.

In my minds' eye, I recalled a tag with a barcode on her backpack—she had checked it onto the plane. Yet it was not too large to fit inside an overhead bin. Perhaps she had stowed something inside she didn't want discovered (I had raised two boys, after all). Marijuana. A glass pipe. Whatever kids used. I had no idea anymore. I hoped it wasn't anything stronger, like crack or heroin. Harry, how could you do this to me? Camille, you bitch, I hope you're enjoying Budapest.

The wine was beginning to have a relaxing effect on my irritation—so much for moralistic worries over marijuana, I chided myself. I was guilty, too, sipping my wine, using my own drug of choice.

Had my granddaughter ever heard a loon? They were calling now at sunset, their weird yodel knitting a circle of songs from woodland lake to lake that I loved. Minnow might be scared.

"What the hell is that?" Minnow emerged suddenly from the shadows. Molly stood next to her, then padded down to the edge of the lake for a drink.

It was not an easy evening. Minnow expressed a litany of disgust with the cabin's eccentricities. I began to wish she'd had to sleep on the smelly old army cot instead of her lovely new bed. She had no idea of the effort I'd made to create a comfortable transition for her. Then again, I knew I was coming across like a harridan.

The battery to her iPod died, and of course her smartphone did not work. The girl amused herself by writing poems until dark, and then wrote more when I lighted the Coleman lanterns. Her introduction to the outhouse went unresolved; Minnow said she didn't have to go. I showed her the metal chamber pot, set it out on the porch where we would each have some privacy during the night, if necessary, and placed a roll of toilet paper on a chair within reach.

"When I came up here with my grandparents, they set up a toilet seat for me in a grove of pines." I figured it wouldn't hurt to back off my bitchiness with a little nostalgia. "The toilet seat was white and wooden, shaped like a regular one, but it had folding metal legs. I was so short that

Grandma Waters had to lift me up to sit on it. She always stayed with me. 'The whole forest is your bathroom,' she told me. 'Isn't that fun?'

"But after I got older and came up here with my parents—your great-grandparents, Minnow—the legs on the folding toilet had been bent and my mother told me to 'go find an old log and let your bottom hang over the edge.' Every log I found was mossy and damp with lichen, and bugs scurried over my thighs. The moist bark was rough on my bare bottom and crumbled so it stuck to me. Pee dribbled down my bare legs and into my shorts. It takes a while to get used to living up here without the usual amenities, but you'll learn to manage. I know you will."

Minnow's response was a sarcastic, "Poor you."

She was still writing furiously in a notebook.

"And another thing I want to share with you is that calendar over in the corner. Look—"

I waited until she eventually gazed where I was pointing.

"It's a calendar from 1927, the year after my Grandpa Waters built this cabin. He was a pharmacist and had a drugstore in Little Wolf. The woman in the illustration is Lydia Pinkham. When I was a little girl, Grandpa taught me some funny songs about her. I realize you're not ready, or maybe even willing, to learn some history here, but I have a lot of memories of Waters Edge, and your dad and uncle Seth spent summer vacations at the cabin, too."

"My silence is my sound," Minnow spoke up. "Could you please let me alone? Can't you see I'm writing a poem?"

It was nine o'clock and almost dark, so I climbed into bed and read for an hour with a battery-operated lamp. I'd placed one on a table next to Minnow's bed, and she read for a while, too. I turned mine out first and snuggled next to Molly, who was already asleep.

"Grandma?"

The voice coming out of the darkness startled me.

"I'm sorry I'm so pathetic but I can't help it. I'm just a waste of space."

I realized this admission could mark a pivotal moment, and I wanted to respond with something especially meaningful, words that would comfort this troubled child and reassure her that growing up was hard, that it would get better, easier. I had never had a daughter, always wanted one, wished I knew a magical phrase. My sleeping pill was kicking in (must cut back on those!), and my muddled mind could not come up with anything life-affirming.

Before I could speak, I recognized the regular breathing and sighs coming from Minnow's bed. The girl was asleep.

The next morning I awoke when I heard Minnow go outside. I glanced over at her bed and saw the calendar illustration of Lydia Pinkham had been deliberately ripped in half. I quashed the temptation to tape it back and decided to let it stay dangling, as it was.

> Then we'll sing, we'll sing,
>> We'll sing of Lydia Pinkham,
> Savior of the human race.
>> How she makes, she bottles, she sells
> Her vegetable compound,
>> And the calendars publish her face.

This kid was not going to beat me down. I was too tough for that.

❧

I didn't mention the calendar. After breakfast, I asked Minnow to give me a hand pushing the boat into the lake, and then we struggled to get the heavy motor down to the shore. I had to figure out how to attach it to the boat and the gas tank, too.

"Haven't you ever done this shit before?" she asked.

"Your grandfather always did it," I replied, sweating hard with the effort. Deerflies swarmed, biting. Molly jumped into the water to avoid them, and she was not yet supposed to get wet.

"There are some chores around here that I now have to learn to do myself. I'd appreciate your help."

Minnow bent down to help me attach the motor.

Molly jumped in the boat, shook herself all over us, and we took a tour of the Celestial Chain—the three lakes tied together by links of the Lost Arrow River. I pointed out LilyPad, Ginger and Lily's cottage on Lake Sickle Moon. Then we came back to Sundog, past our cabin, went on through the tube under the road and into Star Lake. Passing the Saloon, we waved to Ginger, who watched from the porch. I'd never seen the Last Resort from a boat, but I explained its relevance to Minnow. Bud was right in his directions: just come through the tube and keep on going straight.

We suffered through a hard-fought struggle for a few days. Every morning, Minnow went out on the porch to get enough light for applying neon eye shadow, and then she conscientiously arranged her hair in the cabin, using the duct-taped mirror above the basin.

Lydia Pinkham still drooped above Minnow's bed and I made no move to mend the calendar. One day Minnow mentioned it—said, "I hope you aren't upset. It's just a picture of an ugly woman, and she was getting on my nerves." Clearly, she was disappointed that I hadn't made a fuss.

One day I saw her sitting at the porch table and surreptitiously watched as she touched up the "tattoo" under her eye with a blue Sharpie. So. It wasn't real. The crying heart on her shoulder had healed and looked okay. She ran around in her tank top, seemingly oblivious to mosquitoes, but there was plenty of bug repellent around that she may have applied without my knowledge. She said she liked Diet Coke, so I got a six-pack in Antler. She drank out of the can, nursed it for a long time. I knew what was up.

Minnow asked if it would be okay to take out the canoe. She said she'd learned to paddle at summer camp, and I didn't see any reason why not since I could see her anywhere on the lake from the dock. I dug a paddle out of the mess in the lean-to behind the cabin. She promised to use a life jacket and shoved the aluminum canoe into the water.

"If you'd rather take the boat," I said, "I'll show you how to use the motor."

But she was already slicing the silence with her paddle. Molly watched querulously from the dock as if she felt quite left behind.

I went back into the cabin and found Minnow's backpack on the table. It usually accompanied her, even to the outhouse. With her safely out on the lake, I cautiously unzipped the bag and reviewed the contents, making a mental note of how each had been arranged inside. Her now-dead iPod, of course. Her poetry notebook: "Lost in a world full of hate. Pain doesn't hurt, when it's all you've ever felt. I wish I was invisible. Feel my pain, hear my screams, and watch me fade. Not all scars show, not all wounds heal." Well, that was enough of that.

A plastic Ziploc bag held what looked like oregano, but I was certain it was not. And the glass pipe was not for blowing bubbles. I didn't fall off the turnip truck yesterday, as Ginger would say.

Cigarette papers for rolling your own.

There was a bottle with prescription pills for depression. Did she take them? I counted thirty and would check again, when I could.

Her smartphone, which wasn't very smart here at the cabin.

Razor blades. Hmm. A much more serious concern. I would need to check her wrists, see if she cut herself. Hadn't planned on that, needed to do a Google search.

Cheap black and purple hair dye.

A dozen airplane-sized bottles of vodka and rum, which she was mixing with the Diet Coke, I surmised, and another reason (besides the weed) for checking her bag. I would not throw them away, but I might count them again tomorrow too.

Molly was still sitting on the dock, patiently awaiting the return of her new pal. I went out to join her and felt sudden empathy for Minnow. Her parents were busy with their own lives, and she was trying so hard to feel relevant, not just "a waste of space." How much had she revealed in those few words?

Charlie admonished me for using swear words, so I'd always toned them down in his presence. But I distinctly recalled when I learned that Harry and Camille had named their sweet baby "Minnow." I rushed out of Camille's luxurious birthing suite and down the hall of the hospital in a rage. Charlie followed me, sensing the cause of my distress. He caught up with me and pulled me into his arms.

"What the fuck kind of name is Minnow!" I exploded. "Minnow! Minnow Waters. It sounds like something you'd order at a fancy restaurant, like sardines on toast."

I had heard the name often enough; it was Harry's nickname and I'd always hated it. Seth, our oldest son, had been a strong swimmer. Fans of his high school team called him "Big Tuna." But when Harry came along and hoped to match his brother's prowess, his gangly physique was no match and he was christened "Minnow." I felt it was hurtful, but Harry never seemed to take offense. Camille thought it was endearing and "Minnow" became her baby's name.

"Wait until she's an old woman and in a nursing home where they have her tied to her wheelchair with a dishtowel to keep her from sliding out and there's a bib around her neck to catch her drool, and some nurse's aide is going to say, 'I've got to tend to Minnow again, the old fish is slobbering all over herself.' It's an insult to Harry and to my surname, Charlie! I can't understand why you're not enraged!"

"It's *Minnow Waters Lindquist*," he reminded me. "It's your name and mine, too," Charlie calmly patted my back. "She's ours. And she's our grandchild. We also have a responsibility for that little girl."

I could hear her out in the middle of the lake now, humming to herself.

The scent of marijuana floated past me. It wasn't the worst thing, I assured myself. I had a responsibility for that guppy. Dammit. This would take all the empathy I could summon.

⚮

We drove into Eagle River on Wednesday morning to pick up supplies for the fladry and get more water and ice and some fruit and vegetables. I told Minnow I expected her to help with the fence, if she was worried about wolves. "This fence is going to provide us security," I explained.

"Well, I'm sorry Molly got injured, but the wolves were here first," she replied.

I asked if she wanted her clothes washed; I knew she had few changes of clothing in her pack and was, frankly, smelling rather rank in the same old jeans and top. Deodorant was obviously not high on her list of necessities. Was this emo or goth or just plain stubbornness?

"I'm fine," she said. "I think I smell natural, the way a woman's body is supposed to smell."

"And what about tampons or pads; how are you fixed for those?"

"Don't worry about it," she said. "I can take care of myself."

On Thursday morning, Minnow sullenly cut the many triangles of red fabric that we would hang. I laid out the rebar and measured enough wire to provide a circumference that would include the outhouse within the perimeter.

Then Ginger called.

"I know that was a heck of a lot to pay for extra-speedy shipping, but UPS just delivered, and we can get started day after tomorrow if you guys are free."

What else would we be doing? I'd probably need to go into Antler tomorrow for ice and groceries, but Minnow and I had nothing planned for Saturday. I was having my dinner with Bud that evening, but it shouldn't interfere. "It's part of a bargain we made," I explained to Ginger. "The night he drove me to the vet with Molly, he promised me she'd get well. And if she did, I had to go out to dinner with him."

"Oh, one of those," she sighed. "Just so it's not a real date or anything romantic. You've got lots of other stuff to focus on these days, like your granddaughter and our expeditions. So why don't you c'mon over to Lily-Pad with Minnow tonight for supper and we'll put our heads together."

I welcomed the invitation, explaining that we were installing fladry and pounding the rebar into the rocky ground had become a grueling task.

I'd made the comment about the fladry perfectly innocently, I swear, but not more than an hour later, Eric pulled up to my dock with Chloe and Miriam in the boat. Will Davis was with him, too. They'd been meeting at the Inn to consolidate last-minute plans for the symposium in July: "A New Era for the Wolf."

Chloe had never seen the cabin nor met Minnow, so she suggested we watch from the porch while the men tackled the fence. "But Minnow should have a chance to get her hands dirty," she advised.

I was delighted with the opportunity to play with Miriam. The little girl had short, dark hair and bangs, the perfect image of her mother.

"I'm intrigued with Minnow," Chloe confided. "Ginger filled me in on the details. I went through a period of rebelliousness myself and struggled with low self-esteem, so my heart goes out to her. I was wondering if you'd mind letting Minnow spend time with Miriam?"

"Miriam?" I asked, stunned. "Minnow? She smokes pot, and . . . well, I'm not sure I'd entrust her with a child!"

"But she'd be nearby; I'd be in touch with her all the time. Baby monitors, you know. It's just that we could use someone to help—like a nanny—now that we're getting so busy with our summer season."

"You'll have to check with Minnow." I watched her hold a pole of rebar and flinch each time Eric pounded it into the ground. Will looked up at me and flashed a grin.

"Nice man," Chloe said. "We're very fond of him. It's amazing, the number of reservations we've had from fans who are anxious to meet him at the symposium, hear him speak."

"I like him, too," I muttered, but low enough that Chloe couldn't hear.

I fixed a pitcher of lemonade. Chloe had thoughtfully brought along a fresh batch of cookies. When the rebar was in place, Minnow and the men tied the red strips on the wire and joined us on the porch to celebrate the fladry's completion.

"This would have taken us days to finish," I admitted.

"You can thank Ginger," Eric said, setting down his emptied glass. "She's the one who said, 'You boys get your asses over there.' Apparently she wants you in good shape for her Dillinger treasure hunt."

"John Dillinger?" Will asked. "I want to hear more about that."

"I'd tell you myself, but Ginger would embellish it in her own inimitable way," I assured him.

❧

At LilyPad that evening, we found that Ginger's Dillinger research now overflowed a plastic laundry basket. After Boca Burgers on the grill—a nice concession to Minnow—the girl curled up in a corner with her recharging iPod and closed her eyes. Lily and I watched as Ginger reviewed the equipment spread out for display—three of everything. "Maybe now we'll need four of some stuff," Ginger conceded.

"I'm not wearing those disgustipating overalls," Minnow complained.

Each item I had ordered was there, plus Ginger's additional whims. For example, she had uncovered a child's metal detector that a departing guest had left behind. That was deemed Lily's tool. It beeped and was lightweight enough for her to carry along with her hiking stick. Lily had put in new batteries, tried it out, and found two quarters in the fish-cleaning shack just that morning. Ginger winked at me.

"I got this book on eBay called *Buried Treasure*," Ginger added. "And it quotes a man who was a lawyer in Chicago. He said he once represented Patricia Charrington, one of Dillinger's molls, and she confided many confidential details about the Dillinger gang's operation." Ginger began to read from the book,

Including the fact that she had fenced more than a million dollars of negotiable stocks and bonds in Minneapolis the day before the Little Bohemia ambush, selling them for $200,000 in small bills. She arrived in Manitowish Waters just as the G-men were about to descend, and handed the suitcase over to Dillinger, who told her to go to Chicago and find a new hideout in that city. After he fled the Little Bohemia raid, Dillinger met with her and told her he "ran exactly five hundred yards straight north" of the lodge to escape the FBI. Stopping, he got to his knees and dug a trench in the soft earth and buried the suitcase. He quickly covered up the hole and placed dead leaves and twigs over the spot.

"Well that's impressive," I had to admit.

"But that's not all," Ginger continued in a somber voice that would have been appropriate for a television announcer during the funeral of a dignitary: "'There were three large trees, two pines and one oak. It was his intent, according to Charrington, to return to Little Bohemia and dig up the loot he'd buried when the heat was not as intense. But he was killed before that was possible.' A semicircle of trees, just like in the clipping I found with Evelyn's letter," Ginger grinned. She then admitted that she had spent a great deal of time online checking websites for recent posts by treasure hunters who made observations regarding the information that she had just revealed, including this one: "Paper money from that era has most likely rotted by now. Even if it hasn't, it is doubtful that it would still be legal tender. However, it could be worth a lot as historical value to collectors. If you can prove the connection to the gangster it will be worth many times its original value. Proving this connection will not be easy; however, as it was allegedly going to be his getaway money, perhaps there is a possibility that there are some other papers in the stash, such as a passport?"

"Passport?" Minnow said from the corner, obviously listening more carefully than we'd thought. "That's ironic, isn't it?"

As long as she was listening, Ginger took time to explain to Minnow that she was sorely needed in our expedition, because she was the youngest and could provide moral support and carry heavy things. And assist Lily. Minnow begged to stay at the cabin, but Ginger insisted that she accompany us.

"Haven't we been through this before?" Minnow asked. "Am I really that important?"

"Of course you are," Ginger said in a matter-of-fact voice. Now listen to this one:

> According to local legend, in his haste to escape from the FBI that night, Dillinger may have buried a suitcase with more than $200,000 in stolen money somewhere in the area. In fact, *The People's Almanac No. 2* by David Wallechinsky and Irving Wallace lists Dillinger's mysterious suitcase as one of the "great unclaimed treasures of the world."
>
> Although speculation on the likely whereabouts of the buried suitcase has ranged from the area around Little Bohemia to the towns of Woodruff and Eagle River, no concrete historical evidence has ever been found to substantiate its existence. But that doesn't diminish its place in the lore of the Northwoods.

"It's true—you can't prove that it is out there," Ginger announced with a growing twinkle in her eye. "But then again, you can't prove that it isn't, either. I prefer to think it just might be. 'One of the great unclaimed treasures of the world!' How about it, girls?

"Now, the weather's supposed to be nice tomorrow," she added. "No rain in the forecast. Of course we'll have the usual bugs to contend with, but that goes with the territory. Get it? Goes *with the territory?* Oh, Tallie, I can't tell you how excited I am!"

"Thundersnow," Lily announced in an assertive voice. "I just thought of the name to assign to this secret mission. Thundersnow, like when we have lightning and thunder during a snowstorm. It could be that's what they had that unforgettable eve."

"I like the way that sounds," Ginger agreed. "'Mission Thundersnow.'

It has a trace of the mysterious about it, and the power of the thunder as well. What do you think, Minnow?"

"My Chemical Romance," she replied. Then she sang with her iPod, "I don't love you like I did yesterday."

Ginger paused for a moment, waiting for something else. I was embarrassed, certain Minnow was high on something, but at least she was subdued. Then Ginger announced she had permission from Little Bohemia's owners to explore on their land.

"And what about the neighbors?" I asked.

"Most people just go off on their own without a how-dee-doo," the neighbors told her. "So having somebody ask if it was okay they said was real polite."

7

*W*e heard wolves howl that night, but their laments were far away. I cut my sleeping pill in half and slept soundly just imagining our red flags were keeping the place secure—which was what I promised Minnow before I blew out the lantern. Tomorrow we would not have to take a drum along to the outhouse.

After working on the fence, Minnow complained the men pushed her too hard. Eric and Will had given her responsibilities that she had dutifully carried out, and they had shown no surprise or wonder at her incongruous makeup or body art.

Later, when we were alone, I'd briefly floated the idea of caring for Miriam, and she wanted to know more. I could understand the appeal, since it would provide an escape from the confines of the cabin and my constant attempts at camaraderie. But I wanted Chloe to provide the specifics of behavior, responsibilities, and dress, so I didn't pursue it further than saying Chloe had mentioned she needed help.

Minnow's daily makeup and hair routine naturally had to be concluded before we embarked on Mission Thundersnow the next morning. I stuck a baseball cap on my head and put some clean clothes in a bag in my car. After our hike, I wanted a hot shower in preparation for dinner with Bud. Ginger and I had decided that Molly and Minnow would spend the night at LilyPad.

The morning turned out to be wet and cool. Ginger insisted that merely gave us a handicap similar to that faced by anyone fleeing G-men on a certain April night.

"Except for the snow," Minnow said.

"And how cold it was," Lily added.

Despite donations of sweatshirts, fresh jeans, and a plastic poncho, Minnow refused to get properly dressed. She complained about having run out of cigarettes. She whined that she could be carried off by a wild animal and no one would give a shit, especially her indifferent parents, her impetuous grandma, and two meddling old women.

Ginger, of course, had a characteristic comment on the last remark.

"That girl's got too much of what the cat licks it's ass with: a tongue."

Minnow sulked in silence after that.

We decided to dress ourselves in the Saloon so we could begin our trek as soon as we arrived at our location. Insect-repelling shirts with long sleeves went on first and had to be buttoned. Over them, the camouflage overalls were stiff and the metal clips on their straps needed adjusting. I had trouble bending over to pull on my hiking boots and found myself consumed by giggles. The weirdness of it was an expensive and surely a short-lived exercise in comedy. It would have made an entertaining documentary.

We had only three walkie-talkies, so we decided that Minnow would hang out with Lily and share, since Lily was confused by the variety of buttons and dials. I took the compass.

The waterproof ponchos (heavy vinyl) were the final touch to our pre-hike prep, and they went on once we reached Little Bohemia. Then liberal sprays of OFF around our faces, necks, and hands. And after some help getting each other into our heavy backpacks, we were all set to enter the woods.

Minnow was probably the most comfortable of all—the rest of us were already sweating beneath our protective gear before we'd proceeded ten feet from the car. She wore her hoodie and the usual black tank with sneakers and jeans. I encouraged her to wear socks, and she complied only when I reminded her of the fat wood tick I'd recently removed from Molly. Ginger let Minnow take the real metal detector, instead of the kiddie one Lily leaned on like a cane. Minnow's outlook must have improved then, because before we entered the woods, she offered to carry Lily's backpack with her own.

Our strategy was admittedly vague, but Ginger had provided each of us with a map. Lily and Minnow were to stay in sight of the lake, probably to keep them out of the way, while she had specific paths carved out for the two of us. "Look for the three trees Dillinger mentioned," she reminded me. "Two pines and an oak. Or the remains of trees like that, maybe three stumps in a semicircle. Five hundred yards straight north of the lodge.

Ginger conceded that the "straight north" Dillinger declared might have been blurred, by the haste with which he escaped in the dark. So I checked the compass before she and I split up.

Almost at once, the deerflies descended. They weren't so bad when there was a breeze, but the morning was still and damp. Thick undergrowth impeded my progress, and several times I tripped over wild vines. Branches hit me in the face, and water trickled down my neck and mingled with perspiration. Berry bushes reached out and tugged at my pant legs. We didn't get very far.

I could hear Lily telling Minnow she had to go. By the time I reached them, Minnow had unfettered Lily from her poncho, helped her get her overalls down and was holding her hands for balance while the old woman squatted. "I would personally have invested in Depends for her if I knew I'd be doing something this gross," Minnow whispered under her breath.

We managed to get Lily put back together, and I promised them we'd spend only thirty more minutes before calling it a day. Ginger was somewhere out in the woods, measuring every three trees.

I hadn't told anyone, but I secretly carried Bud's dismantled shotgun in my backpack, along with a sandwich bag of shells.

After all the flurry of planning, we'd forgotten to pack a lunch. Our venture took us only a short distance from Little Bohemia, anyway, so we planned to reconnoiter around two o'clock by the car before lunching at Little Bohemia.

I relied upon Molly to help me find my way back. She ran on ahead, and mostly I just followed. Deerflies and mosquitoes had bitten her, and her eyes were nearly swollen shut, but she could sniff the way we'd come, which involved several circular wandering paths that resembled a meditational labyrinth, which we dutifully followed to achieve our return.

I bumped into Ginger, who was musing about Dillinger and which way he'd likely gone and what he'd probably done and who was with him. The gang had broken up into pieces that night, and several had traveled in separate directions.

Then we encountered Minnow, who said Lily was not feeling well. She'd left her lying beneath a spruce tree, where she could rest.

"Who was in charge of bringing water?" I asked. Ginger admitted she was.

"Lily said she felt lightheaded, and I was afraid she'd faint," Minnow added. "So I had her lie down. I'll show you where."

Lily looked pale, spread beneath the tree like a corpse. I pulled out my cell phone to dial 911, but Ginger shouted "No! Then the whole damn county will know what we gals are up to! All she needs is some liquids. The poor thing's probably dehydrated."

"You won't let me call for medical help, yet you're the one who forgot the water," I said coolly.

"I didn't *forget* the water, I left it in the car. Too excited, I guess."

"Um . . . I hate to admit this," Minnow said, "but I have two cans of Leinenkugel's in my backpack. I stole them from the refrigerator at LilyPad last night and hid them in our cooler without Grandma finding out."

"Well, see if Lily will drink a little bit," Ginger ordered.

I held Lily's head up so she could take a sip.

"I'd prefer wine," Lily said. "A delicate chardonnay?"

"Oh for cripes sake, Lily, you give me fits, you know that?" Ginger paced back and forth. "Watching over you is about as tough as stuffing a wet noodle up a wildcat's ass."

Lily laughed so hard at that, beer spurted out of her nose.

"I guess she's still alive," Minnow said as she boldly sipped the remaining beer.

At the car, stowing our backpacks, Minnow was the only one not to suffer blisters on her feet. The whining of mosquitoes had driven every-one nearly mad—the hovering mass in front of our faces, the whining in our ears. Ginger said we'd need to order special socks for next time and she would put mosquito netting on her list.

I quickly announced there would be no "next time" for me. Minnow was of the same mind. Lily mumbled something no one could make out.

Molly drank a bowl of water and was content to stay in the car, curled on her rug with all the windows open. Minnow said she wanted to stay there with Molly, but I knew she must be hungry, as she'd only had black coffee at breakfast.

Seated at our table, Minnow maintained she had no appetite. Lily, now quite revived, mentioned she wouldn't mind a bite. Ginger ordered four hamburgers.

"I'm a vegetarian, remember?" Minnow said.

The order was changed to four hamburgers and one salad.

"I won't eat it," Minnow announced after the waitress left the table.

Uncharacteristically, Lily said, "I think you're basically a nice girl, Minnow, and I appreciated the beer, but I'd like to take you over my knee and give you such a spanking."

"My father would take you to court for assaulting his child."

"Humph," Ginger grunted. "You're not going to go far with that personality—like a turd in a punch bowl."

As her grandmother, I should have defended Minnow, but I whole-heartedly agreed with Ginger and Lily.

"I hope you remember you're not here because it was my idea," I said. "It was your mother's brainstorm, so I doubt that your father would have Lily charged with assault."

"Why can't you crazies see how stupid this whole so-called treasure hunt is?" Minnow asked, harshly. "What do you want to bet that even if there was any cash, the owners of this place found it right after Dillinger left and kept it all themselves. Then they probably kept the rumor going to get people to come here and look. Doesn't that make sense? If I'd been here after the FBI left, I'd have been tearing those rooms apart to find anything valuable that might have been stashed. And as for following the trail, there was snow on the ground, remember? Tracks? Huh? Duh? Why didn't anybody think of that?"

Lily was shivering in the air-conditioning, so we were anxious to be served.

There *was* some validity to Minnow's point. Had we and everyone else been duped by publicity fabricated and advertised by the resort?

"I'm going to wait in the car," Minnow said. No one stopped her, so that's where we found her when it was time to leave. She'd bummed a cigarette from someone and was smoking in the back seat.

Ginger rode in the front seat and was suspiciously silent. Either she was pondering Minnow's declaration or she was already planning another Mission Thundersnow. Surely she must realize that when the search ended today the rest of us would consider our responsibilities accomplished.

We drove back to Star Lake in peace. The old lodge still had rooms above the Saloon for rent, and two large bathrooms, men's and women's, were at one end of the long hallway. I took a welcome hot shower there, dried my hair, and put on the clean clothes I'd brought along. When I came downstairs, I found Ginger and Lily at the bar rolling dice with a group of fishermen. Minnow was seated on the porch, playing with her newly recharged phone. Molly lay next to her on the glider with Babe squeezed in beside.

"Have fun on your date," Ginger commented.

"It's not a date," I muttered, perhaps too stridently.

"It's not a date," Lily echoed even louder. "It's a bargain," she added, "a bargain with a Bud."

Ginger left the bar and walked me to the screen door. "We'll take good care of Molly and Minnow tonight, so you just have a good time," she advised. "But not *too* good. You deserve a night out at least, with all you've had to deal with. Lily and I can deliver these guys back tomorrow."

"I appreciate—" I began, but Ginger interrupted me and quickly brought up searching again for the Dillinger loot before I could get away. I must have pointed to my watch at least a dozen times, but it should not have been a surprise that Ginger had already devised a new plan.

"Since your Grandpa Waters showed so much interest in John Dillinger, did he ever happen to mention that he actually met the man?"

"Sorry," I replied.

"Well, think about it!" Ginger hollered after me. "How come, do you think, he saved all those old clippings?"

The idea was absurd, to even suggest that Grandpa Waters had met John Dillinger! Grandpa Waters was a registered pharmacist and a respectable businessman in Little Wolf. I knew he served on the village board for a while, and even the local school board.

"I want to know more about that," Ginger yelled as I reached my car. "No good deed goes unpunished, you know."

How she thought that applied, I had no idea.

❧

Bonfire, an upscale restaurant that had just opened, was my selection for dinner with Bud. It wasn't the sort of place I'd go alone or take Minnow, so it was a logical choice. I wore a pair of black linen pants with a taupe silk shell and matching silk cardigan, black sandals with a little heel, a necklace strung with small gray and rust-colored stones. I hadn't brought much in the way of fashionable clothing along to the cabin, as there was seldom any need for it. I also went light on the makeup, never wore much, anyway, and there wasn't a lot I could do about my hair—medium brown with roots showing streaks of gray. It was short and easy to scrunch into place when wet, I'd been having it colored but decided summer at the cabin was a good time to finally grow it out and go au naturel. "More age-appropriate," as Charlie, who never appreciated the cost of having it dyed, had frequently hinted.

When Bud picked me up in his truck, of course he noticed the fladry.

"My granddaughter's staying with me, and I wanted a humane way to deter wolves," I said, "because she was afraid. Warden Jensen explained how to do it, and it seemed like fairly inexpensive and easy way to go."

It was almost true. Just a little fib, because I wanted the fladry, too.

He shrugged, smiled, and I had an odd epiphany. He reminded me of the former football player who was an announcer for the pregame shows for the NFL. Crew cut, wire glasses, tall guy. Affable. Warm smile. A big, friendly bear. No wonder I saw him as nonthreatening. And why not? He'd been considerate with Molly, helped me feel more comfortable at the cabin, looked after my safety. I had no reason to distrust him except for his apparent sanction of propaganda that advocated the brutal elimination of wolves.

Bud had to concentrate on following the tracks in the long grass when we drove out the logging road, so I was silent. It occurred to me that I hadn't spoken with Charlie in quite a while.

"This is not a date, Charlie," I mentally sent into the universe.

"Molly's doing okay?" Bud asked, interrupting my meditation.

"She's having her stitches removed next week."

"I'm not going to say 'I told you so,'" he flashed me a warm smile, "but I'm really happy to hear that, and not just because you're having dinner with me."

I didn't expect my dining selection to be so luxurious. Bonfire obviously catered to affluent residents and Northwoods tourists whose accommodations were much more well-appointed than mine.

After I'd been served a glass of wine (Bud had a soft drink) and we shared an order of shrimp bruschetta, Bud explained that in addition to owning the Last Resort he ran an outfitting business, Northwoods Pursuit. He hired out as a guide for hunting bear, bobcat, and coyote. He handed me a business card. When I slipped it in my handbag, I accidentally touched my checkbook with the camera's memory card inside. Reminded of that, I encouraged Bud to tell me more about hunting bear. He was proud to be a houndsman and especially enjoyed his special group of dogs. When the hounds get the bear's scent, hunters search for the tracks. Bear size is gauged according to the size of the toes—there are dime, nickel, quarter, and half-dollar toes and the hind footprint has a large human-like heel.

I said I'd heard he coached football and asked why he'd quit coaching to be an outfitter. Bud paused for a moment and then seemed purposefully equivocal. "I went through a really bad time in my life. You can't imagine how bad. I'm so ashamed that I can hardly talk about it. The community was mostly supportive, but I had to make big changes. I like being with my hounds, out in the woods. I grew up around here and started hunting as a kid, with my dad. So I kind of fell into being an outfitter, I guess."

A pianist at the grand piano was taking requests for romantic music. I was lulled by the wine, the white linens on the tables, the fine china, the soft candlelight.

I could relax. Minnow was being looked after, and Molly was okay.

I was tempted to "innocently" mention the bear bait I'd discovered on my land. But I held back. What if the trail cam I'd destroyed had been Bud's? I didn't want it to be, but I bit my tongue again.

I had not mentioned that I'd met and spoken with Will Davis about the Howlers or the negative effects of wolves. Nor did I entertain Bud with a witty description of our Thundersnow treasure hunt, even though I had a few colorful quips ready to toss in if small talk ran out.

Right now, that seemed disloyal to Ginger. He also hadn't known until tonight that my granddaughter would be with me for the summer. Was I weaving a web of protection or deceit?

Bud was a good-looking guy and seemed genuine. What was it about him that made me feel uneasy? I wasn't quite old enough to be his mother, but when he said he guided hunters out West for cougars, I'd stifled a laugh. If I were interested, he'd be great prey.

Oddly, the phrase "wolf in sheep's clothing" played in my head. I'd mentioned it in our conversation the other day, and now I worried that it might be appropriate.

Finally, Bud helped me out, by mentioning there were different seasons for hunting over dogs and hunting over bait.

"Bait?" I asked, with a faux puzzled tone.

"Bear bait. Sweet stuff, like frosting and pie filling, junk you can get wholesale from places that sell it for that purpose. Whole truckloads. Cookies, jam, cereal. Moldy sweet rolls. You mix it all together and put it where bears can find it. Black bears like we've got up here can't see very well, but they are awesome at picking up smells and sounds."

"And then?"

"Well, you don't want to put the bait where there's a lot of 'mast'— acorns and hazelnuts and berries, food bears naturally find on their own. And you start putting out your bait a couple of weeks before the season opens. Then you should really monitor the place where the bait's at by putting up a trail camera."

"A trail camera?" I enjoyed playing dumb.

Our meals were served then. I had the crab and lobster ravioli, and Bud had the New York strip. I said yes to another glass of wine.

"A trail cam," he explained so patiently that I began to feel guilty. "It's a special camera. Either a still camera or a video camera; there are all kinds and prices. You attach it, about waist-high, to a tree or a fence post near where you place the bait, and anything that moves in front of the lens is captured. Turkeys, coyotes, big game, you name it. Up here we use them mostly so you know when the bears are eating the bait, *if* they're taking the bait, or if wolves are in the area. They used to use film in the cameras but now they're mostly digital."

"So, do *you* use trail cams?"

"I got a couple," he admitted. "They're a good scouting tool. Some guys combine baiting for bear with using hounds, and here in Wisconsin you can put out bait from April to October. You're only supposed to train hounds during the hound season, which is different every year— this year it's during July and August. Then you can run the bear into trees or take pictures of them where you found them. To hunt, you have to be lucky enough to score a kill permit. If you get one, you can shoot a bear in September and the first few weeks in October."

"And you get a kill permit by . . . ?" I asked.

"It's a kind of lottery," he explained. "Only a limited number are issued."

"Have you ever caught wolves on your trail cams?"

"Wolves, deer, bobcats, whatever moves. There's way too many wolves now," Bud explained. "And they're doing too much damage. I know we talked about this the other day, but it's a fact that the population needs to be regulated, and the DNR will agree. I happen to think there should be a season for hunting wolves, to bring down their numbers. Not many big bucks around during deer season the last few years."

"Because of wolves?"

"It has to do with the rut," Bud said, reddening a bit. "The time when the big bulls—the bucks—are in poor shape. They're more vulnerable to predators, then. To wolves. Fawns are at risk, too. And does. Some say it takes 108 deer per year for a single wolf to survive. So, with my outfitting business, I've got to wonder where all those deer are going to come from."

The ravioli was splendid, and for dessert we split a slice of Door County cherry pie, my favorite.

"But isn't it true that when you eliminate your large carnivores, bad things happen? I mean, the deer herd, for example. When wolves were down in number, the deer herd overpopulated the area. There seems to be a balance in nature that has to be maintained."

I had the last word, but that did not mean I'd won.

Bud walked me to the back door of my cabin to protect me from my wolf, which was not very funny, although I laughed to be polite. He held me close, and gave me a shy, tender kiss. Then there was another kiss, more lingering, which I found myself returning. Uncomfortable with my careless response, I broke away.

I wanted him to leave. I wanted him to stay. My body—it was as if a pilot light had been ignited. I felt a rush of physical attraction that I knew I should smother immediately.

"Would you like to come inside?"

Minnow was gone, so was Molly. The cabin was empty.

I struck a match, and two oil lamps cast a soft, romantic glow.

Bud sat on the side of Minnow's bed and said, "C'mon over here. Sit next to me." He punched up Minnow's multiple pillows so the mattress resembled a daybed.

My sex life had ended with Charlie's biopsy for prostate cancer. There was the one last trip to the cabin after that and my surprise gift of our new bed, but that rendezvous had ended with tears of regret from us both.

Well, to be brutally honest, there had been a minor and embarrassing misstep this summer about a week before I drove up to the cabin, when Howard Eberhart had asked me to dinner. It seemed innocuous enough. I had known Howard's wife, and I had not been out in a very long time, so I said yes, dinner would be nice. Howard said he wanted show me a new restaurant in the country. Even better, I thought, in case any of my friends saw us and thought I was not properly mourning my husband by having dinner with another man, even though by then Charlie had been gone for over a year.

I didn't know the evening would involve crossing the Wisconsin River on the Merrimac Ferry (and back again), nor did I expect Howard to respond, when the waitress asked if we were celebrating our anniversary, "This is our first date."

It was chilly crossing back over the river after sunset, and Howard didn't want to sit in the car but stand by the rail and admire the dying flush in the western sky. He asked if he could put his arm around me to keep me warm.

Back in Madison, Howard insisted on showing me his new condo on Lake Monona. It was still fairly early, so I agreed, because one day I might consider selling my house, and buying a condo was a possibility. Howard's condominium was lovely. He and his wife, Stella, had had beautiful furnishings in their Highlands home, and Howard said his decorator helped him select what to keep and what to sell. I took a seat on a deep pink brocade loveseat, a piece of furniture I distinctly recalled having admired many times at Stella's book-club meetings. Then Howard sat down beside me and began to nuzzle my neck.

The amusement I later found while lying in Howard's bed was not something I'd foreseen. Bored? Okay. Self-conscious? No doubt. Guilty? Probably, since Charlie was surely watching his friend, who was undressing in front of me. But I had no idea until Howard disrobed that beneath his shirt he wore a colossal silver cross, the size of a saucer. Size matters, I told myself, and suppressed an impolite giggle. After minimal foreplay, the cumbersome cross smacked me in the face with each of Howard's determined thrusts. At last I could no longer stifle my amusement. I shrieked! My chin bore the whacking pain of his religious zeal.

I turned my head into the pillow and pretended I was overwhelmed with passion, hoping Howard would translate the concealment of my laughter into exhaustion from my rapture and feel proud of himself, the studly Lothario.

After I calmed down, I wiped my eyes and solemnly explained, "I can't see you again, Howard. It's just too soon for me. I'm not ready to become involved."

Only days before I left for Waters Edge, Howard called again. With great relief, I was able to say I was spending the summer up north.

It was still too soon for me, and that's what I told Bud, pulling myself from his arms.

"What are you doing for the Fourth of July?" Bud asked before he said goodbye, and my muddled brain permitted me to truthfully answer, "Nothing!"

Thus, I was formally invited to his annual Road Kill Picnic.

8

*B*ud's truck pulled back up the hill around midnight. He said I should bring my visiting granddaughter to the Road Kill Picnic, too. I knew Minnow would try to resist. "And don't forget Molly," he added. "Our regulars have been asking how she is. They'll be glad to see her healing up so well."

So I agreed to attend with my surly granddaughter, my dog, and a dish to pass. The last was essential; at least there'd be something edible.

Will had suggested that Minnow might enjoy participating in a wolf howl and offered to pick us up one evening to give it a try. I was excited about the idea and hoped my enthusiasm would break down her refusal to go along.

"He can teach you how to howl at a wolf pack, and they might howl back," I said. "There's a good chance that'll happen, because Will knows where all the local habitats are up here."

"If you think it's so cool, go by yourself," Minnow said. "I'll stay here with Molly."

"But Will isn't doing this for me, Minnow; he's doing it for you. So you know what it's like to have that experience. Not everyone has a chance to interact with wolves—it's a gift he's offering."

"Why'd he do that, to get in your pants? No, I take that back, you've already got a boyfriend: Bud. And that's gross, you're so old. Jesus."

"And you're an obstinate brat," I replied. "No wonder you don't have any friends."

"I have friends." Minnow answered, defiantly.

"I mean in-person friends, flesh-and-blood friends, not just strangers you've met on the Internet."

"Shut the fuck up."

That was my cue to go out on the dock with Molly and take some very deep breaths. It was a cool morning, and I was certain that my body was steaming in the early chill.

"Minnow, I want you ready to leave here at 7:30 tonight when Will comes for us," I said when I returned.

"So instead of the Boy Who Called Wolf, I'll be the Girl Who Called Wolf?"

"No, you'll be the girl who learned to howl like a wolf."

"I can't wait," she said sourly. "On My Summer Vacation: I learned to howl."

"You'll also learn to chop wood and clean the outhouse and clear brush before the summer's over," I added. "And it wouldn't hurt to haul a pail of water up from the lake once in a while, either. You might even think about taking a bath. Frankly, you stink."

"Frankly, I don't give a shit."

Will picked us up just as it was getting dark. I hoped Molly would be all right in the cabin by herself, but she was already curled up on my bed and would almost certainly stay there without moving until sunrise. Still, I told her, "Stay."

"I think we'll have good luck," Will said to Minnow, who sat in the back seat with a sullen expression Will couldn't see. "The DNR does these flyovers—has your grandmother told you about them? They 'fly wolves' to track each pack—usually one wolf in each pack wears a collar—and the pilot makes a note of the GPS location. Yesterday, they detected a radio-collared female in the state forest, not far away."

He explained that howling surveys were routinely conducted to determine the general location of wolf packs and that July, August, and September were the best months for howls.

We drove for about a half-hour before Will pulled the car to the side of the road and turned off the ignition.

"Mosquito spray," he said, handing a can of OFF to Minnow and one to me. "As soon as you're out of the car, make sure you're covered. And don't talk—stay as quiet as you can."

We did as he said, although hordes of mosquitoes discovered our presence within seconds and whined around our heads despite the generous amounts of bug spray we applied.

"Okay, now we'll walk along the road for just a little way," Will directed.

"Don't we get a flashlight?" Minnow asked softly.

"No lights," he whispered. "We're trying to be inconspicuous. The moon's almost full, so we should be able to see where we're going."

We followed behind him for around a hundred feet, until he stopped.

"I'm going to do some soft howls," he said, "in case they're nearby."

He then cupped his hands in front of his mouth and made a sound that grew from a low moan to a high-pitched whine. He repeated this five times.

"Nothing," he said. "Now I'll try some loud howls."

He cupped his hands again, and his howls grew to a bold call that trailed into the forest and diminished with a shrill cry of anguish.

I shivered with chills as brief answering howls came from the depths of the woods.

"Pups," Will whispered. "Their howls are shorter and less bold than the adults' because they have less lung capacity. Let's get a little closer."

We returned to the car, and Will drove a short distance toward the pups. This time when we got out of the car, Will asked Minnow if she wanted to try.

"No," she said, brushing mosquitoes away from her face. "I don't want to. I can't do it."

"You can," Will said. "You watched and heard me. Do it. Now."

Minnow glanced at me and then over at Will. We stood there, waiting, as the mosquitoes indulged themselves. Slowly she raised her cupped hands to her mouth. Her first howl was self-conscious and tentative. She brought her hands down. Then, after a deep breath, she raised them and howled again. This time, an entire chorus of wolves began to howl along with her.

"Oh my God!" she said, backing away in surprise. "How many are there?"

"I'd say at least three adults and that many pups, maybe more."

"Can I do it again?"

"Once more," Will said. "Go ahead, give it a try."

Minnow howled again, and again, the same response.

Will gave her a hug, and she sobbed in his arms. He may have glanced over at me in the moonlight, but I had tears in my eyes. I think Will did, too.

A few days later, Eric and a couple pals arrived to remove the old roof. They would seal it with waterproof material and install the new asphalt shingles and skylights. They assured me it would only take a day or so with a small generator and battery-powered tools.

"Could you remove the pot-bellied stove?" I asked. "As long as you're here?"

The behemoth sat in the middle of the cabin and took up valuable space. The guys agreed this was a good time to do so, as they could then cover the hole in the roof where the chimney had been. They'd also haul the heavy stove away. I wanted one of those little compact Swedish stoves that fit unobtrusively in a corner and burned only one log for the entire night.

I'd hoped to burn my moll clothes when Minnow was on the lake, but it had been so hot and I'd forgotten and now the costumes were still hidden at the bottom of the blanket box. I dug out the moll stuff while the men were on the roof. Molls never wore anything like the red five-inch fuck-me heels I'd found at Goodwill, but Charlie took great pleasure in seeing me teeter in them—until the time I lost my balance, grabbed the table, knocked over an oil lamp, and set a stack of paper plates on fire.

If there had not been men pounding right above me and sawing two rectangles that (surprisingly!) let in an enormous amount of light, I could have become sentimental while reviewing the flimsy items. As it was, I sorted the lingerie on the sly so I couldn't be observed.

The moll fantasy was fun. We played it almost every time we were here. Except for that sad final time, of course.

To begin with, we'd drive to Little Bohemia—not speaking to one another during the drive—and Charlie would go into the bar for a drink. I'd wait in the car for at least fifteen minutes. Charlie would wear a three-piece suit, a nice tie. I'd slip into the ladies' room and change in a toilet stall, then cover my sexy new outfit with a trench coat so no one would think anything amiss. Often I'd secretly purchase a sultry new corset or a fancy bustier to surprise him.

I enjoyed the hungry, glazed look in Charlie's eyes when he'd watched me enter. Then he'd join me in the corner of the bar, where I'd found a place to sip my drink (this was usually mid-afternoon, when the bar business was slow). Sometimes he'd sit close and slip his hand under the hem of my coat. He loved to run his fingers up under my garter belt, toward my crotch, where he'd clandestinely touch me, if no one was watching.

When we went back to the cabin, he'd talk rough. Not angry or mean, but a sort of brutal gangster slang. Silly Charlie, he had a deeply suppressed persona. What a paradox. After that, our lovemaking possessed an intense fervor that turned me on, too. The old metal bed creaked with vigorous passion.

It was time to pick up Minnow, so I told the guys I was leaving. Molly and I took the boat and headed toward LilyPad. When I reached the far end of Sundog, where the Lost Arrow River begins, I turned down the motor. The moll clothes were stuffed into an old pillowcase, fixed into a knot. In the bow of the boat, the anchor was a coffee can heavy with cement, tied to a rope. We could concoct a new anchor easily enough, so I tied this anchor to the pillowcase, then heaved my mementoes overboard.

When I reached LilyPad, I heard Minnow telling Lily and Ginger about the wolf howl. "It was totally cool," she said. "The wolves howled back at me like we were having a conversation!"

I closed the door a little louder than necessary, so she wouldn't think I'd eavesdropped on her enthusiasm. Then, after Ginger's and Lily's greetings, I told Minnow that Eric mentioned she should give Chloe a call. So Minnow spoke with her, then hung up the phone.

"She wants me to look after Miriam for her," Minnow said. "And she'll pay me, too. Will it be okay, Grandma? She said I could start on Friday and work everyday."

Was she asking if I felt she was capable, or did she want my permission?

"What a wonderful opportunity," I said, giving her a hug.

"You'll be such a help to Chloe," Ginger offered. "She's got her hands full up there, with the Inn being such a success and all. The place got real popular a lot faster than they planned."

"Miriam will love you," Lily said. And Minnow grinned.

"Of course Chloe will let you take off time for Thundersnow," Ginger said. "She has to understand that we old women need you, too."

Minnow closed her eyes, took a deep breath, then nodded her head.

"By the way," I asked Ginger, "why aren't you working at the Saloon this morning?"

"Lost power last night," Ginger replied flatly. "Happens a lot."

Lily grimaced and spoke up. "When she gets tired of working she goes in the kitchen and flips the lights on and off a couple times, then leaves them turned off. 'Power's gone,' she yells. 'Sorry we have to close. Happens all the time up here.'"

"The *power* will be restored around noon," Ginger coolly replied. "And I think tomorrow morning would be a good time for another Mission Thundersnow, as long as Minnow will still be free. Agreed?"

Minnow was impressed with the amount of new light and fresh air the skylights gave Waters Edge. The stove had been removed, and the vacant area in the center of the room seemed to invite even more transformation. I had been toying with the idea of painting the inside walls with a thin coat of white, to resemble whitewash and obscure the water stains on the walls and the inside of the roof. With Minnow away, caring for Miriam, I could paint for a couple hours and then have a bath or a swim before I determined what I wanted to do for the rest of the day.

Neither of us was crazy about Ginger's sudden inspiration for another Thundersnow. Minnow said maybe it would satisfy Ginger's curiosity once and for all. I wanted to believe her, but I knew how tenacious Ginger could be.

This time Molly was going to stay at the Saloon with Babe, and Eric would keep an eye on them both.

Because she had practiced and mastered the art of Internet shopping, Ginger insisted we were much better prepared for our second outing. In addition to the earlier equipment, she now possessed a machete to hack at undergrowth. And she was not aware of the folding shovel in my backpack, so she'd ordered a folding camp tool that was a combination shovel, sledgehammer, hatchet, pickaxe—all in a handy faux-leather carrying case which she proclaimed a steal at $160. There was also a folding camp stool for Lily to rest on, and a first aid pack that contained emergency disaster gear, including a twenty-piece first aid kit, sanitary pads for Minnow in case she needed them, an extra whistle, utility knife, gloves, ponchos, waterproof matches, and enough food rations for us to have 1,600 calories apiece. This would all go in Minnow's pack—Ginger had ordered a new one for her, and it was colossal.

"Where's the mosquito netting?" I asked.

"Gol dangit, I've been busier than a one-armed paper hanger," she replied. "Hate to admit I forgot. How about using some cheesecloth instead?"

Minnow was still assigned the real metal detector, and Lily was content to use the kiddie one. Again, I carried Bud's dismantled shotgun in my pack. We each had a bottle of water and a plastic bag that contained a sandwich and an apple. But now we'd be wearing baseball caps to hold large squares of cheesecloth on our heads, which would drape over our faces and most likely obscure our view.

We'd planned to leave Star Lake at nine o'clock, but even though Minnow and I had arrived at eight, it took more than an hour for us to get dressed. By that time the sky had clouded over, and it looked like rain.

Minnow helped us with our stiff camo overalls (she still wore her lived-in jeans). Lily had purchased Depends but forgot to pull them on until she was in her overalls and the last button had been buttoned. We had to undress her completely because she insisted that she didn't want to be a burden by having to stop and go to the bathroom in the woods. I suggested it might be a good idea for all of us to wear diapers, but Minnow didn't think it was funny and threw me a snarly look.

By the time we got there, Little Bohemia had a busload of tourists wandering around. "They're all going to see us," Minnow complained. "And we look like a bunch of noobs."

She was right. We would stand out in the crowd with our overalls, backpacks, and associated items. But it was too hot to stay in the car, and Ginger insisted we just ignore them and go about our business.

Our leader had developed a new strategy for this attempt. Lily would go with her, and Minnow would accompany me. Because we were not able to complete the routes Ginger had traced on her maps the last time, we'd begin where we should have ended then and end where we'd begun.

"Remember, three trees in a semicircle," she repeated. "Two pines and an oak. And for inspiration, I want to read you all a little something."

I sighed, then turned the ignition back on so we could use the air-conditioning, since it didn't seem as though we'd be immediately hitting the trail.

Undaunted, Ginger continued. "With all due respect, I came upon this quotation on the Internet the other night: 'A third of the entire budget of the FBI in 1934 was devoted to hunting down this one man. After he was gunned down, Hoover maintained a macabre private museum of Dillinger artifacts, including the gun, hat, pocket change, and eyeglasses that were found on the body that night in Chicago. For the rest of his life, Hoover would refer to these curios with great pride and obvious personal satisfaction.'"

"So?" Minnow inquired.

"So this is a big deal," Ginger replied. "I want to impress that on you. J. Edgar Hoover, the head of the FBI, considered Dillinger to be Public Enemy No. 1, and getting him was practically all he could think about. Now, let's go get ourselves some loot, gals. Oh, and by the way, another thing I read was that newspaper reporters thought the molls were so young that they called them 'mollettes.' That's what Minnow is, our little mollette."

"It sounds like 'mullet,'" Minnow complained.

"A mullet's a fish," Lily said. "Maybe you're a baby mullet. A mullet minnow. I believe I should write a poem about that."

We left the car and put on our packs. This, in itself, garnered a small crowd.

"Who are you?" a little kid asked.

"I'm a frigging mollette," Minnow responded. "Who are you?"

"What are you doing here?" a man wanted to know.

A woman, suspicious, asked "Are you from the government?"

A man: "Four women? You gotta be crazy or something."

"With all due respect," Ginger replied officiously, "our project happens to be a carefully planned government secret. I suggest you give us space to work and keep out of our way, or you could be subject to disastrous consequences."

That warning didn't stop anyone. We set off into the woods with a parade of inquisitive tourists in tow. Lily and Ginger split off as indicated on the map, while Minnow and I plodded on, muttering to ourselves. The tourists split, too.

It was just as hard going as it had been the other day: thick bracken to tramp down, berry bushes tugging at our legs, no-see-ums swarming around our cheesecloth-covered faces, and mosquitoes whining in our ears. I especially hated it when they squeezed under the cheesecloth to get between my glasses and my eyes. Then I'd have to pause, remove my cap, detach my "veil," take off my glasses, wave away the mosquitoes, and invite more of them to settle on my face or fly down my collar.

We still had a few intrepid sightseers following us; the majority had gone with Ginger and Lily, because they moved more slowly.

Maybe six hundred yards from the resort, after we'd turned left and began following the contour of the lake, Minnow's metal detector began to beep.

"Grandma," she said, and took another step. The beeping became louder, more distinct.

"Wave it over the area in a circle," I advised.

She did, and the beeping turned into a loud whine.

"Folks," I addressed our followers, who had thinned out considerably due to bugs, brambles, and the oppressive heat, "we must now ask you to respect our critical task."

Minnow was on her walkie-talkie informing Ginger of the hit. She and Lily weren't far away, but it took them at least fifteen minutes to reach us. They, of course, brought their own rubberneckers along. How could we dig up Dillinger's hidden treasure with inquisitive spectators?

Ginger addressed the crowd assembling around us in a circle: "This has now become a restricted area. Our indications show that it is also powerfully radioactive. If you insist on remaining, we must have you show us picture IDs and sign waivers saying that the United States government will not be held responsible for any radiation injuries that you may receive."

Several people on the outer perimeter began to retreat.

"In addition," she said, "the four of us have ingested classified medicines to prevent us from fatal illness if what we find—and we have good reason to believe this is the case—that this is the target specified by aliens." She waved her map in the air above her head. "I am obliged to warn you, however, that without the benefit of those medications you may all become violently ill. It's my solemn duty as a certified government agent to warn you of this hazard."

"I have the papers for you to sign," Lily said, wriggling out of her backpack. "We're going to need your name, address, social security number, and the names and phone numbers of your current physician and any close family members to be contacted in case of your untimely death."

That did it. The tourists swiftly dispersed.

"Bravo, Lily," Minnow said, giving her a hug.

Ginger was already fiddling with Minnow's backpack to remove the combination tool from its handy carrying case and assemble it. Minnow paced the area with the metal detector, targeting the strongest signal to indicate where we should excavate.

I'll admit it. We were really excited, even though we could not see a semicircle of tress. The signal indicated this was more than a buried beer can or a pocket of loose change. And not very deep. I actually wondered if we'd stumbled upon the real thing.

As it turned out, our targeted objective was easily retrieved. Not far beneath the soil, Ginger came upon a disintegrating leather knapsack. I took the shovel from her and dug around it so we wouldn't disturb the item.

"Looks big enough to hold what we're looking for," Lily said with a note of awe.

"Pretty shallow. Could've been buried in a hurry."

"Where are the three trees?"

"Who the hell cares about the trees," Ginger said. "Pull it out of the hole. I want to see what's inside this puppy!"

"Wait a minute. We have to document our find." Minnow pulled out her phone and took pictures from every angle. Then she squatted and carefully ran her hands beneath the knapsack to loosen it from the soil, in what became a vain attempt to bring it up whole. The leather was rotten, and its contents immediately spilled.

The knapsack had held a cache of ammunition.

"What are these?" I asked, inspecting the bullets that dribbled out of the decaying container.

"Lemme see," Ginger said, holding one of the tarnished objects up to the light. "Looks to me like a .45. That would be ammunition for an old fashioned tommy gun, otherwise known as 'the Chicago piano.'"

"One of the first hand-held machine guns," I explained to Minnow.

"And there might also be some .38 ammo here for the handguns Dillinger carried in his shoulder holsters."

"How do you know that?"

"Research, my little mollette." Ginger was beaming. "Gals, we got ourselves some authentic Dillinger treasure. Maybe it's not the *cash* we're looking for, but for all intensive purposes there's plenty of confirmation that Dillinger hid a *cache* of ammunition in the woods a couple days before the big escape. Could be he wasn't able to find where he buried it, after the snow. Back up, and let's take a few more pictures of our evidence."

We replaced the knapsack on the ground and verified the proof of our discovery once more, from all angles. Then we passed the phone around and had pictures of ourselves taken as we pointed to our loot.

"Remind me to put 'camera' and 'mosquito netting' on my list for next time," Ginger remarked.

In spite of my elation, I felt my backbone begin to slump. Next time?

"Now let's get this wrapped up and take it home and cool off. It's hotter than the hinges of Hell out here, an' I gotta pee so bad I have to swallow to keep from drowning."

"Too much coffee," Lily remarked to Ginger. "You should've worn diapers."

Lily had a clean plastic garbage bag in her pack, and together we carefully placed the crumbling treasure inside, trying not to disturb it any more than it already had been by Mother Nature. Because of the crowd of tourists surely waiting in anticipation of our return, we decided that we'd march in step directly to the car, saying nothing, and return to the Saloon.

"What if we're followed?" Minnow said.

"Then we'll pull over and give 'em another warning," Lily concluded. "This time we'll tell them they have to be photographed and finger-printed, too."

"Alien treasure," I mused. "What might that have been?"

"Who the hell cares," Ginger said proudly. "The last person to touch what we got in that bag was John Dillinger. Stick with me, gals, and I'll have you farting through silk. I'm so dang proud of us and our Thunder-snow find. But let's keep it quiet; we don't want the media flocking up here to interview us just yet. There's still the loot."

"Ginger . . ." I began, and then faded away. Obviously this find was not going to quash her fascination. And we faced another quandary. The batteries in my GPS were dead. And Molly wasn't there to lead us out of the woods.

With the excitement of our trek, we also had ignored the storm building in the west. Now it started to rain, and strong winds threatened to blow us away. Again, I reached for my cell to call 911.

"Put that away!" Ginger shouted. "Put it down! I won't have you calling Fire and Rescue while we're on our mission! Hunker down, this is just a little squall. It'll blow over."

"A squall with thunder and lightning," I called over the wind. "Don't hunker under a tree!"

"There's an old boat," Minnow hollered. "Let's crawl under that!"

An overturned wooden rowboat had been discarded in a clearing surrounded by tall pines. We were already soaked by the time we reached the boat, and it was a tight fit, but at least, crouched together, we had a roof of sorts over our heads. Unfortunately, the storm did not let up until after dark.

"Whose idea was it to call this *Thunder*snow?" Lily fretted, clutching the bag with the ammunition.

"Why is there a discarded boat in the middle of the forest?" I wanted to know.

"It was put here for us to find it," Ginger said with nonchalance. "I think this is the chance of a lifetime for all of us, and I'm not going to argue with Divine Guidance, John Dillinger, or the Powers That Be."

We saw headlights on the road, after we crawled out from under the boat and attempted to stand up straight. "Head for the highway, gals," Ginger ordered, and we were too tired and wet to argue so we wearily followed her determined lead.

"Now, which direction do we go?" I asked, once we'd reached the gravel shoulder.

"We hitchhike," Ginger responded, "and ask for a ride to where we parked."

"We look too fucking weird," Minnow said. "No one's going to pick us up."

A group of kids decided to take a chance. They pulled their beat-up car over onto the shoulder and we climbed in.

"What's up with you guys?" one of the boys asked.

"Yeah, you look really feral!" another chimed in.

"Little Bohemia, please?" I asked. "We'd appreciate a lift."

"You go to school in Antler?" the first boy asked Minnow. "You should wear your grandma's overalls when we have 'Wear Your Camo to School!' It's freaking cool!"

Back at the Saloon, we removed our heavy gear, took hot showers, and ate our sandwiches with hot cocoa that Chloe brought to warm us up.

Then we carefully reviewed our treasure in more detail. Ginger showed us underlined pages in books and other documents that mentioned the buried ammo.

Despite my fatigue, I did feel a sense of pride. Charlie would have been so excited. Grandpa Waters, too. And how cool was it that Minnow, of the newest Waters generation, was involved in the discovery? What would we do with what we'd found? That was a question left unanswered for the moment, but I had no doubts that Ginger would figure it out.

⤟⤞

Minnow reported for work at Star Lake on Friday morning, by boat. I went into Antler for more ice and purchased paint at the hardware store, where I also rented a very tall stepladder that I had to tie to the roof of the car.

By Monday night, I had finished painting the ceiling. It was the worst part of the project, because even with the new skylights, the heat tended to settle up there. I bathed and felt refreshed. My supper consisted of fruit and cheese. Minnow worked at the resort until after Miriam was put to bed—the Inn served a prix fixe dinner every night, with Chloe as chef. Chloe was also a vegetarian, so she was delighted to cook a separate meal for two instead of one.

"How's it going," I asked Minnow after she'd tied up the boat.

"Pretty good," she told me, flopping into the chair next to me on the dock. "I never babysat before. Back home, none of our neighbors have little kids. And I'm an only child, so I didn't know a two-year-old could move around that fast. Or demand so much attention."

"Chloe says Miriam adores you."

"She tried to stick a nail up her nose today," Minnow said. "Chloe and I agreed that I should remove my jewelry next time before I come over so Miriam doesn't hurt herself."

"Meaning . . . ?" I asked.

"The nose ring, the lip rings. She doesn't know about the one in my navel."

I didn't either.

"And she asked if I had any other clothes. She was really polite about it, but I know my stuff must be getting pretty rank, because I heard Ginger washing my jeans and my tank the last time I stayed at LilyPad."

"Chloe might prefer that you wore something less dark."

"She suggested that. She's so nice about it, though. We've been talking about how it was when she was growing up, and the protest marches she went to in Madison and how she wore Eric's clothes to annoy her mother and had her head shaved."

"Please don't shave your head," I interrupted, shocked.

"Don't worry, Grandma," Minnow grinned. "I wouldn't do that. But I told Chloe I'd ask you if she could cut my hair." She tugged at her bangs. "I'm getting tired of this purple shit."

"Whatever you're happy with," I told her, blessing Chloe's positive influence. "It's your hair and your clothes—you'll have to decide."

"I want you to take me shopping," she said, abruptly.

Oh. My. God. Since her arrival in Rhinelander, I had yearned to hear those words from Minnow.

I had not seen Bud since the night of our dinner at Bonfire, and his Fourth of July picnic was almost at hand. Minnow claimed that as a vegetarian she would be totally out of place. I told her she could be of immense help to me by looking after Molly at the Last Resort, because I didn't want the dog off her leash over there. Nor did I expect to eat anything except whatever we brought ourselves. I promised we'd go to the Inn and have a couple veggie pizzas afterward.

"I have to make an appearance," I explained. "That doesn't mean we have to load our plates with garbage; maybe there'll be regular salads and even desserts."

"Maybe salads made from weeds," Minnow suggested.

"Maybe we'll bring a salad as our contribution."

"Ginger says she's going, and Eric will be there too. Lily refused; she says eating road kill is disgusting."

"I suppose if it's venison that's still fresh . . ." I was trying to prepare myself.

"And it's not against the law?"

"A friend of mine hit a deer near Madison with his car, and he had to get a deer tag. But then he could take the deer home and butcher it and put it in his freezer."

"Eeeew. That's nasty."

"Probably not as grotesque as the food at Bud's Road Kill Picnic. I suspect there'll be a lot of hyperbole."

"Yeah, like 'chunk of skunk.'"

"Or 'gizzard of lizard.'"

"How about 'poodles with noodles.'"

"That's not fair. Poodles?"

"I didn't want to say 'slab of Lab' and hurt Molly's feelings," Minnow said.

"Ummm. I could really go for some shake 'n bake snake," I replied.

As it turned out, the Road Kill Picnic wasn't as creative as Minnow and I had predicted. We'd brought a bowl of tortellini salad, fresh from the IGA deli, that we'd scooped into a nice dish and doctored up with sliced black olives, roasted red peppers, and walnuts.

I was surprised to see a fairly good crowd at the picnic, and now that I was not covered with blood or wearing my deceased husband's underwear, the group did not recognize me as the woman whose dog survived a wolf attack a month ago until Bud quieted everyone and announced who I was. There was scattered applause (it's hard to clap when you have a plastic glass of beer in one hand), and everyone wanted to greet Molly, whose glossy brown fur now covered almost all her scars.

Everybody seemed welcoming. Beemer, Dr. Baker's vet tech, introduced me to his buddy, Cooney. "Bet you can't guess where he gets that name from," he grinned. Cooney turned around so I could see that his gray hair was pulled back into a pony tail that, in turn, was attached to a raccoon tail. Beemer then introduced me to more of the other guests, whose names immediately vanished.

There were maybe ten picnic tables on the lawn next to the tavern, which was draped with patriotic bunting. A couple more tables held the makings of the peculiar meal we were expected to eat. Minnow added our salad to the array, then joined Ginger and Eric, who had saved room for us. Red checkered tablecloths flapped in the breeze and provided a festive air.

The woman pouring beer from a half-keg had long, curly blond hair like corkscrews, and she'd tied it with a length of yellow CAUTION tape.

"Who's that?" Minnow asked.

"That's Ruby Rose, Bud's girlfriend," said a woman at our table whose nametag read "My name is Toots." "Girl's got a hot temper, so I'd keep my distance."

I was relieved to know Bud had a girlfriend. Relieved and, I suppose, a little taken aback.

Ruby looked like a pistol in denim cutoffs cut so high that they revealed plump pink buttocks. A tight white tank stretched over what had to be enhanced breasts.

"Has she had a little work done?" I inquired of Toots.

"Honey, you don't know the half of it. Ever heard of 'trout pout'? Look at them lips. She might not be much of a beauty, but Bud sure needs her out here." She leaned over to someone else at the table and asked, "How long was it, Lois, since Bud killed them kids in their car after the football game?"

Lois said, "Six or seven years. He served time in jail and never took a drink since then. All of us felt awful for him 'cause everybody loves Bud. Well, for the families, too, because as you can tell, we're a close-knit community, the regulars. The summer folks, well, I'm talking this way since I know who your family is and you've been here awhile so you're kind of in the middle between summer and regular." It seemed the beer was getting to Lois. "Bud lost his licenses to drive and to run the Last

Resort. He still owns it, but Ruby has the liquor license, so he's beholden to her."

We tied Molly to the leg of our table and stood in the buffet line with our paper plates.

"Hard to fillet them hoop snakes," a man standing behind us said.

His partner agreed, "Yup, all sidewall, no meat."

"Good to see you," Bud nodded as we reached the first buffet table. "This is all safe to eat," he promised. "No one has ever gotten sick after one of our Road Kill Picnics."

"That's because he boils the hell out of everything," Ruby commented dryly.

Placards listed the ingredients in each dish.

"Redneck Steaks Skewered with Bloody Mary Dipping Sauce" were actually venison steaks marinated, grilled, and sliced into strips, skewered with toothpicks. I took two. Molly should be able to down them in one gulp.

"Eating road kill provides you with meat that hasn't been pumped full of antibiotics," Ginger said. I think she was serious, but I could not look into her eyes. "And it's locally grown."

"I've eaten frogs and toads," Eric commented, "and they taste like chicken. But it's pretty hard to find a road-killed frog or toad that's got enough meat to eat. They get pretty flat."

That had Minnow giggling.

An array of grilled sausages called "RATT" claimed to contain remnants of rabbit, turkey, and turtle. Nearby, there was a platter of hot-dog buns, one of which immediately took up space on my bare plate. On second thought, I lined it with ketchup, pickle relish, and mustard so I could have something to nibble and not just sit there like a side-dish no one had ordered.

A Nesco roaster simmering with stew promised porcupine, squirrel, and coyote. I dipped a ladle in and stirred it around.

Raccoon gravy was just that—bits of meat floating in gravy served with a side of french fries. I helped myself to the fries, and Minnow heaped her plate with them.

Barbecued bear. I figured that might be a little tough. The hoop snake man said there were more and more bears killed by cars these days, and it was a shame for all that meat to go to waste.

"Pot Roast of Fox in Red Wine" actually smelled pretty good, but I resisted temptation. Slices of carrot floated on top with baby onions and mushrooms.

Ah. Potato salad. You go right here, beside my french fries. And of course, this delicious tortellini salad with walnuts and olives—you look truly fab.

Back at our table, Eric expounded on the road kill rules when I asked where Bud got all this food.

"Folks hit something by accident, say a raccoon or even a deer, you get a permit from the DNR and you can take it home. Or you can bring it out here, and Bud puts it in one of his big freezers."

"I can't help it," Ginger said. "I got to tell you something that happened when I first came up north. I was just a young thing back then, and it was as cold as a well-digger's ass. Well, I had to have a job, and there wasn't much available so I got a job as a waitress at the old KnockAbout down by the center of town. I found myself a room on the outskirts that was more of a heated shed behind a trapper's house, where there was a bed."

"Heated?" asked Eric.

"If I stoked the stove with kindling, it might melt the frost on the windows," Ginger continued. "But that first night, I walked back from waitressing around twelve. Pitch dark, I didn't have the right clothes, and I was about freezing to death. So I opened the door to the shed, turned on the light, and the whole place was piled high with beavers. Frozen beavers. One stacked right on top of another. Let me tell you, I grabbed ahold of those beaver tails and began pulling them outside, one by one. Warmed me up, too! Finally I went up to the house and knocked on this guy's door. 'What's with the beavers?' I asked, and he said, 'Oh, are them botherin' you? I brought 'em inside to thaw 'em out so I can skin 'em.' I told him they were all outdoors at the moment, and I was going to bed."

Pleased with the laughter her story was yielding, Ginger dug into her barbecued bear with gusto.

"Confidentially," Eric added, "I know fur trappers contribute a lot of the meat from critters they trap to this meal—beaver, muskrat, and so forth; all they're interested in after all, is the pelts."

"How do you know the meat is edible?" I asked.

"If it's road kill and wasn't there the day before when you drove by, then it's probably fresh. In fact, I've heard that road kill with rigor mortis is still safe to eat if the weather's been cold for three or four days."

I asked, "Have you tried this tortellini salad?"

"That's about all I've eaten," he replied. "Is Molly still hungry?"

When his Road Kill Picnic was breaking up and the crowd of regulars was moving inside the tavern, Bud offered to show us where he kept his hunting dogs. Ginger and Eric took Molly back to the Saloon with them. Minnow and I followed Bud through the trees to a group of large overturned barrels that lay on their sides with dogs tied to them on long chains. Most of the barrels had dirty rugs or blankets inside. Seven or eight brindle-colored dogs jumped and yipped with excitement when they saw Bud approaching. The dogs were medium-sized, not as heavy as Molly, but athletic and agile. I remarked that they looked as if they'd be fast.

"Excuse the mess," Bud said, indicating the mounds of feces dotting the landscape. "With the picnic and all, I didn't get down here this morning to shovel the crap away. When they're out hunting, I use a radio collar on the hounds that are running."

Bud grabbed a collar from inside the cab of an old pickup that didn't have any tires. "That way, if a hound gets away from the pack, goes off on another trail, I can track him and find out where he is."

"What's with the tape?" Minnow asked.

"I tape a magnet to the radios when they're not being used. That turns them off and helps them last longer.

"Hi, puppy," Minnow said, reaching to pet one of the dogs.

"Hey," Bud grabbed her wrist. "Not a good idea. These aren't pets. I can't guarantee he won't bite."

He explained that the dogs were originally bred for boar hunting in Germany. "They're Plott Hounds, good hunters and sometimes vicious, as a matter of fact. They can tree a bear like nobody's business. Wish you could see 'em hunt. This one here's my favorite, old Bubba. How are you, Bubba boy?" Bud got down on his knees and stroked the head of a dog with a grayish muzzle, letting the dog lick his face.

"Bubba's been with me the longest, and we're real good buddies. He's my lead dog. Here, you can pet Bubba," he motioned to Minnow. "He got bit on the ham by a bear last year, right here on the hip. But bears are the least of our fears, aren't they, old boy?"

Minnow reached out tentatively and let Bubba sniff her palm. Then she patted his head and he responded affectionately.

The dogs chained to the surrounding barrels yipped and barked like crazy to get Bud's attention. Then he uttered a word I couldn't quite make out—something like "shaddup." And they were silent.

"Wolves are actually more dangerous to my dogs than bears are. You learned that with Molly—they don't like other canines invading their territory. After wolves are done with a dog, there's usually almost nothing left. Last year, during the training period, sixteen hounds were killed by wolves. In fact, I've seen remains where wolves ate the bones and all. They might leave the skull, and maybe the collar, but that's it. I could show you pictures that I guarantee would turn your stomach."

I had a feeling I had seen pictures like that, on my laptop.

"Oh God," Minnow said, covering her mouth in dread. She said goodbye to Bubba and began to retreat to the car. We followed her.

"Molly was just lucky that your grandma scared the wolf away in time," Bud told Minnow. "That's why I gave her a shotgun. Whatever you do, don't take Molly in the woods without a gun to scare the wolves away."

We were all heading up the path now, toward the driveway where the parking lot was thinning out. I could see Ruby clearing the picnic tables.

"I'll teach her how to use the shotgun," I promised Bud. I could see Minnow flinch.

"I know I haven't been around much, getting ready for this picnic and all," Bud apologized, "but I've been spending a lot of time with my hounds, too. The bear season opens in early September, and the official date for training hounds on bears is the first of July. I'm going to use my dogs one day next week, so if you're interested, I'd be glad to take you along to watch how they work."

We were at the car now and Minnow, standing behind Bud, gave me a frantic look and mouthed, "Please, no!"

I said we'd have to think about it, because we had so many fun things planned. That had Minnow's eyes rolling, too. "We're going shopping in Eagle River. And Minnow has a job."

"Besides, I'm against hunting," she remarked to Bud. "I belong to PETA."

"I'll bet you don't eat meat, either," Bud said, teasing. "You brought that pasta salad today, right?"

"I'm a vegetarian. And I won't wear leather or fur."

"I've heard 'vegetarian' is a word for 'bad hunter.'"

"Bud . . ." I didn't want him teasing her.

"I'll bet you eat animal crackers—"

"C'mon, Bud," I was serious now.

"Okay, how about this: A guy has a stick of celery sticking out of one ear, a leaf of lettuce out the other, and there's a zucchini up his nose. He goes to the doctor and asks him what's wrong. So the doctor tells him, 'Well for one thing, you're not eating right!'"

Minnow's face had become set and grim. She opened the car door, slid in, and pulled it shut.

"You were a little harsh," I said.

"I'll make it up if you agree to come along and watch my hounds. Honestly. This isn't something you usually get to see. There's at least twenty-three thousand bears in Wisconsin right now. Last year hunters took out over five thousand. But there were almost a hundred thousand hunters who wanted bear permits."

"Twenty-three thousand bears?" I was amazed at that number. "How big are they?"

"The sows, maybe around 120 pounds. But the males can be up to 300 or more."

What had I done with that trail-cam memory card?

"As I recall, you said you attracted them with bait."

"Where I have my cameras, I do," Bud said. "Sometimes I use a pail of Twinkies. Or stale doughnuts, that kind of stuff."

I gave him a tentative "yes," but when we drove away, I told Minnow that I wasn't really serious. Maybe it was the comment he made about Molly and the vision he'd given me of her lying there, a dead carcass with only a head and a tail. Maybe it was because he hadn't ever said a single word to me about Ruby or told me why he didn't drink.

"His jokes were rude," Minnow added. "How come he thinks he has the right to make fun of me? And that meal was so disgusting. It was a buffet of garbage."

"You're right, that's exactly what it was," I agreed. "In fact, I hope Molly doesn't get sick from everything that was slipped to her under the table. Are you ready for a pizza?"

"Why do they hunt bears, anyway? They don't hurt anybody. Bears were here first, just like wolves."

"You'll have to ask Bud," I replied. "It's probably a macho thing."

"Yeah, the guys get bigger balls if they shoot a bear."

"Or they get furry balls," I said and noticed that I'd provoked a wide smile.

"Let me teach you a little song. One of the verses goes like this:

Billy Black lacked hair on his balls,
And his pecker wouldn't peck.
So he took, he swallowed, he gargled
Some vegetable compound,
Now it's as long as a gy-raffe's neck.

By the time we returned to the cabin, Minnow had memorized every verse of the Lydia Pinkham song, and we were singing duets. The next morning I noticed Lydia's face had been carefully taped back together and was once again staring placidly from the wall.

9

Since our "dinner date," I had given more thought to Bud's comments about how he'd gone through a troubling time in his life and was trying to be a better person. Then I shared with Minnow what I'd been told at the picnic, that he had driven drunk and killed four students and that he'd spent several years in jail. We discussed the need for giving some people a second chance.

"You could see how proud he is of his dogs. I think he wants us to see how well they've been trained and how he uses them," I told her. "One more hike in the woods. How bad can that be?"

So we met Bud at the Last Resort on another very warm and muggy summer morning. We were on time, but he was restless, ready to go with six of his dogs caged and packed in the back of his pickup.

Minnow had been given the morning off; Eric had assured her it was a sight that she would probably never again have an opportunity to witness. She was wary. So was I, but I did like dogs and I was fond of bears. Despite my curiosity, I was privately skeptical.

I told Bud we'd follow him in my car. "It'll take a half-hour or so to get there," he replied.

"I'm still not in with this," Minnow complained as we took off after Bud who was whipping his truck on down the road. "I think it's cruel to hunt bears with dogs, and I still think Bud's a jerk."

"You know I'm with you on dogs tracking bears, but maybe we'll gain some factual evidence to back up our opinions.

"The bear-hunting season," I explained, "lasts about five weeks and has a few quirks—like placing bait in the woods to lure bears to a spot where you then know they're likely to be. And I guess some hunters use both. Bait and dogs."

"What do you mean by bait?" Minnow wanted to know.

"Anything sweet, mostly. Trucks bring barrels of leftover stuff up here. You can find ads for bear bait in the small local newspapers. Bears can't see much, but they can apparently hear and smell especially well."

"So does anybody hunt bears without bait or dogs? What about bows and arrows? That would seem more fair."

"Not sure, Minnow," I told her. "I'm just along for the ride like you are. Bud said that during the hunting season, the houndsmen have to trade who starts the season with those using bait. This year, I guess the hounds get to go first. And, by the way, baiting bears is banned in all but nine or ten states."

"Is hunting bears with hounds banned, too?"

"No idea. But Bud's an outfitter, and hunters pay him a lot of money to guide them and be assured of killing one."

"How much does he charge?"

"I've noticed in ads in sportsmen's magazines that most guides around here charge about $500 per hunt. But some offer deluxe packages that can run as high as a thousand dollars. First, the hunter has to get a license from the state. It's called a 'kill tag.' You get that by lottery. If you want more information, you could ask Will Davis. I'm not sure I understand all the details."

We were traveling pretty fast, and if I hadn't been chasing Bud, I'd have needed a GPS to show us where we were going. "Do you see any road signs? For all I know, we're already in the UP."

"You Pee?" Minnow repeated.

"Michigan's Upper Peninsula. People who live there are called 'Yoopers.'"

We turned off the highway and kept to the dirt tracks that led far into the forest. Two other trucks were waiting. They also carried dogs in cages. Bud introduced us to his friends. In the group, I saw Beemer, the vet tech who worked for Dr. Baker, and his pal Cooney wasn't difficult to spot with his raccoon ponytail.

The men talked among themselves for a while. There seemed to be some kind of argument before they went off without their dogs.

"You wait here a few minutes," Bud told us before he left. "We're going to check for bear signs before we release the dogs. It'll probably take about twenty minutes or so. Don't think I've left you stranded in the forest, okay?"

Minnow and I remained in my car. We tried to tune in the radio, with little success. I caught a brief weather forecast mentioning a cold front and thunderstorms, but I had no idea of where we were or where the station was.

The dogs were restless and irritable until their owners returned. Within ten minutes, Bud appeared at my driver-side window and said they were good to go. Minnow and I got out of the car to watch.

When they were released, the dogs abruptly began yipping and howling, and we had to run to keep up with them when they caught the scent. The dogs then began to bark differently—excited, short, sharp barks that lasted for maybe a quarter mile.

"We could see bears at our bait site from quite a distance away," Bud explained.

"How many bears?" Minnow wanted to know.

"A sow and two cubs," Bud said.

Minnow slowed her pace.

Ahead was a large oak tree, which the hounds circled, yelping now, squealing urgently, some of the dogs furiously scratching at the bark, trying to climb the trunk.

"They're gone," Bud explained. "Must've spooked 'em."

An overturned barrel at the base had been filled with what looked like jams and jelly and pie fillings. It had holes on the sides and a concrete block on top so it couldn't be tipped over. Bud had to yell now to be heard above the dogs.

"That's the bait, there in the barrel. It attracts the bears to this location. Sometimes wolves show up at this spot too, and that can cause trouble if a dog catches a wolf scent and goes after wolves instead of bears."

"Because the wolves will win?" Minnow yelled back.

"You got that right," Bud said.

There was a great deal of commotion.

"Look," Bud shouted above the swarming turmoil. We looked where he indicated and saw that the hounds had run a black cub up into the branches, where it hugged the trunk, trembling and panting. Guffaws, elbowing, and pointing ensued among the houndsmen, who passed around cans of beer and popped them open as they boasted about the superiority of their dogs.

"Grandma," Minnow cried, clutching my hand.

Bud's dogs bounded and howled with the others, all crazy with lust. We tolerated a few minutes of this before Bud said, "Well, that's the way it goes. No point having you hang around any longer. I'll walk you back to your car so you don't get lost."

I was ready to go.

He left his dogs still circling the tree. We said thanks and goodbye, but as we were getting into the car, we heard a rifle crack.

"What was that?" Minnow asked.

"Didn't hear a thing," Bud said.

"You're lying," I cried. "One of your buddies shot that cub!"

Minnow tripped and fell on the ground in her haste to run back to the tree. Bud tried to catch up to her, but Minnow was much faster.

The cub was on the ground, surrounded by cheering houndsmen who shouted their approval as their dogs wrenched and tore the live bear apart. Bloody flesh mingled with black fur.

Minnow began screaming. The guys yelled at Bud to get her the hell out of there.

Bud grabbed Minnow by the shoulders and roughly jerked her back.

"This is just to give the hounds a little taste," he assured Minnow. "Makes 'em better hunters. But you shouldn't be here. What they did, it's kind of against the law."

I noticed Bud's dogs were feasting on the cub. Even Bubba. And Bud did not make a move to pull *him* away.

Sickened by the sight, I vomited in the bracken and had to wipe my face on my sleeve. Minnow hugged me and, weeping, hid her head on my shoulder.

"Let's get out of here Grandma, please!" she begged.

"It's a rough sport," Bud apologized. "I shouldn't have invited you along. I promise I didn't know that would happen with the cub."

"Why do you shoot bears, anyway?" Minnow asked. "What do they hurt by being alive?"

"We've got too many. Just like wolves."

"How many wolves?" I screamed back at him. "How many bears? How many goddamned mourning doves? How many foxes? How many deer? How many is too many, Bud? How many is so many that you want to kill them all? Next thing you'll want shoot at birdfeeders. Jesus."

I'd had it with him. It all seemed to be about numbers and killing.

My phone rang in the midst of this rage. I saw it was Ginger, probably full of arrangements for our next damned adventure. I clicked my phone off without answering. I was so consumed with anger I couldn't even speak.

On our way back to Antler, Minnow was rigid with fury. I know I drove way too fast and we were just lucky we didn't get lost.

"It's like he was leading us to the slaughter," Minnow mourned, and I agreed; I didn't know if I'd ever be able to erase the carnage from my memory. I'd never forgive Bud for exposing my granddaughter to that sight.

"I grew up enjoying the sight of little black bears up north," I told her. "It was such a special treat to go to the dump at twilight. Those were the days before plastic garbage bags and recycling, when people threw leftovers and other trash on a pile at a place known simply as The Dump. Sometimes there were old stoves and ironing boards and other junk there, too.

"Grandpa Waters would drive his big black Buick in slowly, with the lights turned off, and we'd roll up the windows so the bears wouldn't smell us or hear us, and we'd wait. The car would get stuffy, but it wouldn't take long before one bear and then another would pad out of the shadows to root around in the garbage."

"Like we had to eat at Bud's road kill thing."

"Sort of. Anyway, it wasn't unusual to see a bear pick up a tin can and lick whatever was inside. Or a jelly jar. We thought they were cute. Eventually it got really hot in the car, but we couldn't make a sound or they'd run off; bears are very shy."

"Did you ever see wolves?" Minnow asked.

"Never. There are notes in the cabin journal that your great-grandpa Waters heard them howl in the 1920s, just after the cabin was built, but I don't remember hearing them when I was a kid. The wolf population had pretty much died off by then because you could hunt wolves year-round and collect a bounty. A lot of folks up here today are pushing for another hunting season for wolves.

"I think it was during the 1980s that I started hearing about wolves up here again. There were only a couple dozen. And now, because they're a federal endangered species, the wolf count has grown to over eight hundred. I can understand the need to get wolves off that endangered list and control the increasing population, but I don't want guys like the ones we just left back there in the forest, killing wolves. There has to be a better way. Will Davis and other experts are working on that."

We stopped in Antler for groceries and ice. When we got to the cabin, Molly was interested in all the dog smells we carried. Since we'd been talking about bears and bait—and because I was still really pissed off—I decided to risk showing Minnow where I'd found the bear bait in our woods. We were going outside the fladry, whose boundaries had become our comfort zone, so I took the shotgun along. I also showed her the remains of the trail camera and said I intended to have the photo card printed, one of these days.

"What if it was Bud who put the bait there?" Minnow asked.

I didn't think he would risk the chance of being discovered. But Minnow added that Bud didn't have any way of knowing I'd be coming north this summer.

Her comment seemed logical but annoying because I'd wanted to trust Bud and he'd seemed to try so hard to be my friend and help me out. Of course, I didn't reveal it to Minnow, but there was the romantic interlude I'd shared with him, and whatever happened with that? Was it *all* a con?

We were sweaty and sticky with bug spray, so Minnow went for a swim before she took the boat over to care for Miriam in the mid-afternoon. Early in the morning, I'd filled the sun-shower—a four-gallon flexible plastic bag that absorbs heat from the sun—and it had been warming on the dock since then. Now I clumsily carried it out back, where I hung it from a branch on a birch tree. I was sheltered from the lake, so I took off my clothes and bathed in a nice, warm, comforting spray.

While my eyes were closed and my hair was sudsy with shampoo, I heard a vehicle approach. It paused while someone got out to open the fladry gate. Damn! I couldn't clip the water off because I couldn't see the valve, so I called out, "Just a minute!" while I quickly rinsed my hair. Blindly (soap in my eyes), I groped for the towel I'd hung somewhere nearby.

"Who is it? Molly?" She hadn't barked, so it had to be someone she knew.

"Take your time," I heard Will Davis call. "I can't see anything because of the trees."

Liar. He could see me perfectly well. He may even have heard me singing. Immediately, I sucked in my stomach, just in case.

Will didn't mention it afterward, when I'd put on some clothes and called to him that I was "decent."

"I phoned, but there was no answer, and as long as I was in town, I decided to drive out," he said. "I didn't know if you'd had your radio on to hear about the weather. There's a line of powerful thunderstorms heading this way, and a tornado watch has been issued for this part of the state."

The humidity had become oppressive. Despite my shower, I was covered with a veil of sweat. A thin line of dark clouds lay close to the western horizon. Right now, everything was eerie and unnaturally still.

"I'd also like you to take a quick look at my speech. It's the keynote for the symposium. I need at least ten minutes cut from it, but I can't be objective anymore."

Will noticed all the changes in the cabin and said he could see I hadn't been sitting around like a lady of leisure. The new Swedish stove had been installed and I had only finished painting the walls a few days ago. I'd outlined with tape the messages written on the walls, so when I painted, the notes remained, as if they were framed.

"I like this one," Will said, reading aloud:

> I came here on crutches with a hot water bag,
> I leave fit to take on Jack Dempsey.
> —W. T. Garrettson, Milwaukee, July, '29

I'd also placed the dog photos in a frame with a mat separated into squares so they formed a nice collage. Minnow had carefully printed each dog's name underneath the appropriate picture. He paused to study them and commented on the space I'd left for Molly.

Will ran his hand over the now-white two-by-fours and paused to admire the mirror I'd purchased at an Antler antiques shop—it had a border of twigs, a bucolic woodsy style. Below it, the basin was now supported by a bentwood plant stand.

"Updated bathroom, I see," he remarked.

"Only this part of it," I said. "The outhouse can use some work."

He was in need of a haircut—white curls now touched the collar of his chambray shirt. I felt an incredibly strong need to run my hands through those curls. I could hear Ginger's admonition—"Girl, you're getting as horny as a two-peckered billy goat"—and pulled myself together.

When Minnow and I came back through Antler, we'd stopped for groceries. I'd checked my e-mail at the library and was relieved to learn that Howard Eberhart's urge to come up and check on my safety had abated. There were a few more angry missives from Howlers that I deleted without reading. A note from Camille: "Enjoying Budapest. Hope Minnow is not too much of a nuisance. You must try the baths when you visit this city!"

I'd picked up more ice and some frozen lemonade at the IGA, and now I fixed cold drinks. We sat on the porch, where I read through Will's speech and pointed out a few places he'd lapsed into terms that might be a little too dense for his audience. At least they were impossible for me to comprehend.

"I keep forgetting to give you something," I said and went inside to retrieve the memory card from my purse. "Can you get this printed for me, somewhere other than Antler?"

Will slipped the envelope in his shirt pocket.

Then I told him about our upsetting morning. I had to wipe away tears as I recalled the ravaged cub. Will said bear hunting was sometimes brutal and that he could not condone hunting with hounds. "Sometimes you'll find a hunter who'll take his dog over to the other side of his truck and dispatch it right there if it's not being aggressive."

He filled me in on the state's strict fines and penalties for shooting a bear out of season. No wonder the guys were mad at Bud. What we'd witnessed was even more egregious than I'd thought.

Eventually, Will began to gather his things. It was six o'clock by then and already so dark that I struck a match to light a lantern. The ominous clouds were closing in.

"Are you going to be all right when it storms? Where's Minnow?"

"She's at Star Lake," I said, and at that moment my cell phone rang. Ginger said Minnow was going to spend the night with them at LilyPad.

151

The crowd noise in the background seemed unusually loud for the Saloon. She said they were busy but added, "I tried to call you earlier. Big storms coming tonight Tallie, so you take care!"

This old cabin had been standing for how many years? I assured her Molly and I would be okay.

After she said goodbye, I wondered, if the storms were going to be *that* threatening, why hadn't she asked me to stay at LilyPad, too?

I tuned in my battery-powered radio before Will left. The tornado watch for Lakeland County had now been changed to a tornado warning: strong supercells had been spotted on radar.

The daylight was developing a sinister, sickly greenish color.

"What's for dinner?" Will asked. "I might stay a little longer."

"You're joking."

"No, I'm not. I won't get halfway home before these storms move in. Might as well wait them out. Keep you company, at least."

"I can do a fruit salad . . ."

"I've got groceries in my truck. Let's see what we can cobble together."

We ended up sharing a bottle of red wine, a steak, an orange and avocado salad, and a loaf of crusty bread, which we topped off with fudgy brownies.

Meanwhile, the thunder in the distance was growing. There was a breeze out of the west and a threatening whisper in the pines. Molly, who had recently become more afraid of storms, stuck to my side like Velcro. When the winds and rumbles grew even louder, she began to whimper and pant.

Will closed the windows and skylights to keep the rain from blowing in. My radio reception went to hell, of course. Nothing but static that we couldn't even hear above the roar of the storm.

Trees began to snap and crash. Shattered branches released the fragrance of fresh pine. Rain swept by in sheets so thick we couldn't see the lake.

I usually enjoyed the sound of an approaching storm and would linger in bed in the morning if I heard one moving in. But tornado watches and warnings were definitely something else. I'd always been terrified of tornadoes. They were numerous around Little Wolf when I was a child, and Grandpa Waters would call afterward when the sun came out to ask if I'd like to ride out in the country with him to view the damage. I grew up with a fear of having my tornado-whipped panties snagged on a barbed wire fence and pointed at by motorists who'd say, "Hey, look at that!" as if it were the worst misery I could experience.

"Come over here," Will said, seated on the side of my bed. He put his arm around me and pulled me close. "Are you afraid?"

"Are you?"

"I was more comfortable during dinner."

We laid back against the pillows, and when lightning cracked really close (I'd been counting "one Mississippi, two Mississippi") and thunder rocked the cabin, we instinctively joined in a protective embrace. Molly, shivering, tried to squeeze between us. We hugged her, too; the three of us huddled against the tempest.

It seemed as if the cloudburst had paused directly overhead, because the lightning and thunder did not seem to move on. Winds gusted so heavily the walls of the cabin creaked. I was aware of the tall trees above and around us, bending to their limit. For the first time, I missed the old metal bunk bed and the shelter the top bunk gave those crouching on the lower one. I was mighty glad I'd had the roof replaced!

After the storm calmed a bit, I reluctantly released myself from Will's arms to check my watch with my flashlight. Nine o'clock. The sun should be setting soon, but it had been alarmingly dark since seven.

"You're not going to start for home in this downpour, are you?"

"Are you extending an invitation to spend the night?"

I had an extra bed. And his dogs would be okay—he'd called a neighbor earlier to ask her to close the windows and let the dogs out. "I really wish you'd stay," I said. "This is a pretty scary storm."

Hail began tapping the skylights and soon clattered, scattershot, on the roof. The deluge continued. Thunder came and went.

We said goodnight around nine-thirty. It took a great deal of convincing to assure Will that I'd prefer Minnow's twin bed and that he'd be more comfortable in the larger, double one. Molly gave me a strange look when I crawled beneath Minnow's quilt, and she chose to sleep next to Will as if to say, "This is *my* bed, too."

Will only removed his jeans and his prosthesis. "Hope this doesn't freak you out," he said, before slipping beneath the sheets.

I didn't know how to react to that remark. Of course it wasn't upsetting, except for knowing the suffering he must have experienced before and after losing his leg.

"I sleep in my deceased husband's underwear," I replied. "I hope *that* doesn't freak you out."

As I blew out the last lamp, I could hear Will calming Molly with tender assurance. With no curtains on the windows, each flash of lightning was vivid. Would this storm never end?

"At least it'll be a lot cooler tomorrow," Will remarked. "This is a strong cold front moving in."

I had trouble falling asleep. The cabin cooled off as the temperature fell outside. Molly usually kept me warm, burrowed by my side on nights like this.

I took the quilt from Minnow's bed and covered Will and Molly. Then I slipped silently, cautiously, into bed next to my dog.

"Cold?" Will asked from the other side of the bed.

"A little. The extra quilt will help."

"You're safe now, Natalie. We survived. Everything's all right."

His reassurance seemed like a blessing. Across the foot of the bed I touched his one leg with mine, in gratitude. It also warmed my cold feet.

Will was up and fixing breakfast when I awoke. I lay there with my head on my pillow, watching him. Bacon had never smelled so good to me. He'd made a whole pot of coffee—I usually only made a cup at a time. My clock said six—but the sun was up, and Molly must be outside.

He'd even put a log in my new little stove, to warm the cabin.

"Good morning," he said, bringing me a mug of coffee. I sat up while he plumped my pillow.

"Forty-nine degrees outside, according to the thermometer on the porch. No wonder the winds were so strong last night—we hit ninety-eight yesterday."

"What's that hanging out of the back pocket of your jeans?"

"You mean this?" He pulled out a pair of red lace bikini panties and wriggled a couple fingers through the slit crotch.

"Molly was carrying these around. I figured you didn't want her to chew them up."

I pulled the sheet over my head. They must have fallen under the bed while I was hurriedly packing my moll clothes.

"Charlie liked them," I said, my voice muffled and my flushed face hidden from view.

"Your Charlie was a very lucky man," Will remarked.

I hope there aren't any trees down across the road," I finally offered after a few long minutes and several grateful gulps of coffee. Will was seated at the table, tuning in the radio for storm reports. A couple tornadoes hit in the UP and there were multiple reports of damage.

"I hope you have a chainsaw."

"Yes, I do. And gas for it, too."

"Then don't worry," he said. "I'll go out and take a look."

I put on a pair of sweatpants and a sweatshirt, and we had bacon and eggs before Will went outside to check for damage.

I heard the sound of the chainsaw, but it didn't last very long.

"Looks okay," he said when he got back. "Better check out my own place now."

I didn't want him to go. I wanted him to climb back in bed. He looked even more desirable now that he was scruffy and needed a shave. His eyes—his eyes—damn, I felt like Billie Frechette. It was as if his eyes could see right through me. And if they could, then he was able to read my thoughts.

He left his groceries with me and I walked with him out to his truck.

"I envy you," he said, "all the happy memories you have of Waters Edge. And your good marriage was part of it."

"One of the benefits of hospice was that Charlie and I found a lot of time to reminisce about the past and talk about my future. His biggest concern was always that I still had a lot of years left. I had to promise that I would get on with my life. As I know you realize, that's more easily said than done."

Will took both of my hands in his and raised them to his lips.

"Thank you, Natalie, for an unforgettable night."

I could feel the slight rasp of a day's growth of beard. Damn! I so wanted to place his face between my palms, bring it close to mine.

After he left, I allowed myself to linger in a state of bemusement for a little while. I hugged the pillow he'd slept on and inhaled his scent.

I wasn't especially pleased when Ginger and Lily docked their boat out in front. Minnow walked up to the cabin.

"We're on our way to the Saloon but wanted to make sure you were okay."

"I was worried about you, too," I said. "Everything safe and sound at LilyPad?"

"We lost power, that's all, but we thought about you over here, all alone. Everything okay?"

I said nothing, just nodded, but a little shiver of pleasure lingered from the warmth of Will's arms. We'd slept together. Sort of. Literally. Not amorously. But memorably. *An unforgettable night.* Did women my age have crushes? Whatever it was called these days, that's what I had. Madness, perhaps. Charlie would have liked Will.

Ginger waved from the boat and hollered, "That was one helluva humdinger, didja hear it?"

"I didn't lose any power," I joked, then beckoned the women inside for coffee. I knew Ginger was eager to see the changes Eric and I had made.

"Sure makes a big difference to have those skylights," she said. "Cozy, too, with that brand-new stove. And the white walls are nice. Looks European, almost. Now you need a fresh new set of windows. The ones with the knobs that crank the windows in and out are nice."

"Are you going to sew curtains?" Lily wanted to know. "I have a sewing machine."

"Not curtains," I said. "But I've been thinking about getting a small generator so I could have enough light to see when I clean. Maybe use a vacuum cleaner, too. Then again, it might be scary to see what the place actually looks like!"

"I'd like a toilet," Minnow added, "more than lights. You can get composting toilets that burn up all the . . . stuff."

"She's been reading our catalogs," Ginger said. "Those ones we used to order our hiking supplies. And by the way, it's time we plan for our next Mission Thundersnow."

I shook my head and sighed deeply. "Ginger, we've already hit a big jackpot. We haven't even decided what to do with our bag of ammunition!"

Why had I forgotten to tell Will about the relics we'd found? He would have found the last expedition very amusing. But it also would have revealed more about the ridiculous pursuit I'd consented to engage in.

"This is absolutely, positively the last Thundersnow you can count on me for," I stated firmly. "I'm beginning to wonder why I let you talk me into such a preposterous scheme."

"It was for the Waters legacy," Lily reminded me.

"For Grandpa Waters," Ginger echoed. "And Evelyn Frechette. Remember that letter I showed you and the clipping that fell out of it?"

"I don't think it's so awful," Minnow announced, which caused the rest of us to look at her in wonderment.

"I mean, it's historical, right? We proved John Dillinger did bury a cache of ammunition, just like his gangster friends said. And if we'd find buried treasure, well . . . maybe I wouldn't have to go back to New York and my sucking other life."

"What would you rather do?" Ginger asked, serious now.

Minnow was silent. "I'm not sure," she said, "but anything besides that."

The day turned out to be rampant with callers. After Ginger and Lily left with Minnow, a woman from the Antler florist hiked her way down the hill and called out through the screen door.

"I have a floral delivery for Natalie Waters."

Molly barked an audacious welcome, so the woman placed the bouquet on the steps and quickly jogged back to up her car. I had no idea how she'd found us.

Flowers from Will, I wondered? That would be nice.

But the basket of pink and yellow roses, yellow and lavender carnations, carried a handwritten note.

Truly sorry about yesterday.
Hope we're still friends. Bud.

And I had another visitor: Warden Jensen. He asked about the location of bear bait on my property, which I gladly hiked back into the woods to show him.

Then he wanted to know if I had the photos from the camera I'd destroyed. I told him they were currently being developed.

He asked if I knew exactly where the houndsmen shot the cub.

I realized Minnow must have contacted the DNR and filed a report.

"I can't give you the exact directions," I said. "But I could show you how to get there."

"Do you have time to go with me right now?"

"Can I bring my dog?"

10

I've grown to love these lazy mornings of meditation, evocative private thoughts, sitting on the dock on a quiet Northwoods lake with my dog and my pen. This morning the still water reflects the haze lifting from it like so many ghosts that materialize and evaporate. I would like always to awaken to this calm world, the wilderness in which I find a kind of primal comfort pressing in on all sides. Soon, the sun on the lake will be like a morning fire—blazing, blinding.

Being here this long gives me an idea of what it would be like to live here year-round. Silence and solitude. No police or fire sirens. No train whistles, no threats of random crime. But no library five minutes away either, or post office or shopping mall. Here there are hours spent driving, and in the winter the snow can be five or six feet deep." It's like going through a tunnel," Ginger says." At least you never have to worry about going off the road!"

I think I can just be content to be one of the" summer people" and spend weeks in this landscape so dear to my heart. I love the reassuring snore of my dog at my feet, her occasional snuffle and the odd, large sigh. What causes her to feel so resigned?

Chloe called yesterday to confirm details for this weekend's wolf symposium. I volunteered to help in the *kitchen, so I'll be able to hear Will's speech. I knew she needed a hand. And she mentioned that one of Bud's hounds has gone missing! His favorite, Bubba. Apparently someone cut his chain. Who would commit such a reprehensible act?*

⟋⟍

When the symposium, "A New Era for the Wolf," commenced Saturday morning, I had been in the Inn's kitchen since four-thirty, working with Chloe to get a casual breakfast for those who were up in time for pastries and coffee before the morning workshops. I regretted not being able to attend several of the discussions:

> An Investigation into the Use of Self-Medication in Captive Wolves: Do Wolves Select Plant Chemical Defenses to Protect Themselves from Disease?
> Ethiopian Wolves: Rabies and the Afro-Alpine Ecosystem
> Large Carnivore Conservation in Europe and the UK

"This is the third conference we've had here, but it's the largest by far," Chloe said. "Over a hundred registrants! I'm so grateful you offered to help, Tallie. At last night's welcome reception I met people from all over. They said the workshops and their leaders had been a big draw, but Will Davis is so popular! He seldom appears in public. and he's sold thousands of books."

The Inn supplied thirty double rooms, and the old cottages down by the lake were also filled. I imagined motels and resorts all around Antler were taking up the slack.

A wolf howl (of course) was scheduled for later tonight, with school buses that would haul the would-be howlers into the nearby state forest. Tomorrow morning, Sunday, there was one last gathering before the farewell lunch at noon, at which there'd be an opportunity for everyone in attendance to meet Bruce Bartlett, a painter of wolves, whose work would be displayed at the Inn, and Anthony Brewer, who photographed wolves—his work would be exhibited, too.

Everyone had enjoyed their breakfast, and they were now tucked away in various meeting rooms. The luncheon buffet was ready, and girls from Antler, hired for the weekend, dressed in clean jeans with dark blue Star Lake Saloon T-shirts, were setting up the spread in the Inn's two-story dining room of pale varnished logs and so many floor-to-ceiling windows that it seemed you were right outdoors among the trees. Buffet tables were crowded with sliced ham, smoked turkey, three kinds of cheese, homemade rolls, tomatoes, fresh green salad, pickled beets, you name it. Ginger had insisted that we include fresh cheese curds, so she had gone to the factory in Cedar Springs to purchase them this morning, warm, squeaky and salty, right out of the vat. I'd already nibbled more than my share.

Down by the Saloon, Eric had a pig already turning on the spit for the evening's spanferkel. Crocks of homemade sauerkraut had been fermenting in the wine cellar for weeks, and Chloe and I would have German potato salad and apple pies ready for dessert. Ginger would serve six kinds of beer, all Wisconsin artisanal microbrews.

Minnow was playing with Miriam somewhere on the grounds. Chloe had given Minnow a dark blue T-shirt so she'd look like the other girls, and she was thrilled.

I'd parked Molly with Lily and Ginger, who were at the Saloon. She'd probably lie on the porch swing with Babe and sleep all day. Of course Lily never "tended bar"; she was more like Ginger's lady-in-waiting—doing the waiting, and she seldom drank anything stronger than iced tea.

So it seemed peculiar when Lily burst into the kitchen just before noon and breathlessly announced that Bubba had been found.

Climbing the hill caused Lily such distress that she had to sit down and place her head between her knees. We couldn't understand what she was mumbling, she was so unnerved.

"That's great, isn't it?" I asked, but Lily shook her head.

"Take your hands away from your face," I told her. My own hands were involved with massaging a bowl of buttery piecrust. "We can't hear you!"

"Dead," she said flatly. "Bubba was killed. Devoured by timber wolves."

"Who told you that?" Chloe demanded. "Somebody at the bar?"

"A fisherman got bait at the Last Resort, and Ruby told him."

"Shit." That was Chloe. I muttered something similar, because I knew how heartbroken Bud must be.

But Lily? Why was *she* so distraught? I didn't think she'd ever met Bud or his dog. The intensity of her agitation didn't make sense.

Ginger was still down at the Saloon. Convention guests who'd arrived the night before found its quaint porch perfect for sitting and nursing a beer. I wiped my hands on a towel and made a call down to Ginger to verify Lily's news and warn her to keep an eye out for unusual activities later on. No telling what might happen if the Howlers knew about Bubba's attack and decided to attend Will's lecture en masse.

Ginger agreed that all hell might break loose among Bud's friends when news of Bubba's death circulated. Then Chloe called the sheriff to warn him of a possible disturbance and asked if he could spare a deputy for the afternoon. I was so shaken that I poured half a pitcher of water onto someone's lap while refilling glasses, and Eric left the pig to comment on the irony of the juxtaposition of events. Disturbing vibes were definitely surfacing.

It was nearly two o'clock and time for Will's keynote speech by the time we had the tables cleared and the kitchen straightened up. All the apple pies I'd baked were cooling, and the fragrance was extraordinarily enticing.

Grateful for a brief pause to go into the audience to hear Will, looking like an old granny with my apron and hairnet, flour smeared on my face, I tried to be unobtrusive and sat in a folding chair next to the kitchen door. Immediately, I noticed unregistered guests leaning against the back wall with arms crossed and belligerent expressions. Bud was not with them, but Beemer and Cooney and Bud's other bear-hunting buddies were. Howlers. Chloe, standing beside me, whispered that the deputy had arrived.

Will was introduced and warmly welcomed by the crowd. I had not seen or spoken with him since the night of the big storm. He wore black jeans and a black long-sleeved T-shirt. His white curls had been trimmed. In one hand he carried a pair of reading glasses, which he slipped on.

I slept with that man, I thought. And then I amended that reflection because I hadn't really *slept* with him in a carnal manner, but we'd both slept. In the same bed. I smiled to myself.

A table next to the lectern held stacks of Will's most recent book, fresh from the publisher. *The Wolf: Restoring Nature's Balance.* After lengthy applause, Will began his talk and PowerPoint presentation by saying, "No matter where you find wolf conservation efforts, you'll find the politics of wolf management. Wisconsin is not an exception."

Then he explained the history of Wisconsin's wolf population and went on to discuss what was happening around the globe.

"The Mexican gray wolf is another example; an important part of the Southwest's ecosystem. It's been extinct in the wild since it faced a wholesale slaughter by our government and ranchers in the first part of the twentieth century. Right now there are only about fifty Mexican gray wolves, as a result of reintroduction efforts. Montana and Idaho are already pressing to allow public wolf hunting.

"But it's not just here in the United States. Take the Tver region of Russia, where a bounty of $50 is offered for every wolf, pup or adult. Once a hunter applies for the bounty, he can do whatever he wants with the pups—sell them to zoos or circuses or to people who want to have a pet wolf. If he can't find a buyer, the hunter can kill the wolf. Bulgaria also offers a bounty.

"Then there's the Arabian wolf, a subspecies of the grey wolf that lives in one of the most extreme environments on earth—the arid and semiarid areas of the Middle East, where it inhabits mountainous areas, gravel plains, and desert fringes. They need large home ranges, which they patrol constantly, and they escape the heat by digging deep dens and burrows. They cannot survive without water, so they do not wander far into the great sand deserts."

"Fuck them Muslim wolves," someone suddenly shouted from the back of the room. "Let the camel humpers worry about 'em."

Will ignored the heckler and continued. "The Arabian wolf was once found living throughout the entire Arabian Peninsula, but now it can only be found in small clusters of southern Israel, Oman, Yemen, Jordan, Saudi Arabia, and possibly in parts of the Sinai Peninsula in Egypt. To see this wolf in the United Arab Emirates, one would need to visit Arabia's Wildlife Centre in Sharjah."

"Who the hell gives a crap about them!" another man cried. "We got too many goddamn wolves right here in Wisconsin that we need to kill!"

"In Ethiopia, the World Wildlife Federation is working with the Ethiopian government on implementing a regional resettlement plan for the rare Ethiopian wolf—"

Will attempted to continue, but the turmoil in the back of the room was growing. As Chloe and I watched along with the rest of those in the dining room, the Lakeland County sheriff's deputy approached the intruders and asked them to exit.

"Murderer!" one of them pointed at Will. "Wolves are slaughtering our hunting dogs and our pets. Next thing you know, it'll be our kids. Who in the hell do you think you are?"

"Yeah, we heard you got one of your legs torn off by a wolf!" another guffawed. "Who are you to talk, you stupid fuck?"

That's when things began to really get out of hand. The registered attendees looked around uncomfortably and began to rise from their tables as if to leave. They attempted to ignore the Howlers, who continued to shout. Then one of the Howlers turned over the reception desk; another threw a heavy glass vase of flowers into a window, and an enormous pane shattered, scattering shards everywhere. Some conference-goers ducked for shelter beneath their tables.

When the Howlers began throwing anything they could grab hold of toward Will at the front of the dining room, it was evident that the deputy could not round them up on his own. Eric and several of the more muscular conventioneers attempted to help. Awkward punches were thrown. Men ended up wrestling on the floor, on broken glass. Chairs were overturned as the uneasy crowd rushed to get out of the way or to move in closer for a better view. Chloe and I took cover in the kitchen and watched the confrontation through a crack in the door.

Outside a siren sounded as another squad car pulled up. Finally, the Howlers were arrested, handcuffed, and taken away. The dining room was in absolute disarray. Chloe was in tears.

I wondered, uneasily, if the Howlers knew that Minnow had contacted Warden Jensen with information about the cub. Or that I had shown him where I'd found bait on my property. And that I'd destroyed the trail cam. Had I unintentionally helped ramp up their antagonism?

I slipped out a side door and ran down to the Saloon, which was locked, of course, because Ginger and Lily had gone up to the Inn to hear Will's speech. Now they were probably helping Chloe and Eric clean the dining room, as I was aware I should be. But the porch was open and blessedly empty except for Molly and Babe, both dogs flopped and snoring placidly on the squeaky glider.

I wedged myself between them and leaned over to hug them, trying to stop shaking. They remained unmoved by my presence. Sweet Molly, sweet Babe—I stroked their velvety ears and tried to match my rapid and shallow breathing to theirs.

Poor Chloe and Eric, who were so earnest and hardworking and had devoted their efforts to making this event a success. Poor Bud, who'd lost old Bubba, his favorite hound. Poor Will, who had to endure the disgrace of a mob of miscreants.

I hugged the dogs even harder and buried my face in their fur. If the bar hadn't been locked, I'd have poured myself a glass of wine.

I've been looking all over for you," said Will when he opened the door to the porch. "Only got a few minutes—we're taking an hour to straighten things up and settle everyone's nerves."

He squeezed next to me on the already crowded glider, and the Labs adjusted themselves to drape themselves over our laps.

"I want to give you these pictures from your trail cam. I had them processed in Minocqua so nobody would be recognized. A couple nice action shots of you," he teased.

I thought he was going to tweak my cheek in jest but he brushed flour from my forehead and my chin.

I stuffed the photos in the top pocket of my apron before I whipped off my hairnet and put it in there, too. I was sure I had raccoon eyes from my tears and smeared mascara.

"I wish that hadn't happened," I said, "up there."

Will just shrugged and stroked Molly's head. "Well, it gave the audience a firsthand glimpse of the heated emotions that the presence of wolves can exacerbate. I've got to get back." He shifted Molly's body, gave my arm a friendly squeeze, and stood.

But Ginger and Lily were coming up the steps. Ginger asked Will if he'd like a drink, and he admitted with a sigh that he wouldn't mind a beer. So he resumed his seat, and after Ginger brought his beer, she began to lobby for the next Dillinger expedition. I couldn't believe her gall.

"Not right now," I pleaded. "Ginger, that's the last thing on my mind!"

"Oh, calm down, Tallie. What happened just now, well it's about as important as a pimple on a gnat's ass."

"John Dillinger again," Will said, with more enthusiasm than I wished.

So Ginger launched into the next chapter, including the discovery of the buried ammunition. I reminded Will that he had to get back to the Inn.

"I do," he said. "Sorry." He drained the rest of the bottle and handed it to Ginger. "But I'm very interested in hearing more about what you've found."

Ginger offered to walk with Will back up to the Inn. I was no longer paying any attention to her. I was hugging Molly and Babe and thinking about Bud and the fact that it was so very coincidental that my dog was wounded by a wolf and Bud lost his favorite hound to the same kind of predator.

Lily sat at a table, calmly dealing a game of solitaire. Ginger must have slipped her a Xanax or two.

"I'll be back in a few minutes," I told her. "Watch the dogs, okay?"

I grabbed my keys from the kitchen and headed over to the Last Resort. This was the first time I'd been in the tavern since the night of Molly's attack, and Ruby was there, serving beers to a half-dozen men.

"Is Bud around?" I asked,

"How come you weren't here with your lady friends the other night?" Ruby asked with a smirk. "Never had 'em stop by for one of our shitty pizzas."

I honestly didn't know what she was talking about. Presumably Ginger and Lily had ordered a pizza at the Last Resort. Kind of odd, since they'd claimed their pizzas had an inedible cardboard crust.

"I want to offer Bud my sympathies about Bubba."

"You looking for him, he's probably down with the rest of his dogs," Ruby replied. "But don't go feeling too sorry, okay? Those guys claim a lot for a good hound that's been killed by a wolf, and the state'll pay 'em, too."

Then Ruby added, with a genuine touch of sympathy, "I hear you had some kind of a ruckus over at Star Lake just now. Sorry 'bout that. Those idiots were here all morning getting 'ammunition' for their brawl. They're none too happy about you and your dealings with the game warden, neither. Be careful with them," she said and firmly grabbed my arm. "I'd watch out if I was you. I mean it!"

I could feel my face turn red, so I just said, "Thanks," and left.

It didn't take long to walk down to where Bud kept his hounds. I saw him right away, seated on Bubba's empty oil barrel holding a length of chain in his hands.

"Bud," I said, causing him to look up sharply. "I heard what happened, and I wanted to let you know how sorry I am."

"He was a good old boy," Bud said, nodding. He took a rumpled handkerchief out of the back pocket of his jeans to blow his nose. "Didn't think I'd get so emotional," he apologized, clearing his throat.

At this point, I had nothing more to offer. I was ill at ease with his grief, but recalled how he'd held me in the vet's office so I went to him. Bud put his arms around me and sobbed on my shoulder like a little kid.

"I should've put him down after last season, but Bubba lived to hunt. He was stiff with arthritis and going blind. I thought maybe he could have one more good year, following the pack. But I knew when I took him out, that day you and Minnow came along, his hunting days were done. He wasn't aggressive. He'd gone soft, unsure of himself. Whoever cut this chain did me a big favor, in a way. Somebody else put Bubba out of his misery so I didn't have to."

I was patting him on the back and making soothing sounds, but questions were building in my mind. When did Bubba go missing, and where was he found? What shape was he in? How did they know for sure it was a wolf that got him? And who did Bud suspect had cut the chain?

"I got a good idea who did it," he said, as if sensing my thoughts. "Goddamn Beemer. He and his buddy Cooney were out in the woods and mad as hell I brought you guys along. In fact, Beemer's the one who shot that cub. I never told you. Pissed off at me ever since. He's probably going to lose his hunting privileges for three years and pay one heck of a fine."

"Because I reported him?"

Bud took a deep breath, pulled away from me, and lit a cigarette.

"Beemer had a nice little shady business that he ran on the side. No way you'd have any suspicion of that, but that cub wasn't shot just so the dogs could get a sample. You can bet Beemer got in there and pulled out the gallbladder first.

"He used to work with me when I started taking clients out to get bears. And when they got one, Beemer always offered to clean out the bear for them free of charge, so they wouldn't have to get their hands dirty. I thought that was a nice gesture. Helped me get a lot of clients, too. Wasn't a year or so before I discovered that Beemer was stealing the gallbladders, drying them and selling them to China. Matter of fact, I wouldn't be surprised if Beemer's strewn bear bait in a dozen different spots around here. If you told me he killed the bears, slit 'em for the gallbladders, and let the carcasses rot in the woods, that wouldn't surprise me either."

"What's the deal with gallbladders?" I asked, mystified.

"The Chinese use 'em for medicine. Don't know much about it."

He seemed to be getting uncomfortable, so I made a move to go.

"Where did they find Bubba?" I asked him then.

"That's another thing," he said, looking off to the side. "How could a blind dog run that far away?"

"Did Beemer know that Bubba was blind?"

"I hadn't told anyone yet. His eyes weren't all that cloudy, and I wanted to see if he could carry his load with the pack. You're only allowed six hounds on a hunt, and Bubba was taking up the space of a younger dog."

Just as I was giving Bud a goodbye hug, Ruby came down to join us.

"I'm leaving now," I told her.

When I started up the path, I detected a flash of green among a group of pines and took a closer look without trying to be obvious. It looked exactly like the handle of a bolt cutter we had hanging in the lean-to at our cabin. One summer, I forgot to bring the key along for the lock on the boat, and Charlie had to go into Antler to buy a bolt cutter. The sight of it made my stomach lurch.

Ruby fell in beside me.

"He's having a hard time of it. Worse than I figured, but the guys brought Bubba around this morning, and honest to God, it was just Bubba's head and collar and backbone, not much of him left at all. Before Bud got a good look, I wrapped Bubba up quick in heavy plastic and put him in the freezer. Dr. Baker will have to check the remains and get him signed off on Monday with the DNR and the other guys. No way we could get it all done today, and I didn't want Bud getting even more worked up than he already is."

"You say 'the guys,' brought Bubba in. Who were they?"

"Strange you should ask," Ruby said with a harsh laugh. "The same ones that caused that row over at Star Lake today. Quite a coincidence, huh? Bunch of real brainpower there."

When I returned to help with the spanferkel, Will had finished his presentation and folks were milling around. Eric's rotating pig garnered a lot of attention and the aroma was fantastic. Minnow was on the porch of the Saloon, swinging with Miriam and reading to her. Ginger was listening to the story, and Lily was playing solitaire.

"So how's everything over at the Last Resort?" Ginger asked, avoiding my eyes.

"I heard you and Lily stopped by for pizza the other night," I replied. "I thought you told me their pizza wasn't very good."

"I thought it was fine," Lily replied, staring at her layout of cards. "But the pepperoni gave me heartburn."

The women, including Minnow, who fussed unnecessarily over Miriam, seemed noticeably uncomfortable. Maybe I shouldn't have mentioned the pizza; it was really none of my business. Anyway, I didn't have time to hang around. It was already five o'clock. Cocktails were at six, and dinner was scheduled for seven; Chloe would be looking for me, and I didn't want to let her down.

❧

Minnow had put Miriam to bed, and when I left the Inn, Chloe said she was heading there herself. It had been a very long day. I was wiped out, but I assured Chloe I'd be back to help serve breakfast the next morning in a dining room that now had plenty of fresh air. Because it would be Sunday and the final day of the symposium, the breakfast buffet wasn't scheduled until nine o'clock. We were serving egg stratas that were waiting in the refrigerator, all set to bake.

So it was around eleven o'clock when I finally got back to the Saloon, where Ginger said she and Lily were heading out soon and I assumed Eric would be taking over the tavern duties. That was not unusual, as Eric usually held the ten to two o'clock shift. It wasn't very busy; those who wanted to "get a snoot on," as Ginger put it, were interested in something more than a beer bar on a long, winding gravel road that didn't see much traffic in the way of other folks to drink or play pool.

"Sit down, Tallie. We gotta tell you something," Ginger ordered. She was wringing her hands.

"If it's about the next Thundersnow expedition, this is really not the time," I said. "I'm so tired, honestly, that I can barely stand up."

"Then sit down," Lily ordered. I was stricken by the unusually harsh tone of her voice.

"Let's go inside," Ginger offered. So we went in the bar.

"A cup of iced tea?" Minnow asked. "Herbal? Lemon Zinger?"

I agreed that would be fine.

We sat around a pub table, one of those high bar tables with tall stools. Minnow brought my iced tea and served the same to the others, including herself. The bar was empty. Even Eric was not there.

"The Saloon's officially closed tonight." Ginger said. "Private event. There's plenty of beer up at the Inn."

I sipped my cold glass of tea, and although I was dead tired, I was now anxious and annoyed.

"Okay, about the pizza," Ginger began. "You're right, we went over there."

"That was the night with the tornado warning, when I stayed at LilyPad. I contacted Warden Jensen," Minnow admitted. "I didn't want you to know, because I wasn't sure you would approve. I told him about the bear cub. And the bear bait you showed me, on our land."

Wearily, I admitted that I was aware of that. "So if that's all you have to say, then I really would like to go."

"It's not all," Ginger interrupted. "Back to the pizza, okay?"

"The pepperoni gave me heartburn," Lily repeated.

"I know it did, sweetie," Ginger told her with an affectionate hug.

3

Cry Wolf

Never trust a woman or an automatic pistol.

John Dillinger

11

"Can this wait for fifteen minutes?" I begged. "I have to be back here early tomorrow morning, and I'm really, really tired."

Clean towels were stored in a closet near the communal bathrooms in the lodge above the Saloon. I'd planned for a hot shower and had stuffed a flowered cotton shift in my bag. I threw the shift over my head and came downstairs clean but barefoot, to confront three faces with strained expressions.

"Okay," I said, climbing back up to my seat at the pub table. "Does this have something to do with a bolt cutter with green handles that's supposed to be hanging in our lean-to?" I asked Minnow. "Because I spotted one just like it, flung under the trees at the Last Resort not far from Bubba's kennel."

Minnow cleared her throat. "Well, what happened was—"

Ginger interrupted, "That night when we got a pizza—"

"Go ahead," I said, encouraging them to spit it out. I was exhausted and impatient and didn't much give a damn.

"Ginger called you from there to tell you about the storm. And we provided a commotion so Minnow could cut the chain." Lily sputtered.

"Cut the dog's chain?" I repeated, but Ginger was already explaining the elaborate script they'd devised to divert Bud and Ruby's attention. "First we played the jukebox. Loud. Country and western. Put five bucks in. Lily said she didn't want the pepperoni pizza, but I insisted, and then Lily made a fuss like we planned, so I asked if they could manage a half-and-half, but Ruby said the pizzas were frozen either one way or the other, with pepperoni or without, and we said why couldn't they just crack 'em apart and make one out of the two parts, one side pepperoni and the other side plain. Ruby got hot and bothered and yelled at us. Just like we wanted."

"Pepperoni gives me heartburn," Lily explained, soberly.

"Minnow?" I already knew the chance this opportunity had given her.

Minnow nodded, tearfully. "I didn't know the wolves would get him."

She sobbed into some napkins while I slid off my chair and helped myself to a beer that I didn't bother to pay for and didn't want.

"The other dogs barked, but Bubba didn't run off," she sniffled. "He followed me back to the parking lot, really calm, and laid down by the door to the tavern. Like he was waiting for Bud."

"Anybody leaving the bar would've seen him," Ginger added. "When Lily and I came out after eating our pizza, it was already storming. We saw Bubba lying by the door and thought we failed. Our plan was for him to run away."

"We didn't want Bubba to die," Lily added, "just make Bud have to look for him."

"I made sure he was wearing a tracking collar," Minnow said. "Bud told us if any of his dogs wandered off he could always find out where they were, because of those special collars. I even peeled the tape off the magnet, so it would work."

"And the point of this was . . . ?" I asked, testily.

"Bud made us see that little bear get shot," Minnow sobbed. "I wanted to pay him back."

"He didn't *make* us watch it," I retorted. "And he's aware that Warden Jensen was alerted."

There was a long, painful moment of introspection.

"Were you aware that Bubba was almost blind?" I asked. "That might be another reason the poor dog felt more comfortable lying near the tavern door, a familiar place where he felt safe."

"We're so fond of Minnow," Lily said, brushing the girl's hair from her forehead. "She's like a granddaughter to us."

"Of course we know she's *your* granddaughter," Ginger added quickly. "But when she told us what Bud had subjected you to, we just wanted to help."

"*It wasn't Bud's fault . . .*" I tried make that fact clear.

"Do you have to tell him I did it?" Minnow's eyes were red and swollen.

I'd had enough.

"Yes, she's *my* granddaughter, and Bud admits he mishandled the hound episode. It was a very unusual coincidence—and even if he suspected there was a possibility that what happened *might* happen, I'm positive he didn't intend for us to see it. Remember, Bud Foster helped me with Molly. I'll always be indebted to him for that.

"Ginger, I'd hoped you'd be a much better influence on this child. And Minnow . . . there's no way I can sanction such malicious behavior on your part. I don't know what to say except I'm ashamed of all of you and wish you had the *slightest* notion of how deeply you hurt that man. When you lose a dog you love, it's the equivalent of losing a family member."

I had never seen three more despondent people.

"I'm not a child," Minnow mumbled.

Ginger squeezed her closely. "Of course you're not," she murmured. "You're a beautiful young woman."

I took the beer back behind the bar and dumped the contents into the sink, watching the foam dissipate. Then I threw the bottle in the sink, too—the loud jolt of glass against metal was gratifying.

"We'll talk more about this tomorrow," I promised. Molly trailed behind as I stomped up the hill to my car. I drove us both to my cabin, took an Ambien, and we went to bed. Ginger and Lily could handle overnight arrangements for Minnow.

When I got up to let Molly out around three o' clock, the fladry safeguarding my cabin and protecting us from wolves was on the ground, destroyed.

I came across the trail-cam photos the next morning when I returned to the Star Lake Inn to serve breakfast and dug into the pocket of my apron to pull out my hairnet. My mood had not improved with the few hours of sleep I'd been able to steal, and now I pulled the snarled hairnet over my equally snarled hair and opened the envelope.

There were more than a dozen pictures. The exposures were not sharp, but each carried a printout of the temperature, the phase of the moon, the time and date. Color pictures were taken during the day and infrared at night. Most were not of interest—a fisher, a fox, several of deer—all were inquisitive about the bait. There were several photos of a black bear, two of wolves. One of me investigating the lure—not a good hair day, even wearing a baseball cap—and a couple of me with the shotgun trying to figure out what to do. Then I came to the photo with the earliest date. Without a doubt, it was the man who'd placed the camera there and was caught admiring his work. Of course I recognized him.

"Coffee?" Chloe was bustling around the kitchen. I hadn't been doing my part.

"Yes, please," I said, taking the mug she offered. "I'll need a couple of these."

"Minnow spent the night here," she said. "Miriam was excited to see her so early this morning."

"I should explain—"

"Minnow filled us in. Right now we have some hungry folks waiting in the dining room. Let's move."

Somewhat chastised, I began dishing up servings of egg strata and fresh fruit salad.

"Grandma?" Minnow was standing behind me. I didn't bother to turn around. I knew this had to be serious, because she almost never called me grandma, so I softened my stance a bit and asked what she wanted.

"I've been thinking—because now I know that Bubba was blind, and because when I saw him last he was waiting by the door of the bar—well, you know those men who caused all the trouble here yesterday? Ginger said they were in the bar when she and Lily had their pizza that night."

"And?"

"Well, maybe they came out of the bar and took Bubba with them. Because I don't think he ran away like we wanted. Honestly, I really don't. When he followed me he was like, limping, like his joints were sore. You were right, he didn't want to go anywhere. And maybe, because those guys were mad at Bud and wanted to get back at him, they could steal his dog."

"Bubba had been completely devoured by wolves, Minnow. Ruby said there was almost nothing left."

"I've been thinking about that, too. Eric says it wouldn't be impossible to make it look like it was a wolf attack. We should ask Will. He's here for breakfast because there's that presentation later on, by those artists."

I was handing over plates of egg strata as fast as I could and still there were waitresses lined up.

"I'm busy right now, Minnow."

"Anyway, Ginger said she'll invite Will over for supper tomorrow night and we can ask him about it then."

After the resort was abandoned later that afternoon, the atmosphere was almost eerie. All the guests had checked out, and the cleaning crew was at work. Chloe refused to clean the rooms and the cottages; she, her mother and Ginger had once tidied the cottages by themselves, but now, with the success of the Inn, they could afford to hire outside help.

"I'm too old to scrub toilets," Ginger said. "Always used that excuse to take it easy," she chuckled. "My job was to count out those little bars of Ivory soap."

We sat in Adirondack chairs on the lawn, our feet up, hairnets off, aprons in the laundry. I'd placed the photos in my bag for safekeeping. A plate of leftover roast pork and sauerkraut sat on my lap. I'd eaten the food with my fingers, which Molly was now licking, so I dropped the plate on the grass for her to nibble the leftovers. Minnow and Miriam were sacked out on a blanket in the shade with Babe. I felt myself beginning to doze. With the symposium over, I had other problems to sort out, but they could wait their turn.

Chloe, smiling at the girls, turned to me: "Miriam really loves spending time with Minnow. I don't know what we'd have done without her help this summer."

I told her I was amazed at the change in Minnow's appearance and behavior and appreciated Chloe's role as a "big sister" and helping her feel comfortable there. I added that my Madison renters were leaving at the close of the summer session, toward the end of August. Minnow's parents hadn't exactly been in close touch during their European sojourn, but I presumed she'd have to fly back to New York in two or three weeks.

"When I came up here in June, I had absolutely nothing planned," I confessed. "And look how busy I've been!

"If you hadn't dropped off that box of old Dillinger relics in the first place, we wouldn't have had our thrilling expeditions," Ginger said. "Our Thundersnows."

I paused momentarily, for a mental kick in the butt. Then I continued, attempting to downplay Ginger's constant topic. "Waters Edge has been beautifully transformed. If we put in running water and electricity . . ."

"Or even a generator," Eric offered.

"A generator would help with refrigeration," I agreed. "Then the place would be pretty livable any time of year. My sister Max will be here after Labor Day, and she's going to be stunned at how much the place has changed."

"It's been good to get to know you again, Tallie," Ginger said. "I think your lucky stars brought you here to us this summer."

That was surely a reference to the beat-up old sign at the entrance to the resort that said "Thank Your Lucky Stars." It came right after the sign that announced, "This Is It!" Hal Larkin must have had some sense of humor.

⊱✕⊰

One of LilyPad's features that I most admired was a large screened porch that led out from the dining area and was cantilevered over a flagstone patio, which had stone steps to the lake. There was a metal daybed on the porch, where Minnow slept when visiting (I envied that, too—the sense of sleeping safely outdoors), and a generous round wicker table with six matching chairs. Ginger said she preferred a round table so she could see everyone at the same time.

On Monday night there were five of us: Ginger, Lily, me, Minnow, and Will. I was the last to arrive, having spent much of the day futilely trying to repair and replace my fladry. We'd had a dry July, so the rebar was hard to pound back into the solid ground. I'd had to run into Antler for more wire, then hurriedly bathed in the lake, and I was so sweaty that any makeup I tried to apply slid off my face. I knew I must have looked ghastly, but I didn't care. My life would be getting back to normal pretty soon, whatever "normal" meant. After this I'd probably never see Will Davis again and maybe not Ginger or Lily. Or even Minnow.

I sipped the cold beer Ginger served and snacked on cheese and crackers. "What've you been up to?" she asked. "Looks like you've been rode hard and put away wet."

"Thanks for the compliment," I said. "I feel like that."

Reluctantly, I admitted that our fence had been wrecked. "I've decided it's not worth replacing."

"The wolves are probably immune to it by now," Will agreed.

"Why bother?" Ginger agreed. "You seen any sign?"

"Sometimes I hear them howl at night. Molly's so used to it, she doesn't even perk up her ears."

"Ask Will what I told you," Minnow said, kicking me under the table.

"Go ahead," I replied. "It's your guilty conscience, sweetheart."

I was still working out whether or not Bud should be apprised of Minnow's role in Bubba's disappearance. I was still working out a lot of things.

"Could somebody make it look like a hound got killed by a wolf, even if it didn't?" Minnow asked Will.

He glanced over at me with tacit comprehension. I hadn't found an opportunity to clue him in.

"Sure, that could happen," he replied. Minnow looked visibly relieved. "But the two most common things that kill hounds are bears and other dogs."

"It needs to look like a wolf did it," Minnow insisted. "How would you do that? I mean, like, if you had a dog you wanted to . . . to get rid of?" Her voice cracked at the end and faded.

Ginger backed her chair away from the table, trying to change the subject. "Anybody need another beer? Crackers? Cheese?"

"Ginger, it's okay. I really want to know," Minnow insisted.

Ginger sat down.

"There are a couple ways that can be done," Will replied. "You could find a road-killed deer and drag it into the middle of a wolf pack area in the woods—you can get maps from the DNR that roughly indicate where the packs are. Then tie the dog to a tree. After a few nights, your dog would look like it had been part of a wolf attack, even though it had been staged or set up to look that way."

"Oh . . . God," Minnow was pale.

"I agree, it's pretty awful. Why do you want to know?"

Minnow's stared at her hands, tightly clenched in her lap.

"Or you could kill the dog some other way," Will advised.

"Like faster, with a gun?" Minnow asked.

"I wouldn't use a gun," Will said. "It's coldblooded to consider, but you could hit the dog in the head with a bat or a pipe and then let other hounds go at it right away. Tear it apart. Then if you dropped it off in a known wolf area long enough for the wolves to feed on it—consume enough of the smashed skull or brain—it'd be hard afterward to tell what actually killed it. Nine times out of ten, wolves would get blamed."

"And how long would that take?" I asked. "Would you need a week, or would overnight be enough?"

"If you had a map that indicated wolf habitats, then it wouldn't take very long. Just a night or two."

Pause. An uneasy silence.

"Are we talking about Bud Foster's hound?"

Minnow spoke up in a choked voice.

"It's my fault Bubba was killed."

In chorus, Lily and Ginger reassured her multiple times.

"No it's not, sweetie!"

"How'd you know Bubba would tangle with a wolf?"

"We're as guilty as you are, Minnow, honey."

"Don't you go worrying again."

"Bud told your grandma that Bubba was blind and was ready to be put down anyway."

"Okay," Will sighed. "I think I get the picture. How'd you do it?" he asked Minnow, "How'd Bubba get loose?"

"With my bolt cutter," I replied with a snap.

"Where's it at now?" he inquired.

"In some pines, not far from Bubba's doghouse," Minnow replied.

"Don't you think it would be a good idea to get it out of there?"

Will got up from the table, motioned for Minnow to follow, and we heard his truck leave LilyPad. When they returned, they put the bolt cutter in my car. I felt acute relief, both for having the tool back and for Will's compassion toward Minnow. There was no way to tell whether or not he approved of her actions, but he was considerate about her distress. And mine too, I surmised.

"Okay, folks. Grub's ready," Ginger announced. She had prepared barbecued spareribs, and we settled once more at our places on the porch.

"I thought we invited Will to inform him of our Thundersnow endeavors," Lily said as she delicately spread her napkin on her lap.

"Indeed we did," Ginger replied. "And we shall. How much do you know about John Dillinger?" she asked Will.

He admitted that he'd seen the recent movie and had once visited the museum at Little Bohemia.

"Remember, Will's from Minnesota," I said. "He didn't grow up knowing that Wisconsin's Northwoods was a convenient hideout for Chicago gangsters."

"Al Capone had his own favorite resort," Lily said, "at Couderay."

Ginger added, "From what I've read, it was popular knowledge that the guy who owned Little Bohemia had a lot of underworld connections in Chicago, if you know what I mean." She retrieved a file from a banker's box at her feet. "That's why Dillinger and his cronies ended up here in the first place: Emil Wanatka, the owner, had a restaurant in Chicago where his customers were gangsters, racketeers, bootleggers, and every single victim of the St. Valentine's Day Massacre. So that gives you an idea of the connections that hooligan already had."

I often tuned Ginger out when she got on that subject, as I was doing now. She so relished recounting her research into the FBI's kerfuffle and loved to festoon it with embellishments and treasured details. I hoped she was not going to regale Will with tales of Dillinger's extensive penis!

"And right here's the picture of the body when it was taken to the morgue," she was saying. "So that's how the rumor began."

Too late.

Minnow offered, "I've been reading a book of Ginger's that said it wasn't Dillinger who was shot with the Lady in Red after all. Supposedly he had plastic surgery, but the eyes on the corpse were the wrong color and there was a screw-up with the fingerprints. And then in 1963, a man claiming to be John Dillinger sent a letter with a picture of himself to Emil Wanatka, saying the picture and the letter should be displayed with the other stuff in the museum because they were proof that John Dillinger was still alive. The man said that after the shooting he moved to Hollywood and lived under an assumed name."

Will was intrigued by that information, and I was stunned to learn that Minnow now took an actual interest in the story. Ginger said Billie Frechette hinted at some kind of mix-up but never went into detail. "So here's the book Minnow got from the library, and it sounds like it might be true. Could be that J. Edgar Hoover was so determined to get Public Enemy No. 1 that he substituted a proxy for the real thing. Of course we might as well agree that by now the letter writer is dead, if he *was* Dillinger."

"Which means," I said, "that we can keep the loot. When we find it."

I was being sarcastic, but it only served to launch Ginger into a detailed narrative of our expeditions.

"About those bullets we found, according to a 2007 magazine called *Treasure Legends,* an 'informant' said 'Dillinger cached ammunition behind the lodge when they first arrived.' And as for the loot, that same 'informant' said he overheard Dillinger mention an amount of *$210,000* in small bills, buried in a suitcase five hundred yards in the woods behind the lodge. The $10,000 was his cut from their last bank job before they went to Little Bohemia."

Ginger was now well into her rotation. Yes, I'd invested a considerable amount of money in my hiking boots, my backpack, and those god-awful camouflage overalls. Maybe if I left everything at the cabin, Max could use them for tramping through the woods; we wore the same size. I'd have to be sure to leave her a note about the wolves and warn her not to let her dog run free. Maybe she could put the fladry back up; the wolves might have forgotten about it by then.

I'd finished eating. And I wasn't listening. It was like hearing Ginger recounting a familiar fairy tale. Her voice assumed a "once upon a time" tone that made me very sleepy.

I *was* extremely tired. After the weekend's activities and then this morning's physical exertion, I felt myself nodding off at the table.

"I apologize, but would you mind if I took a short nap?"

Ginger told me to just go ahead and relax on the daybed while she entertained Will. I lay down and heard the voices in the background, but it was as if I were floating away like a cloud. I could hear her filling him in, including all the funny parts. Minnow joined in with Lily, and they laughed. I marveled at this as I began to drift off. I heard Will ask a few questions and make some suggestions before he wished us good luck.

I must have slept for an hour. When I awoke, Will was seated in a nearby chair, resting his bad leg on an ottoman. He told me Chloe called. She'd found one of my apple pies stuck away in a cooler and wondered if Ginger would like to serve it for dessert. So Ginger and Minnow headed over to Star Lake to get it. Lily was upstairs in her room, taking a nap.

"Do you think Ginger is letting Minnow drive her around?"

"That appears to be the case."

Then he said I looked too comfortable and wondered if I would make room for him to lie down, too.

"This thing chafes my thigh sometimes, so I like to take it off when I can."

I moved over while he removed his prosthesis. "Thanks."

"What will they say when they come back and see us 'in bed' together?"

"Do you care?" he asked, sharing my pillow.

I caressed his cheek with the palm of my hand. He turned and kissed me tenderly while I grabbed his curls in my fist and held on.

"I have to give it serious consideration," I said. "Do that again."

You've been quiet today," he said later. "Are you really just tired, or is something wrong?"

I admitted that I'd checked my e-mail at the library when I went into Antler for fladry supplies. "Minnow's parents have made arrangements for her to return to New York on Friday. They've enrolled her in a very strict private girls' school, the Woodbridge Academy. I checked it out on the Internet and it's one of those schools where she'll have to wear a soldier-like uniform and be subject to harsh discipline. Harry said they're determined to break her of her bad habits and teach her to be respectable."

"You haven't told him how well she's adjusted?"

"I've sent them occasional e-mails. They weren't available by phone in Budapest."

"No wonder she doesn't want to go back."

"She has no idea what's in store for her out there, Will. I'm sick about it. I don't know how to tell her. We all know she doesn't need that kind of rigorous correction. Okay, maybe she acted up before she came out here, but she's proven to all of us that she's a good kid. Chloe has given her a lot of responsibility with Miriam this summer, and she's demonstrated that she's trustworthy and conscientious—except for the incident with Bubba. But the plane ticket's reserved, and her parents are expecting her."

"Apple pie for everyone!" Ginger sang. "And à la mode, if you want it! Get out of bed, you sleepyheads! There's no snooze button on a cat who wants breakfast!"

"What did she say?" Will whispered in my ear.

"It's a Gingerism," I whispered back. "Never mind."

12

I tempered my grumbling this time because Minnow seemed so enthusiastic about the expedition. And Ginger sincerely promised, "With all due respect," that no matter the outcome, it would be our last.

I'd suggested that to avoid a plague of tourists we should begin at dawn. At this time of year, that meant we gathered at the Saloon at four o' clock.

The weather forecast was for a nice, cool sunny day; the kind those who visit the Northwoods in summer cherish and about which they boast, "This is why we're here." We all wore our insect-repelling shirts, though we hoped a cool breeze would keep the bugs at bay. Sleepier than usual, we checked off Ginger's ever-increasing list of supplies. This time, instead of layers of cheesecloth we wore mosquito veils like beekeepers' hats. We added one more walkie-talkie, so each of us would have our own. We spent much time learning how to dial into the same channel and practicing how to contact one another. Lily had a problem understanding that the red button must be pressed with her thumb to speak and she would have to lift her thumb to hear the answer.

"Pushing red means talk, and letting go means listen," Ginger told her. Lily argued that it should be the other way around, because red meant stop.

Lily insisted on carrying the crazy camp tool with sledgehammer, hatchet, and pickaxe. She proudly revealed that she'd pulled on her Depends before her overalls.

I had the GPS in my pocket, along with a compass, and in my pack was a new Baby Glock pistol that I substituted for Bud's weighty shotgun. They were all impressed with the pistol, though I had yet to fire a single shot.

We each also carried a canister of pepper spray.

Minnow took Eric's video camera and the metal detector and at the last minute decided to stick the bolt cutters in her pack, "just in case." Nobody asked her what she meant by that, but I figured she intended to burden herself with penance for the Bubba episode.

This was Wednesday. I had yet to inform her that in two days she'd be flying home. I hadn't told Ginger or Lily, either—procrastination and my own misgivings. The thought of my granddaughter confined to a rigid private girls' school made me cringe. Harry and Camille obviously did not know their daughter; no wonder she'd claimed she'd been emotionally deprived. Now that I had grown to love Minnow, I tended to agree.

Will had warned us that we should be careful in the area we'd targeted that day because a pack of wolves had recently been spotted there. So we had drawn up a plan. If I saw a wolf, I'd fire my gun and the other women would hear the shot. If Ginger and Lily (who were to stay together) saw a wolf, they'd blow their police whistles and get out the pepper spray. Minnow would go with me and yell if she saw one.

We began this final quest behind Little Bohemia, as always. This early in the morning, the parking lot was blissfully empty.

Ginger repeated her mantra to look for "three trees in a semicircle." They probably did not even exist as rotten stumps anymore, but that didn't stop her from repeating the same phrase.

"Now, one of my sources says the loot consists of $200,000. Another says $210,000, and another goes as high as $270,000. These are all guesses, of course, and we might find a burlap bag with five bucks. But give it all you've got, gals—we've invested our own time and money in this scheme. So far, so good, but you all know this is the end of the line. After what we dug up last time, I got a feeling we'll hit the jackpot."

She was, as always, a remarkable inspiration. Minnow gave me a discreet elbow in the ribs.

Molly was perky and ready to go in the fresh early morning air. The long grass was still damp from overnight rain. My overalls, soon soaked, clung to my legs. We were making very slow progress through rampant berry bushes, thick bracken, and large, coarse ferns. I was having a hard time negotiating the tangled shrubbery, and when I heard Molly yelp, I was alarmed.

"Another wolf?" Minnow asked.

"No idea," I replied.

The dog had apparently been tracking a trail of her own, and when we called her to come she finally appeared behind us on our trampled path, but submissive, shaking her head, whining with pain. Every few steps she'd pause and paw at her nose.

As she came closer, we saw her muzzle was thick with porcupine quills.

I asked Molly to hold her still while I found the multiuse tool in my pack (another of Ginger's last minute whims that now did not seem like such a goofy impulse) and explained that porcupine quills were filled with air.

"If we cut them off, the suction that helps hold the quills in place is lessened and we should be able to pull them out with a needle-nose pliers."

"How do you know that?"

"We've brought dogs up north for years."

"Is there a pair of those pliers you need on that thingamabob?"

"I guess we'll soon find out."

I managed to cut the quills—there were at least a hundred, but it could've been worse. Then I let Minnow pull them out with the pliers that, indeed, were a part of the "fancy doodad," as Ginger called it. I had peroxide in my first aid kit, which I applied liberally to Molly's poor snout.

"I'll take Molly back to the car," Minnow offered.

"Good idea. I'll wait here until you get back."

The stupid beekeeper's hat made it difficult to see, but it did keep the biting flies from swarming around my face, although their constant buzzing was a form of torment the CIA might want to employ.

"Why do deer flies always bite you on the top of the head?" I asked Minnow when she returned.

"They like to hide in your hair," she said. "I researched them on Ginger's laptop. Deer flies feed on the blood of mammals. They also transmit disease."

"Enough," I replied. "Too Much Information."

"Skeeter One checking in," crackled from my walkie-talkie. That was Ginger's handle. What an idiotic game. We might as well have paint-ball guns or laser swords.

"Skeeter Two," I replied. "Roger." Minnow smirked.

"Test . . ." the rest was static. We recognized Lily's voice.

"Still doesn't have the hang of it," Minnow said.

"Apparently not," I agreed.

"Red still means *stop*."

We slogged on, now in deep forest where we encountered moss-covered rocks in the damp shade and had to be careful not to slip.

"Skeet . . ." static. It was Lily again. "Ginger . . . can't . . . log." More static. "Ankle."

"Shit."

"Should we turn around?" Minnow asked.

We paused to consider that, when we heard voices. Men's voices. Just ahead of us.

"Lily," I said calmly, "if you can hear me, stay right where you are. Don't blow your whistle. Repeat: *do not blow your whistle*. Stay quiet for five minutes. Do you read me?"

"Roge—" Static.

Minnow was already slithering ahead from tree to tree with Eric's video camera in hand tracking her progress. She beckoned me to move forward but placed her finger to her lips.

I drew close enough to see a man in camouflage bending over something. Minnow handed the camera over to me so I could get a close-up view.

I had a brief glimpse, but then through the viewfinder I watched as Minnow silently parted the branches in front of her. She stealthily made her way to a small clearing where two men were standing. Beemer and Cooney were digging a hole. Beemer, who, Bud said, had shot the little cub. Beemer, who had a big business selling stolen bear gallbladders to China. Beemer, who . . .

I moved the camera slightly. Cooney was doing the digging. Next to him lay the carcass of a full-grown wolf.

The men were going to bury the animal.

"Minnow," I whispered a warning, but of course she couldn't hear me.

"You sure Bud'll believe this is the one that got Bubba when we hand over the collar?"

"A wolf *did* get the goddamned dog, you idiot," Beemer said. "Just not *this* wolf. A wolf's a wolf, for chrissake."

"So we hand him the collar and a hunk of Bubba's fur and say we got it where we found Bubba's corpse?"

"It wasn't a corpse, dickhead. Jesus, how many times—"

I had the video camera focused on the two men and that's when I saw Minnow move into the scene. Beemer spotted her at once.

"Well, *hello there*! Lookit what we got here, Cooney. This is the little snitch who's staying with Bud's new girlfriend, Tally-ho. We heard you ladies were snooping 'round Little Bo."

"What's going on?" Minnow asked, innocently.

"What's it look like?" Cooney asked.

"Like a dead wolf," Minnow replied. "You guys shoot it?"

"Shit, no. You got any idea what kind of crap comes down for killing a fucking wolf?"

"We wouldn't be that stupid," Cooney said with a grin, "Five thousand bucks? Hunting rights—"

"Shut up," Beemer told him.

Please, Minnow, I mentally whispered, don't say anything more. Just get out of there.

I felt my leg brush against her backpack; she'd dropped it at my feet.

"You're the one who shot that bear cub," she told Beemer.

I squirmed with pain.

"And you must be the little twat that turned me in," Beemer said. "What're you doing out here by yourself?"

"I was hiking with my grandma, but she went back to Little Bohemia for breakfast. I'm supposed to join her there."

"Well, you're not gonna," Cooney said, crawling in the dirt to rummage around in a paper grocery bag. "Here, Beemer—want some o' this here duck tape?"

She made a mild attempt to get away, but Beemer caught her arms and held them behind her back. I knew she was strong enough and fast enough to escape, but the girl had guts. She knew I was capturing every moment, every word.

Beemer held her tight and told Cooney to get the box cutter so they could rip the collar apart and get out of there. Cooney rummaged around in the bag and said he must've forgotten to get it out of the truck when they carried the carcass over.

"Okay, dumbfuck. You watch this little bitch while I'm gone," he ordered Cooney. "Won't take me more than a few minutes, but I gotta take a leak."

Cooney roughly grabbed Minnow's arms while Beemer trotted away. "When're you gonna see a doc?" he called after his pal. "You must have a prostrate the size of a tennis ball!"

I couldn't stand when people mispronounced that word. It took all my strength not to yell out "*prostate*, not *prostrate*." Minnow saw me behind the tree and met my glance, then quickly looked away so Cooney wouldn't notice.

"Your peter gone to Ireland yet?" Cooney yelled.

"It's 'Dublin,' you cretin," Beemer yelled back. "And you can go to hell."

"That's 'Irish arthritis,'" Cooney told Minnow with a harsh cackle. "Your peter goes to Dublin."

He was still laughing at his joke when I put the camera under one arm to make a note of the GPS location and wrote it on the palm of my hand with Minnow's blue Sharpie, which I carried in my pocket. Back to the camera:

Through my viewfinder, I observed the most bizarre action.

Cooney had Minnow pinned face down on the ground, and he was sitting on her back. He fished a cell phone from his shirt pocket and began dialing a number. But he couldn't see the number pad, so he had to dig out his glasses from the other pocket. He was still squinting at the phone when Lily moved into my frame of vision. I held my breath as she sprayed him liberally with pepper spray, then lifted the folding camp tool in sledgehammer mode and whacked poor Cooney smack on the side of the head. She hit him again, after he fell to his knees. He never saw her.

I dropped the camera and was immediately on the scene.

"Where's Ginger?" I asked Lily.

"Tripped over a log." Lily was breathless. "Couldn't make the talkie-walkie work. Followed your path. To tell. You."

Minnow was on her feet and ready to go. "We've got to get out of here," she said. "Hurry up!"

I was in the act of applying duct tape to Cooney's eyes and mouth and binding his legs, taking advantage of his state of confusion. He was not unconscious but dazed and bleeding where one eyebrow had been split. As soon as Lily caught her breath, we fled as fast as we could. I picked up the video camera on my way, and Minnow grabbed her backpack.

Then I paused.

"Wait! Minnow, I need the bolt cutters!"

She removed the tool from her pack, and I told them I'd catch up. Minnow assisted Lily back to the resort, through the ferns.

The wolf's radio collar was made of several layers of heavy-duty material, with an outer belt of some kind of tough plastic. I probably could've been more efficient cutting it off if my hands had not been shaking. I hoped Beemer's *prostrate* was making him pee like a mouse.

Finally. I had the collar cut through and pulled it from the wolf.

"Poor wolf," I said, gently petting its ruff.

And then I ran, stumbling, in my haste to get the hell out of there.

Back at Little Bohemia, Ginger was waiting with Molly, sitting on a bench with her ankle resting on a stump.

"What happened to this poor puppy's snout?"

"Get in the car. Quick!" I handed the wolf collar to Lily, then propped Ginger by one of her shoulders, and Minnow took the other. Lily, exhausted, shuffled up ahead and opened the car doors. Molly was the first to get in.

Cooney only knew Minnow had been there; he hadn't seen me or Lily. And he hadn't known what hit him when Lily took him down. Still, I thought I needed to tear out of the parking lot. Would they notice the missing collar?

Minnow explained the situation to Ginger.

"Lily was on her way to find you and tell you we had to leave," Ginger says. "I couldn't stand the pain. But it's lots better now, with all this hullabaloo!"

"We need to hide Minnow," Lily said. "She's radioactive!"

"You better watch out, Tallie, they might come around the cabin looking for her," Ginger said. "Let's see if Chloe will keep her undercover for a couple of days."

"That's all she has," I announced, soberly. "Minnow's leaving for New York on Friday."

The vehement chorus of "NOs" made my steering wheel wobble.

"Her tickets have been purchased; the reservation's been made. Her father sent me an e-mail. She's flying out of Rhinelander on Friday."

Minnow began to wail.

"We'll just see about that," Ginger said, comfortingly. "Let's take one catastrophe at a time. What are we going to do about that wolf collar, Tallie?"

"I gave it to Lily—"

"I've got it," Lily assured us. "Stuck it in my Depends. Figured if the bad guys frisked me they'll never want to look down there."

13

Since the sheriff arrested Beemer and Cooney at the Inn during the wolf symposium and they'd already spent time in jail, I thought it unlikely they would now follow us back to Star Lake. We found some antibiotic ointment for Molly's nose, then changed from our damp clothing and sat on the porch of the Saloon, discussing our next move. Ginger eventually had a call from Will, enquiring about our treasure hunt; I could hear her on the phone in the bar filling him in on our wild encounter and our current and illegal possession of a tracking collar for a depredated wolf.

"Minnow's going to spend the night with Chloe and Eric," she informed him. "They insist."

Then Ginger summoned me, "Will wants to talk to you," and handed me the phone.

"Why did you remove the collar?" he demanded.

"Beemer and Cooney were going to cut it off for devious reasons," I replied. "I overheard their intentions, and I thought by taking it, I would screw up their plans."

"It's a serious offence," Will warned.

"We're going to hand the collar over to Warden Jensen tomorrow," I added, "with plenty of details on what we saw and what we heard. The collar will help prove their duplicity."

Then he wanted to know if I was returning to the cabin. I told him I had to stay there because my fence had already been destroyed and if I left the cabin vacant it might be reduced to ashes by morning.

"I don't like having you there alone," he said grimly.

I wasn't crazy about it either, but I had Molly and a phone and a gun.

"I'm coming over." He was insistent.

I knew if Beemer and Cooney made a foolhardy move, it would likely take place at my solitary cabin. I'd welcome Will's presence.

Back on the porch, Ginger held an inconsolable Minnow. I had yet to inform her of Woodbridge Academy, to which she'd been condemned. Molly and Babe were nervous in the charged atmosphere and paced back and forth, going to one person and then another.

"I really liked the girls from Antler who waited on tables here last weekend," Minnow sobbed. "They told me they have a cross-country ski team at their school. They have a 'Wear Your Camo to School Day.' I want to do things like that. I wish I didn't have to go back to my asswipe family and that suckadelic school. Why can't I stay here?"

"Minnow . . ." I cautioned, only because of the "asswipe."

"Oh, take it easy, Tallie," Ginger admonished. "The girl's just suffered a shock. Your heart would be broken, too, if you were fourteen and your folks treated you like Minnow's did, sending her out here at the last minute to a place she'd never been. I'll bet they're going to stick her out of the way for a second time, now."

"There is a *new* school involved," I mentioned. "A private girl's school. An academy, actually. Harry said—"

Minnow began a fresh round of bawling. I couldn't bring myself to offer the gruesome details. How could my own son be so inconsiderate? Or was it Camille's idea? Would I be a terrible grandmother if I didn't rescue Minnow from her own parents?

Chloe dropped off a tray of sandwiches and homemade potato chips. Minnow tearfully told her that she had to leave Star Lake. "I'm going to have to break it to Miriam," she cried. "She's going to miss me so much after this summer, and I'm going to miss her, too. I want to watch her grow up!"

When Chloe went back to the Inn, I walked with her and expressed my gratitude for guaranteeing Minnow's safety. Then I explained

Minnow's imminent situation, including Woodbridge and how her parents wished to make her "more respectable."

Chloe agreed that would be an emotionally damaging ordeal.

"She's undergone a radical transformation this summer because you trusted her," I said. "That's been of more benefit to Minnow than any Woodbridge discipline."

"Let me talk to Eric," Chloe said suddenly, with a quick embrace. "Maybe we can work something out. She's been so loving and so competent; we don't want to let her go, either! Miriam adores her. And for me, it's been like having a younger sister help out, not only with babysitting but all the other odd jobs around the resort."

Before I went back to the cabin, I called Harry from the landline at the Inn. The entire crowd gathered around to listen in. Chloe would speak with him eventually, and then Minnow would have her turn. But I wanted to be the first to inform my son that—subject to their approval of course—his daughter would prefer not to return to New York this autumn. She chose to stay in Wisconsin, and, what's more, she had a job.

Harry put me on speakerphone so Camille could hear my message.

"Yes, Minnow has a job and a place to live," I repeated, "as a nanny. In fact, she's been working all summer at the Star Lake Resort. She can enroll as a sophomore at Antler High School." To Ginger's chagrin, I added, "And she's been learning to drive."

There was stunned hush at the other end of the line.

Chloe said afterward that Harry and Camille were surprised that they weren't asked for "references."

Minnow wondered why her parents were not distressed, since they hoped she'd be prepared to enroll in a big-name college, like the offspring of their friends.

"There's nothing wrong with schools in Wisconsin," I said. "They were good enough for Harry and Seth and would be excellent schools for you. Let's see how the next year goes. There are also excellent private colleges here, up north."

I ran upstairs to shower and wash my hair. So much had happened in such a short time that I dropped the soap three times. The shower was so small that once I got stuck when I bent over to pick it up.

Will was already at the cabin when I arrived, but I didn't see his truck. He said he'd hidden it in the trees so any interlopers would presume I was alone. For that reason, he said, we probably shouldn't grill our dinner outdoors or eat on the porch. He'd brought a cooler with cold fried chicken, fruit salad, and half a chocolate cake. His daughter had been visiting, and these were leftovers from last night's meal.

"Where's the collar?" he asked right away.

"I think Lily still has it," I said. "Why?"

"Because I could show you how to disarm it, in case the DNR does a flyover."

"How often do they do that?"

"Once a week, I think. Maybe they flew wolves a day or so ago and you'll have a window."

"We were going to turn it in right away this afternoon, but things got a little out of hand. Ginger turned her ankle out in the woods and Lily had heart palpitations after her attack on Beemer and Minnow was upset because she found out she was supposed to return to New York on Friday and I had to call my son . . ."

"Never mind," Will reassured me. "Slow down. I'll help you hand it over tomorrow."

My mind was sprinting as fast as I was speaking. I couldn't have been more excited if we'd uncovered Dillinger's buried loot.

It was time, I decided over a second slice of chocolate cake, to fill him in on Charlie's fondness for Dillinger and Grandpa Waters's vast collection of clippings. I began by explaining the red lace panties that Will retrieved from Molly the last time he was there. I refrained from the intimate nuances of Charlie's favorite amusement, but explained my suspicion that since my husband was a banker, he may have found that impersonating one of the gangsters gave him a bad-boy thrill.

"Ginger claims Grandpa Waters may have known Dillinger, but that's completely absurd," I said. "There was the bread box of Grandpa's clippings—and I have no clue why he kept them, but Charlie, like Ginger, found the stories fascinating. It was kind of a contest between the two of them; who knew the most details about which heist, and so on."

"Dillinger never knocked off the bank in Little Wolf?"

"I'd certainly have heard about it if he had!"

Will was silent while he apparently considered all he'd heard. "Let's brainstorm the possibilities of a connection with your family," he suggested, "just for fun."

We pushed back our chairs, and he poured us each another glass of wine.

"Grandpa Waters was a pharmacist. I know that he and Grandma traveled, but this was their favorite place for vacations."

"Chicago gangsters came to up north to 'cool off.'"

"The *New York Times* recently ran a story about our state being the historic 'refuge of choice' for bad guys on the lam. In fact, it's hard to find a northern resort that doesn't boast 'Al Capone slept here.' Back then, some private resorts even had armed guards and barbed-wire fences."

"Capone was convicted . . ."

"In 1931. I don't know why that date sticks with me," I confessed. "I'm terrible with dates. His brother, Ralph, had a hotel and bar somewhere nearby."

"So your grandfather could've purchased bootleg liquor from Ralph Capone?"

"If he drank alcohol. Grandpa Waters was a strict Methodist."

There was a pause while we both speculated other hypothetical situations.

"Billie Frechette, Dillinger's girlfriend, grew up on an Indian reservation not very far from my hometown," I suggested.

"Kind of weak," Will replied. I agreed.

"Tell me more about Billie," he said.

I summarized what I knew, but I had to admit that when Ginger got deep into her Dillinger lore I often disregarded most of what she said. So I had few details to add to what he'd already been told.

But Billie, whose name was really Evelyn, was a frequent summer visitor to Star Lake with her last husband, and Ginger got to know her then. So much of what Ginger's passed on to us has been from actual chats she had with her.

"Minnow got interested in gun molls," I said, "and I know she made some notes on Billie Frechette, from what Ginger mentioned privately and books that Ginger collected."

Minnow's journal was on the bench next to her bed. I paged through until I came to the page headed with Billie's name.

"Dillinger made eye contact with a hard, piercing stare," it said. Just like Will. I couldn't read that to him. But I did summarize the remainder of Minnow's notes, adding that Billie's father was French and her mother was half-French, half-Indian. The French ancestors had been fur traders from Canada. Her father died when she was eight years old. She moved to Chicago to live with her sister, and during Prohibition, no Indians were allowed in speakeasies. After she met Dillinger, the other gang members didn't want anything to do with an Indian. And she seldom laughed aloud but smiled to herself, as if amused by private thoughts.

She took Dillinger to Neopit and showed him where she'd grown up on the reservation. There she was seen wearing a diamond engagement ring Dillinger gave her on Christmas Eve 1933 and a diamond-encrusted platinum wristwatch. Billie once said: "A lady has to have considerable baggage when traveling." I would agree with that.

"A complicated woman," Minnow had written. And then there was a note in the margin about the small pup that Dillinger gave Billie on January 19, 1934. A Boston Terrier.

I recalled Ginger mentioning Evelyn's remarks about being given nice clothes, jewelry, and a little dog.

"When Little Bohemia was raided, she wasn't there because she was in a federal prison in Michigan for harboring a criminal," I told Will.

"After her release—after Dillinger's death—she toured the country with a vaudeville presentation about her experiences. That's kind of sad."

"What kind of dog did you say Billie had," Will asked.

"A Boston Bull Terrier."

Will got up from the table and wandered over to the frame in which I'd placed the photos of the dogs of Waters Edge.

"These were your family's dogs, right?"

"Right."

He removed the frame from the wall and brought it over to the table.

"What about Little Beau? Isn't this a Boston Terrier?"

We heard you ladies were snooping 'round Little Bo.

"Just this morning, Beemer and Cooney referred to Little Bohemia as 'Little Bo,'" I replied. "Maybe it's a coincidence. Common shorthand in these parts."

"'Little Beau.' 'Little Bo.' This could be your missing link."

"But how would my grandparents end up with Billie Frechette's dog? That's too bizarre."

It was getting dark by then, and Will asked about the cabin journals I'd mentioned. "You said your grandfather asked everyone who stayed here to record their visits."

I opened the Campfire Marshmallow tin, showed him the worn composition books, and, at random, selected an entry in Grandma Waters's handwriting:

May 31, 1941. Mr. and Mrs. Russell Waters left Little Wolf at 4 p.m. Thursday, May 29 for Camp. Had supper at Tomahawk and stayed overnight with Christophersons at Minocqua—very nice place, $1 each. Had a time trying to get breakfast as every restaurant was jammed to the doors. We finally went to Woodruff and were served nicely. Bought few supplies at Antler and had Bob's young friend take us to camp, arriving at 9 a.m.

May 30th. I caught 8 perch for dinner, good sized ones. Cold and cloudy.

May 31st. We are going to row out. It is foggy. Some rain in night. Saw five deer in back of cottage. Russell killed two "porkies."

"I think that's pretty typical," I said.

"Go back earlier," Will said. "At least ten years."

In Grandpa Waters's handwriting, I found this:

May 17, 1930. Les Hubbard and Russ Waters arrived at 10:45 a.m., coming here from Pine Lake Camp. No fishing as season not open. Cleaned up camp, worked on dock. Went up the trail to salt the sheep—saw 2—Froze hard last night—snowed at daylight. Radiator on car froze up solid as was pump on Marmon car. Colder this a.m. (May 18). Last night a buck deer appeared opposite the large pine tree at the south window—remained there snorting and stamping his feet for twenty minutes. Leisurely he turned away snorting with disgust, evidently, and walked up on the hill at rear of cottage where he snorted for over ½ hour. He was in gray coat and without horns. Weather was cold and raw.

The journal entries were in pencil, and many were badly faded. I needed better light.

My best reading light was fastened to the head of my bed, so we pushed the pillows back, added Minnow's, and reclined together while we paged through more of the oldest journals. Will closed his eyes while I read aloud—I accused him of dozing, but he said he was imagining what it was like up here in the 1930s. "Pretty much the same," I said. "Lydia Pinkham's calendar was nailed above Minnow's bed in 1927."

I was surprised to find an entry for April 21 and 22, 1934. It was in Grandma's hand and said that Sunday, April 22, they had snow. They visited a sick friend near Manitowish Waters, stayed overnight at the cabin, and they—something I couldn't make out because of the faded pencil script. Damn!

On May 19 and 20, 1934, my father came to the cabin with a friend:

Driving up from Little Wolf just to see if cottage was ok and to collect rent from Dillinger. Warm, balmy—water high. No fishing as season does not open until Sat. next. Saw plenty deer, fish jumping, some beaver moving around. This is not a fishing trip but just a trip for inspection and rest.

I knew the "Dillinger" mention was a joke. I paged ahead and came across another entry for July 7 to 10, 1935, written by my father. He'd driven up with two other friends. There was much detail about fishing (pickerel, black bass, perch), and the days were hot and sunny.

A trip to town Tuesday night furnished an interview with two of the individuals that worked with the Federal men in rounding up Baby Face Nelson and Dillinger at Little Bohemia. Carl Christensen at Rest Lake Inn can tell an awful story, stop in and see him. Fifteen bullet holes in him from a machine gun of Baby Face Nelson. Weather awful hot and water awful high so fish not biting but a good time was had by all.

"Finally," I told Will, "there's a mention. But not a very helpful one."

I passed the journals over to him and said it was his turn to read; my eyes burned from attempting to decipher the washed out entries. There were other journals, I told him, but from more recent years; I'd only grabbed the earliest. He paged through, but visitors mostly mentioned wildlife they'd seen (grouse, ducks, deer, beavers, loons), fish they'd caught and eaten, and the weather.

Relaxed now, feeling safe, I closed my eyes to listen. It wasn't long before I was sound asleep. I was not aware when Will clicked off the reading light.

It must have been much later when I awoke to howls of wolves.

"Will?" I said.

"They're fake," he murmured. "I heard a trolling motor. Beemer and Cooney are probably out behind the cabin trying to annoy you."

I told him it was a good thing he'd hidden his truck, but I wondered where the men had docked their boat. He said it sounded like they'd left it in the area west of the cabin where there was a small, sandy beach.

"How'd you know they'd come here tonight to harass me?"

"It's Minnow," he said. "They assume she has the collar, and they want it."

"She *doesn't* have the collar."

"They don't know that!"

A heavy rock then landed on the roof of the cabin. And another. More phony wolf howls. Molly ran to the door, barking.

"What if I sneak down to their boat and disable their motor?" I wondered softly.

"And that will accomplish what?" Will whispered, annoyed. "You want these guys hanging around here all night?"

"No! I want to scare them off and then have them struggle to get away."

"I don't get it. What's the point?"

"When they can't take off, they'll panic and think their lives are in danger!"

I was out of bed by then, slipping on a pair of black sweatpants.

"I just need to know one thing."

I grabbed Minnow's black hoodie and zipped it up.

"And that is?"

"How to wreck their outboard motor so it won't start."

"Natalie, listen to me. You don't want to do this."

Molly's continued barking was at least masking our dispute.

"*Yes I do*," I said sharply. "Those two guys are despicable, and they need to know I mean business."

"You seem to think this is a made-for-TV comedy," he argued. "This isn't a joke. You're right; they're criminals They're also drunk and have a lot riding on what's happened. I can't let you endanger your life."

I pulled on black socks and searched for my orange sneakers beneath the bed.

"You *can't let me?*" I echoed Will after I crawled back out, my voice rising. "*Can't let me?* I saw Beemer with the dead bear cub, and I can prove they shot that wolf. Right this minute *I'm* responsible for my actions, *not you, Will Davis,* and if you don't tell me how to pull the plug on their outboard, then I'll just cut the line from their motor to their gas tank."

"Shhh," Will said. "Hey, Natalie, calm down!"

He grabbed my arm and drew me next to him, seated on the bed. "Let's think this out. If you cut their gas line, then you'll be sinking to their level. You'll be damaging private property. That would be foolish."

I was near tears, rocks were still landing on the roof and, a couple had hit the skylights. Molly wouldn't stop barking, and the guys were howling with a wild, drunken frenzy.

"There's a little thumbscrew on top of the gas tank," Will said calmly. "You know, where it's filled?"

"I know where that is," I said. "I forgot to open it once, and my outboard motor stalled."

"Right. You can tighten that screw. But be careful, okay? If I have to, I'll do what I can to keep them busy while you make your way to their boat. From behind the cabin they can't see where it's moored, because of the trees."

"Then when I get back, I'll take the shotgun and pretend to shoot at them. They'll run for their boat, and it won't start," I said.

"No, it'll start—but they won't get far before it stalls."

"And then they'll have to row to get away."

I tied Molly to a table leg so she wouldn't slip out of the door with me. Through a crack in the rear screen door I could figure out the approximate locations of Beemer and Cooney by listening to their dialogue with each other and the threats supposedly thrown at Minnow.

"Get off our property and let us alone," I shouted through the screen.

"Whatcha gonna do, sic your wild-ass Labrador on us?"

Drunken laughter.

"I don't know what you want, but whatever it is, it's not here."

"Oh, yeah? Well, we wanna talk to the girl. Send her out. We got a message for her."

Immediately, I exited the porch in front, crouched, and headed in the direction of their boat.

"We got something to show the kid," Beemer hollered.

"And I got a helluva headache," Cooney said in a lower tone of voice. This sent Beemer into a fit of hysterics.

"You got a headache," Beemer repeated. "That's a good one. I'm gonna turn over and go to sleep."

"Yeah, I got a headache," Cooney replied. "Damn right."

"Fucking A. And you don't even know what happened!"

"Something came at me, like I told you, I was blinded—"

"*You was blinded—*"

"Burned like hell! Mace or something. I don't know where it come from."

"You got an assload on your head, that's what you got!"

Throughout this exchange, Molly was yipping and barking and straining to get free. I found the thumbscrew on the gas can and tightened it hard.

"I'm back," I spoke softly when I entered the front door. "Give me the shotgun."

Will had assembled the gun. "Keep up the chatter."

"Look," I shouted out the back door, "I know who you are."

"And we know where you live!" they responded. "And we know what you stole."

It sounded as if their voices were closer now.

A sudden blast from my shotgun silenced them. A second blast.

"I said, 'Get out of here,'" I yelled while Will handed me more shells, "I'm not kidding."

We could hear the men stumbling and crashing through the woods as they hastily made their way to their boat.

"Start the motor, Cooney, while I shove us off," Beemer yelled.

The motor grumbled, and the boat rushed away from the shore, then it sputtered to a stop.

"What the hell. Change places with me, you fuckwit."

Beemer had no success with the motor, either.

I figured it was time to fire another shot.

"Row like hell. The bitch means business."

"You're damned right I mean business," I hollered after them.

Will and I had to stifle our laughter as we followed the swish and clatter of their slow journey across the lake.

"Voices on the water carry a long way on a quiet summer night," I commented to Will.

Molly, frightened by the shotgun, was hiding beneath a chair. I freed her, and she immediately had to go outside and pee.

We could still hear Beemer and Cooney. Their progress was slow, but Will surmised they were nearing the tube, where they'd probably parked their truck. I took off Minnow's hoodie, kicked off my sneakers, and slid off my sweatpants before I crawled between the sheets and into Will's arms. Molly, worn out by the raucous episode, obediently followed my order to *stay* on Minnow's quilt.

❧

We were still in bed the next morning when Ginger and Lily pulled up to the dock and came indoors. They seemed unsurprised to see Will lying next to me, although I had been careful not to tell them that Will was spending the night.

"With all due respect," Ginger announced, "it's time for you guys to get up. Ten o'clock. Rise and shine! Daylight in the swamp!"

Ginger lit a fire under the teakettle and measured coffee into the French press.

Lily, unblinking, came over and stood next to the bed where Will and I were still entwined. She waved the wolf collar over us and said, "We better turn this in immediately or hide it someplace safe. Bud came over to the Saloon last night and said Beemer and Cooney were making the rounds of all the bars, spreading a rumor that you shot a wolf, Tallie."

"Bud thinks they want to frame you," Ginger said. "There's reports that you killed that wolf because it's the same one who attacked Molly. This is the way they're going to get back at you."

"How would I know if it was the wolf that got Molly?" I complained. "Plus, *we* know they intended to tell Bud that wolf was the one that got Bubba."

"Change of plans, I guess, after Cooney got clobbered," Ginger replied.

"Excuse me," I told the women with impatience, "could we please have some privacy? *With all due respect?*"

"All the privacy you want," Ginger said. "Lily and I will enjoy our coffee out on the porch. But you better get up and get going 'cause we got work to do. Minnow will be here any minute. I gave her a call."

"And she's coming here, how?" I asked.

"In the Star Lake pickup. Don't get your undies in a bundle, she's a good driver." Ginger shot back.

"I wouldn't mind some coffee," Will admitted. He was sitting on the side of the bed attaching his prosthesis.

I muttered. "I'm not wearing anything."

"Hear that? Hear that sound?" Ginger let the screen door bang while she ran down to the lake. "It's an airplane."

Lily ducked her head inside to tell us, "I'll bet they're flying wolves."

"They'll pick up the collar, Natalie," Will said softly. "You've got maybe an hour before Warden Jensen shows up. He might have the sheriff with him, too, if Beemer and his buddies have any remaining credence with the law."

"And I'll bet anything there's a dead wolf behind the cabin," I said. "By the way, I never told you whose photo was on the trail-cam pictures you had developed."

"So tell me, who was the guy that placed the bait?"

"Beemer, of course. When we have a moment, I'll give you a lesson about the medicinal properties and value of dried bear gallbladders in China."

14

Will handed me the wolf collar and said it was disarmed so we could hide it without the signal being tracked. "That might buy you some time," he said, "but if I'm asked, I'll swear I wasn't involved."

We all agreed and said we'd turn the collar over to Warden Jensen as soon as possible. But we'd hide it for now, so Beemer and Cooney wouldn't spy it, in case they showed up.

Will then said goodbye and that he'd be in touch.

After last night, I wanted a more amorous farewell, but our audience was growing. Minnow had arrived. I saw her speak briefly with Will before he drove off.

I explained the conversation Will and I'd had about "Little Beau" and proposed that, since the dog's name might possibly be a diminutive of "Little Bohemia" which was in close proximity to the site where the dead wolf was found yesterday, it might be fitting to hide the collar where Little Beau was buried. Just for now. Who'd think of looking for it there?

We trooped out to the pet cemetery and found Little Beau's burial place among the others. A large granite stone had always marked the tiny dog's grave. The stone was somewhat buried in the soil, and when we managed to heave it aside a surprising object was revealed beneath: a circular disk of metal. More hasty digging (with our hands; we hadn't thought to bring a shovel) and we discovered the top of a cover to a very large jar. There was a screw-on cap and a wire handle, and the jar seemed to be enormous.

"Maybe it's our treasure!" Lily clapped with delight.

"And why on God's green earth would John Dillinger bury it way out here, I wonder?" Ginger hooted. "Seems like a pretty long jaunt for a man who's running from the law. Unless, of course, Tallie's grandpa *was* a pal of his." She cast me an expectant glance, her eyebrows raised like question marks.

We took turns digging up the glass jar with our fingers and ultimately pulled it out. It said "5 gallons" on the front, and a spread-winged eagle was impressed in the glass on one side. Beneath the jar, in the earth, we could see a disintegrated blanket that partially enveloped the skeleton of what must have been a small dog.

Minnow broke a branch off a balsam and somberly pulled it over the cavity, speaking words of comfort to Little Beau.

Ginger proudly carried the jar inside the cabin, as it was beginning to rain. Lily said it was the sort of pickle jar that used to be on the main counter of the corner store when you purchased one pickle at a time and the grocer would fish it out for you. The jar must have been at least eighteen or nineteen inches tall and ten inches wide; it would have held dozens of dill pickles. She felt inspired to compose a quick poem:

> Your taste buds will tickle
> With a crisp dill pickle
> And it's only a nickel
> So please don't be fickle.

Ginger wiped the glass with damp paper towels and we could see bundles of yellowed envelopes stuffed inside. The most visible of these had a return address, "Waters Pharmacy." I recognized my grandfather's writing: "To Whom It May Concern."

To our tremendous frustration, we could not get the corroded cap unscrewed! We each took a turn.

"Should we take a hammer to it?"

"No, Lily," I replied. "Let's keep it intact."

Minnow then discovered that with all the excitement, we'd forgotten to put the collar in Little Beau's grave!

Before we could decide what to do with the collar *or* the pickle jar, Bud knocked at the porch door. He'd come by boat.

"Oh for goodness sake, come in out of the rain," Ginger said. She took her time welcoming Bud while Lily stowed the pickle jar inside the new Swedish woodstove and secured the glass door.

"Coffee?" Ginger asked. Bud sat at the porch table, where I joined him after quickly rinsing my muddy hands with lake water in the basin. I hoped he wouldn't notice the dirt still embedded beneath my nails.

"I wanted to let you know I'm going to be gone for a couple weeks," he said. There was a client who wanted someone to accompany him on a fishing trip to the Boundary Waters. "I know the area pretty well, and he's paying me good money to go."

"I think it's a good idea to get away for a while," I told him.

"Did Ginger tell you Beemer and Cooney are on the lookout for you?"

"They know where I am, Bud. They were over here harassing me last night."

"It's my fault for taking you and Minnow along that morning. Beemer got fined two grand for that, and now he can't hunt for three years. He's crazy mad. I didn't say anything, but he suspects you turned him in."

Bud looked tired. His eyes were red, and he may have had a shower but he'd gone without a shave for several days. The clean short-sleeved cotton shirt he wore was buttoned wrong. I reached across the table to adjust the buttons for him.

Bud took my hand. "I'm worried about you and Minnow, because there's no telling what those nimrods might do."

"One thing they did want to do," I confided, "was show you a wolf they killed and convince you think it's the one that got Bubba."

Bud put down his coffee and rubbed his eyes. "Sure," he said, after a moment. "That makes perfect sense. I'm not even going to ask where you picked up that information, but I told you I thought Beemer was involved."

The cabin was proving to be a popular gathering place. Molly was busily sniffing and welcoming everyone. A couple hours had passed since the plane had flown over the lake, so we weren't alarmed when DNR warden Dave Jensen arrived. Ginger was preparing her fourth pot of coffee. Warden Jensen introduced us all to the wolf biologist, who'd brought along a receiver because they'd traced the radio collar of a missing wolf to this address. He also had with him a sheriff's deputy, who was ready to make an arrest.

Ginger bustled around and settled all the men indoors at the big table, including Bud. "Now, just where is that collar signal right now," she asked Warden Jensen with a straight face.

Jensen indicated the biologist, who admitted he'd lost the signal, but during the flyover it had unquestionably been located at this spot. "The pilot got the strongest signal right above this cabin, and we believe the collar is somewhere in here."

"Also," Warden Jensen added, unable to look directly at me, "Natalie, here, was reported by an anonymous source as having recently killed a wolf. The carcass was discovered this morning near the tube that leads from Sundog into Star Lake. Do you know anything about this?"

He finally gave me a glance.

"What the hell!" Bud exclaimed. Cooney and Beemer were peering through the screen door in back. They announced they had the very same wolf in the back of their pickup and they had found it just where the warden said it was.

"I wish you'd have left it where it was initially encountered, so we could take photos and have an accurate location for our report," Warden Jensen admonished.

"We can put it back," Cooney replied. "No problem with that."

Beemer cuffed him on the head.

"If those bozos are the ones making the accusations, they're liars," Bud reported.

"What was my justification for shooting this wolf?" I asked. "It's true that Molly was attacked, but I have no desire to kill any wolves as retribution."

"What if that was the same wolf that killed Bubba?" Bud spoke up.

Beemer and Cooney, who were standing outside in the rain, backed away from the screen door a couple of steps.

I thought it might be helpful to welcome the men inside. The little cabin was nearing full capacity. Molly wove between multiple bodies. Cooney's right eye was swollen shut and the side of his face was bruised from Lily's blow. Many voices spoke at once, and I was the only one who saw Minnow slip out onto the front porch and sneak away.

"I think it's time you all shut your flytraps and listened to what we got to say!" Ginger shouted. Everyone was quiet.

"With all due respect, and for reasons that shall remain confidential since they're not relevant to this case, my friend Tallie Waters and I and Lily and Tallie's granddaughter Minnow Lindquist were hiking in the woods behind Little Bohemia early yesterday morning."

Beemer and Cooney started to make a move, but the sheriff's deputy glared at them and they resumed their seats at the table, where they'd been ordered to sit.

"I sprained my ankle." Ginger lifted a cuff of her jeans to show everyone the elastic bandage. "Meanwhile, Lily here informed the others of my injury by walkie-talkie. Tallie and Minnow were ahead of us by a ways, and they encountered a couple of men who were attending to the remains of a wolf."

There were murmurs and mumbling among the crowd.

I saw Minnow standing by the front door with her backpack. Perhaps she'd only gone out to the pickup to bring it in.

"These men were up to no good, I can tell you that. They were plotting to blame the death of Bud's hound Bubba on that wolf and tell him that's why they killed it. Tallie and Minnow had nothing to do with it, I swear."

"You can't prove nothing," Cooney said, "'cause you weren't there."

"No, but I was," I replied softly.

"And so was I," Minnow said. "You know I was there. And I have substantial proof."

Minnow reached in her backpack and retrieved Eric's video camera. Warden Jensen, the sheriff, and the wolf biologist watched the footage.

"You sure Bud'll believe this is the one that got Bubba when we hand over the collar?"

"A wolf *did* get the goddamned dog, you idiot. Just not *this* wolf. A wolf's a wolf, for chrissake."

The room was silent as the camera broadcast the men's voices. The video footage, remarkably clear, included the conversation with Minnow, the men tying her up, and Lily's bold battering of Cooney's head. We watched the video again. And again.

"I have a GPS location for that," I told the warden. It was still written on my hand in indelible marker.

"Excuse me, Warden?" The wolf biologist spoke up. "This is unusual, but I'm now receiving the collar's signal."

The group left the cabin and followed the indication that was broadcast. Minnow was the only one who wasn't surprised to see the collar on the dead wolf in Beemer's pickup. Obviously it had been cut, but no one asked about that. Afterward, Minnow told us she'd put it there. "Before he left this morning, Will showed me how to restart it, just in case we wanted the collar to work again."

I gave Warden Jensen the trail-cam photos taken on my land. Meanwhile, Beemer and Cooney were led away to jail by the deputy, who also confiscated Eric's camera as evidence.

Bud got in his boat and started the motor after I hugged him and wished him a successful fishing trip.

"Now I won't worry about you and Minnow while I'm gone," he said. "It seems to me you two are pretty capable of looking after yourselves."

"Wait a minute!" Ginger came running down to the dock with the pickle jar.

"Could you please open this for us?" she asked.

The pickle jar had been securely wrapped in a bath towel.

Bud had a wrench in his boat, and while Ginger hugged the bottle firmly to her chest, he was able to get the corroded cap to budge.

Lily was hopping with joy in the wet grass with Minnow. By the time we went back inside the cabin we were all soaking wet and breathless from doing our happy dance.

15

To Whom it May Concern

I, Russell Waters, R.Ph. wish to affirm that my wife
Margaret and I were unintentionally involved in matters
regarding the escape of John Dillinger from Little Bohemia
Lodge on the night of 22 April 1934.

"Quiet," Ginger shouted harshly as Lily and Minnow applauded
with delight. "Let Tallie read what her grandpa had to say, for God's
sake! And I think we better all sit down. My heart's about to leap out of
my throat."

We had come north for an early spring visit to make minor
repairs to our cabin, and on Sunday, Margaret and I visited a
friend who was ill with influenza. Because it was Sunday, he
had been unable to procure a medication I happened to carry
in my valise. As we were leaving their home, our car was
commandeered by Mr. Dillinger and friend. I was asked to drive
the men to Antler, where they might obtain a faster car, but
in fleeing mine they left behind a leather valise that matched
mine in every way except color: theirs was brown, and mine
happened to be black. This was a simple mistake to make in
the dark, and we did not discover the mix-up until we returned
to the cabin. Since the men were carrying firearms and seemed

to be in a great haste, Margaret and I felt it would be unlikely that we could overtake them to make an exchange.

"I knew it! Didn't I tell you I knew it?" Ginger crowed. "I just knew your Grandpa Waters met John Dillinger, Tallie. Imagine that. He and your grandma helped Dillinger escape! Woo-hoo!"

"There's more," Minnow said soberly, peering over my shoulder. She took the letter from me and read aloud:

We stoked the fire in our stove. I opened the alternate valise to see if it held anything of value. We discovered a Boston Bull Terrier pup that had apparently been stuffed inside for safety's sake.

We all went, "Awwww," and Lily said, "Little Beau?"

"That makes perfect sense," Ginger clasped her hands to her lips. "I'll bet it was the little Boston Bull Terrier that Evelyn asked Marie Conforti to take care of while she was in prison. One report said there was a little bulldog with Marie at Little Bohemia, but she said it ran away from all the noise. I'll bet when her boyfriend, Homer Van Meter, escaped with Dillinger, he took the pup rather than risk the wrath of his moll!"

"Ginger, will you please *shut up?*" I asked. The rest of us were waiting impatiently to hear the remainder of the letter.

Minnow continued.

The valise also contained a great deal of money, in the form of silver certificates. Margaret and I decided it would be appropriate to return the money if we could determine how to contact the men. The next day, however, upon learning what had occurred at Little Bohemia, we felt it might be more prudent to turn it over to the FBI.

At the risk of appearing to be in cahoots with gangsters, I made several unsuccessful attempts to access J. Edgar Hoover. He was extremely unpopular with the general public at that time and difficult, if not impossible, to reach.

After John Dillinger's death, Margaret and I buried the certificates in this pickle jar in an easily accessed wooded area near our cabin. Now, many years later, we are burying the little dog here—whom we've learned to love and named "Little Beau."

"So what about the 'three-trees-in-a-semicircle' theory and the buried Dillinger loot?" Minnow inquired, handing the letter back to me. "Didn't I say the owner of the resort spread those rumors to get more business?"

"Emil Wanatka had lots of friends," Ginger agreed, "and the tourists are still coming. He did a terrific PR job. Whatever goes over the old sow's back goes down around her belly."

Lily asked, "What does a pig have to do with this?"

"What goes around, comes around, my dear," Ginger remarked with a grin.

Lily had been counting the cash in the remaining envelopes. "It's all here," she reported, "Two hundred and ten thousand dollars."

Ginger added, "With all due respect, there would definitely be interested buyers for these bills, especially if you could document their provenance."

"And not get arrested for trading stolen goods," Minnow added.

"Well, that too," I had to add with a smile.

"Or we could just spend it as it is," Lily offered. "$210,000 divided four ways is pretty nice."

I was not known for my math skills, but Lily's quick calculation came to $52,500 apiece.

"But they're silver certificates," I reminded them. "Those aren't in circulation any more. Charlie and I liked to put silver dollars in the boys' Christmas stockings every year, and sometime during the 1970s the government stopped issuing silver dollars for them."

"These might be worth more than face value," Lily surmised with a sly smile.

"That's almost certain," I replied. "One of Charlie's friends belongs to a numismatic group, and I can ask him what they're worth."

"So how will we unload them?" Ginger asked. "This is a lot of loot!"

"eBay," Minnow answered. "We can set up anonymous accounts and sell a few of them at a time."

"And not get arrested for trading stolen goods," Ginger added.

"There's still another letter," I announced.

Everyone fell silent again while I resumed reading from a somewhat newer envelope with a darker shade of ink:

Addendum to previous letter: This is to inform whomever it may concern that our granddaughter, Tallie, often expressed great interest in the snapshot of Little Beau. The earlier letter will have explained his origin, which her grandmother and I would now like her to know.

"I knew that picture looked familiar," Ginger interrupted. "I'd seen it somewhere before."

"Shhhhh," Lily whispered, "Zip it, Ginger! Isn't that what you're always telling me to do?"

When Tallie visited Waters Edge with us as a child, we developed the habit of occasionally motoring over to Star Lake Resort by boat shortly after supper. She accompanied us in her pajamas, ready for bed. While Margaret and I played a simple game of rummy on the porch with friends, she was often looked after by a woman named Evelyn Tic, who took an affectionate interest in our Tallie. Evelyn, ironically, had been the original owner of Little Beau. I gave her a matching snapshot of the pup.

"Oh. My. God." Minnow said. "Billie Frechette! Grandma!"

"For mercy's sake, I can't stand the suspense," Ginger shouted. "Read faster, Tallie!"

"Calm down, you two—can't you tell Tallie's about to cry?" Lily replied.

You may not recall, Tallie, but Evelyn liked to hold you on her lap on the glider and read your storybooks aloud to you. She never failed to treat you to an Eskimo Pie. Because our visits north often coincided with those of the Tics', Evelyn was delighted to watch you develop into a smart and happy child, as she had never borne children of her own.

And that was all there was.

I don't know why I never noticed that!" Ginger exclaimed. "Of course we had a lot more bar business in those days, and I had to spend most of my time serving drinks until late at night. Evelyn never mentioned you, but sometimes she said she felt so bad about never having had kids. Maybe she said that after she held you on her lap and hugged you and had to let you go."

"I remember the Eskimo Pies," I said. "They melted faster than I could eat them, and the chocolate crust would slide way down to my fingers. Somebody must have helped clean the chocolate from my pajamas."

"Billie Frechette," Minnow said, "Wow, Grandma, that's way, way cool!"

I wished Grandma or Grandpa Waters would have been able to tell Charlie that I'd been cared for by an actual moll of John Dillinger's when I was a child. Yes, tears were welling in my eyes and running down my face.

"We have to share our *fantastic* news with Chloe and Eric," Minnow announced.

"And Will," I added.

"Of course," Ginger agreed. The women decided to head on over to Star Lake. "Let's give him a call right away and find a bottle of champagne."

We agreed to keep our discovery hush-hush, until we decided what we were going to do and how we would do it. The safe at Star Lake seemed like a secure place to store the cash.

I told them I'd follow with Molly; I needed a few moments alone. All three squeezed in the pickup, and I watched Minnow drive away.

Will and I had placed the oldest journals on top of the newer ones last night before we went to sleep. I opened the Campfire Marshmallow tin and dumped all the notebooks on the table. Now, on the top, was the journal in which Charlie had recorded his final visit to Waters Edge.

Usually when we opened the cabin, the most recent journal was the first thing everyone reached for. We wanted to read all the fun details on what previous guests had experienced and note whether there were instructions to put out mousetraps or watch for carpenter ants or get another full tank of propane. Since my arrival, I had purposely avoided the final journal. Within a few weeks I'd have to make my own entry there for this summer, following Charlie's:

All my yesterdays at Waters Edge have run together. I have found solace here, and healing, and I have had the benefit of memorable times with my wife and our sons. My visits will most likely cease when we close the front door and insert the big padlock in its latch, this afternoon. My past is over. My future is irrelevant. My present is all that matters. Before we leave I will walk out onto the dock with my beloved Tallie and our dear Molly to stand at the edge of this beautiful lake. A loon may call; an eagle may fly above. The past may offer something to inform my present, but that one moment of farewell will be unique; not like my past at all.

Author's Note

There *is* an actual Star Lake, Wisconsin, in the Town of Plum Lake, Vilas County. Its history commenced with a prosperous lumbering industry; now tourists and sportsmen enjoy the beauty of the area. Hinz's North Star Lodge, a lovely resort with exceptional dining, was built in 1894 by early lumbermen as the Hotel Waldheim, and it resembles my imaginary Star Lake Lodge—which incorporates the fictional Star Lake Saloon of this book and its predecessor.

One very early incarnation of the Hotel Waldheim advertised, "The climate in this section of Northern Wisconsin is clear and bracing, the drinking water is pure and a health-giving tonic. This County is a cure for insomnia." Those of us who find solace and comfort in the Northwoods would agree.

Natalie's cabin on Sundog is almost an exact replica of my own family's cabin near Mercer, built in 1926. And the Mercer Library is the model for the Antler Library.

Many of these real places, however, have been modified by imagination to become pretend places in a make-believe setting, and the characters (except for John Dillinger, Evelyn Frechette, Homer Van Meter, Baby Face Nelson, Patricia Charrington, Emil Wanatka, Marie Conforti, and Carl Christensen) are not based on anyone in particular.

Little Bohemia Lodge, still in business, is located only a short distance from Star Lake, on a lake named Little Star. It no longer rents rooms, but the cuisine is excellent and the Dillinger museum remains a curious attraction.

The lupine derives from the Latin *lupinus*, "of the wolf" or "wolf-like," as *lupus* is the Latin name for wolf. The plants, which grow in sandy soil, grow to a height of one or two feet with a spike of loosely arranged pea-like blossoms that vary in color from dark blue to white, and they are the only food for the caterpillar of the Karner blue butterfly. The symbolic meaning of the lupine flower is "imagination."

For more information on Wisconsin's wolves or to participate in a wolf howl, contact the Timber Wolf Alliance at http:// discoverycenter.net.